PROJECT DUKE

DUKES AND SECRETS
BOOK THREE

MARIAH STONE

Cover design by Qamber Designs and Media

Editing by Beth Attwood

Proofreading by Laura La Tulipa

GET A FREE MARIAH STONE BOOK!

Join Mariah's mailing list to be the first to know of new releases, free books, special prices, and other author giveaways.

freehistoricalromancebooks.com

ALSO BY MARIAH STONE

MARIAH'S TIME TRAVEL ROMANCE SERIES

- Called by a Highlander
- Called by a Viking
- Called by a Pirate
- Fated

MARIAH'S REGENCY ROMANCE SERIES

- Dukes and Secrets

VIEW ALL OF MARIAH'S BOOKS

Scan the QR code for the complete list of Mariah's ebooks, paperbacks, and audiobooks in reading order.

1

London, 1813

The heat emanating from the cup of tea in Lady Calliope's hands wasn't enough to fight off the chill running up her spine. Nor was the warm June air in the sunlit yellow sitting room of her home, Sumhall Place.

William King, the Marquess of Huntingham, sat across the tea table from her, holding her captive with his cold glare. Even with her grandmama, her brother Preston, and his wife of two months, Penelope, present in the sitting room, her heart raced with a panic she hadn't felt since she was twelve years old—the last time she'd seen William.

What a mistake it was to allow William's visit, she thought. And yet, she couldn't alert her family of his true nature, or it would expose her dirty secret. The secret William possessed.

"We all heard about your dear papa," said Grandmama, cocking her perfectly styled, regal head of silvery-gray hair as she scratched behind the ear of a fluffy white Persian cat lying on her lap. Despite the caress, which Miss Furrington usually loved, the cat didn't show a single sign of her usual bliss, instead staring at Huntingham with wide, dilated eyes. Calliope quite shared the sentiment. "How terrible for you. For your whole family, dear William."

William, that was how she had known him then. Though her grandmama had used the name, this man was William no more. Gone from his face was the softness of a fifteen-year-old boy.

Instead, the pleasingly angular face of a grown man stared at her, with high cheekbones and big brown eyes framed with dark eyelashes. His wide, attractive mouth—lips tightly pressed together, a slight, ever-present curl in his upper lip—hinted at arrogance, and the lines around his mouth spoke of harsh judgment. His square jaw was shaved immaculately, and the whole was framed by thick, dark brown hair in a fashionable windswept style.

Though he was undeniably handsome, the immaculate surface hid a cold interior. Giving her much-needed strength of spirit, the memory of another man caused heat to rush through her. Only a few days ago, she was swaying in the arms of Nathaniel, the Duke of Kelford, at the Royal Navy ball. Golden-haired, tall, muscular, and gorgeous, he'd been striking in his navy uniform. She couldn't help but feel like she was flying in his arms. Like her heart was full of butterflies fluttering their wings. She had burned under the intense gaze of his turquoise eyes, and her skin had tingled under his palms. If only that charming rake were sitting across the table from her now rather than this snake...

William's broad shoulders showed his strength, and he had the muscular thighs of a horse rider. But Nathaniel was much larger, with bulky muscles under his uniform—not many gentlemen were built like him. Calliope's eyes dropped to William's large hands. One of them lay on the handle of the intricately carved chair, casual and relaxed. And yet she knew how cruel that hand could be. How much pain it could cause. A shiver ran through her at the memory.

And her eldest brother, Spencer, was not here to defend her honor like he had back then, the only one who knew anything about what had transpired.

"Grandmama," said Preston with an apologetic smile. "It's Huntingham now."

"I know," she said, petting Miss Furrington. "Huntingham, I hope you forgive my informality. It was meant kindly. Our families used to be great friends."

Another shiver slid down Calliope's back. All that was true...until their families fell apart—because of her.

Preston nodded his black-haired head, an expression of genuine sadness clouding his dark eyes. "I am sorry, too, Huntingham. Our fathers used to be great friends and neighbors. I remember him well."

Sitting on the sofa by Calliope's side, Penelope, who had quickly become one of Calliope's best friends, narrowed her eyes as she scanned Calliope with concern. Penelope looked gorgeous with her pretty dark blond hair and immaculate purple silky dress worthy of the duchess she now was. But what made her even more beautiful was the happiness that practically radiated from her, just as it did from Preston.

Huntingham nodded without a twitch of grief. "Quite. Papa will be dearly missed."

Grandmama opened her mouth to say something, but Huntingham wasn't finished. "While we're all still grieving, however, I cannot afford to wallow in my feelings for much longer." He glanced at Preston. "Grandhampton, I'm sure you understand as you inherited your own title quite recently and know all the responsibilities." He offered Penelope a shadow of a cool smile. "You found a wife very soon after your mourning period was over, as you should have."

Preston's eyebrows drew together, and the corners of his mouth turned downward, giving away the tension he was not supposed to reveal on his usually collected face. His and Penelope's union hadn't been a regular wedding as people believed. Preston had married her to avenge Spencer's assumed death, thinking he was ruining her father. But the woman he had thought his enemy had become his greatest love.

"Quite right," he said politely.

Huntingham continued. "Now that I am the next marquess and the mourning period is over, I must do the same as you and find a wife."

As he said the word "wife," his heavy gaze settled on her again, and an icicle was dragged down her back. Wife... she...to him?

This would be it; she would lose it right here. She'd jump to her feet, embarrassing herself and her family, and run out.

But she didn't let herself fall apart.

Calliope had an odd sensation of stepping out of her own body, watching herself as if she were another guest. The cool and collected lady didn't show a trace of distress that raged within her soul. Her pristine white teacup didn't rattle against the saucer as she placed it back on the table. Her back was perfectly straight, her head was held high, and her legs didn't fidget from the urge to jump to her feet and run. She even managed to suppress the need to breathe as deeply and as quickly as she could. The only indication of her turmoil may be the color of her cheeks, but Penelope was a little flushed, too, no doubt from the summer heat in the room.

Preston scanned the man quickly, his eyes estimating. "Forgive me for speaking so frankly," said Preston, "but I must admit, I am surprised by your visit today given there was no contact between our families for years."

The marquess's upper lip curled in a fleeting expression of anger. He wouldn't tell them, would he? No, surely he wouldn't. But even if he kept his silence—as he had for all these years—he could still hold that information over her head like the blade of a guillotine.

"Yes, you were at that boarding school in Scotland," said Huntingham, putting one long leg over the other. Heavens, he was tall. He may be even taller than her brothers; although, no doubt, not as well-built as them. "So you didn't know that your deceased brother and I had a disagreement."

From September, she and her family and the whole world had thought Spencer was dead. Then from June, they had searched for him for weeks never knowing if he really was dead or alive. If he really had been press-ganged or not. Calliope's gaze fell on the large intricately carved chair by the fireplace, which Spencer favored, and her chest hurt from how much she missed her eldest brother. Had he been there, William wouldn't have dared to show his face.

Spencer, who'd been eighteen then and had been practicing boxing for years, had, with only a few precise and masterful hits, split William's lip, giving him a black eye, and, based on the speed with which William had run away holding his side, broken one of his ribs. The King family had never returned to Grandhampton Court.

"What was the disagreement about, if you don't mind my asking?" asked Preston.

William's warm brown eyes felt icy cold when they landed on Calliope once again. He didn't reply, eyeing her, trapping her in the torturous memory of the day that had changed the trajectory of her entire life.

The day when long curtains had swayed as a warm

summer breeze flowed between the open French doors in the library. The day when she had felt the smooth leather cover of the book she wasn't supposed to go near at the age of twelve. The first day in her life when she had felt that way—burning, aching, and touching herself in the most intimate place as she imagined the brown-eyed boy doing things to her that she was reading about...

And then two strong hands had ripped the book out of her fingers... And the brown eyes staring at her weren't only in her imagination anymore. Two fingers had stroked her neck, making her quiver in a wonderful surprise—

And then a hard, painful pinch at the base of her neck had wiped it all out in a cold, prickly shock. And the eyes had turned from warm to angry, disgusted.

And he'd uttered a single word that made her soul shrink and shrivel in upon itself.

"Whore."

Calliope shuddered with the memory, clutching the skirt of her pastel-green muslin gown.

"The disagreement..." said William King slowly, his gaze like sharp claws digging under her skin. "I can't recall. Can you, Lady Calliope?"

For the first time he addressed her, and her throat clenched tightly, her lips so rigid she couldn't move them. This wasn't her. No one did that to her. She was a strong, intelligent woman who planned to become an investigator, to fight crime and look for lost people. How could one person make her feel so dirty and insignificant?

And yet, the place at the base of her neck where William had pinched her burned. It was as though she was in shackles she couldn't break.

He likely sensed her distress, the corners of his thin lips moving up in a barely noticeable, satisfied smile.

"I can't recall, either," she said finally. Her voice had never sounded so quiet.

William nodded, his shoulders dipping as he visibly relaxed. A triumphant look on his face showed her he knew he owned her. One word of what he'd witnessed, one word and he'd cause a scandal that would forever blacken her name and the name of her family.

"Must have been a simple misunderstanding," William concluded. "What does it matter, anyway? I believe our families can be friends again like we once were. In fact, I wonder if our families can be bound by ties deeper than friendship."

Silence fell on the room. Calliope could hear the clock ticking in the hallway. From behind the open windows, a horse trotted, and the wheels of a carriage rattled against the cobblestones. Grandmama stilled, her eyes wide, her mouth slightly open. Penelope's hand stopped, her teacup midway to her mouth. Miss Furrington raised her head, her ears erect and directed at William. Preston's dark eyes widened in an expression of pleasant surprise. He'd been searching for a husband for her for weeks.

Preston straightened in his chair, his lips stretching in a smile. "I quite wonder the same. The line of the Marquess of Huntingham is old and respectable. Sister, don't you agree?"

A husband was the last thing Calliope wanted. Any husband would completely disapprove of the plans she had for her life. Even her brothers were convinced that starting a sleuth agency was dangerous and had to be stopped.

But William was worse than just any husband. If he had pinched her for reading a dirty book, what would he do to her when he owned her as a husband?

She had to defend herself. She couldn't let herself be trapped into marriage with someone like him.

Calliope's throat felt as dry as paper. She swallowed what

felt like a rock and tried to force herself to speak. Losing control for the first time since seeing William, she shifted her leg, knocked the tea table, and her teacup and the saucer went flying to the floor. William made a sharp movement towards her to grab it.

The teacup shattered with a tinkling crash.

Miss Furrington leapt to her feet, arched her back, and hissed fiercely at William, then sprang at his hand—the very same hand that had pinched Calliope—biting it, digging her sharp claws into it.

He jumped up and screamed, waving his hand, Miss Furrington's white coat and tail swaying like a large fluffy muff.

"Miss Furrington!" cried Grandmama, darting forward to retrieve the cat.

"Oh no!" cried Penelope, jumping to her feet, as well.

"Damnation!" muttered Preston. He grabbed the cat, who clung tighter to William's hand, still hissing. When Miss Furrington was finally coaxed to release her claws, bloody scratches covered William's hand, and he clutched it to his chest, his brown eyes wide and dark. With a guilty satisfaction, Calliope thought he looked quite as he had back then, after Spencer had beat him up.

Miss Furrington leapt from Preston's arms, leaving white fur on his pristine dark coat, and curled up on Calliope's lap, watching William with a warning.

"I am ever so sorry, Huntingham," Grandmama said as she rummaged in her reticule and retrieved a handkerchief. "Miss Furrington is never like this. She must be in distress as Sumhall is her new, temporary home until Lady Calliope marries."

When Richard—Calliope and Preston's brother who had been living at Sumhall with Calliope—had married and left for his honeymoon two days ago, Grandmama and Miss

Furrington had moved in to ensure propriety for an unmarried young lady.

William took Grandmama's handkerchief and wrapped it around his hand, staring at Calliope with barely hidden anger.

"You must have your physician look at your hand," said Calliope, staring at him directly and stroking the warm, soft fur of her little defender. "Right away."

He didn't look away, drilling her with a now positively murderous gaze.

"No," he said, taking his seat. "Something as minuscule as a cat's scratches won't dissuade me from my mission."

"I do apologize, Huntingham," said Preston, going to the servants' bell and pulling it.

"Nonsense," said William. "Do not think twice of it."

Grandmama took her place as well, her sharp gaze on Calliope and on Miss Furrington. "That cat surely does love you, dear," she murmured.

"Let us return to the question your brother had asked, Lady Calliope," insisted William. "What are your thoughts on renewing the friendship between our families?"

"Friendship is one matter," Calliope said. "As of 'deeper ties,' brother, don't you think we should wait until Spencer is back before considering such decisions?"

The shadow of Preston's smile fell off his face. Of course, it wasn't clear if Spencer was ever going to be back. It was the spoken agreement within the family that they were treating him as if alive but lost and were doing everything in their power to retrieve him. Should Spencer return, Preston would remain the duke, as the title wasn't reversible, but their family without Spencer was like a body without a limb.

Besides, knowing what had transpired all those years ago, Spencer would never let William marry her.

William's face paled, and the intense clawlike gaze was

wiped from his face. "Is your brother not...dead? Forgive me for such an indelicate question."

"We're sure he's alive," said Calliope, giving William the coldest stare she could muster. "And we're looking for him."

"So you do not know if he is alive or dead? Or where he is?" asked William.

"We do not," said Preston. "But, as my sister said, we're doing everything we can to retrieve him. And, Calliope, I don't think we need to wait for Spencer's return to make decisions about your future. I know you don't wish to find a husband, but Huntingham is not a stranger. You've known him your entire life. Were you not friends before?"

Calliope raised her eyebrow at William. "Indeed, we *were*. Every year we spent summer months all together, given that the marquess is the same age as Richard."

"Then I am sure I could persuade you to change your mind," said William, his stare on her again. "To be friends again. To forget the misunderstanding."

He was lying. She could practically smell the judgment, the resentment, the mocking amusement. She could not understand for the life of her why someone like him, a marquess, rich and noble, would want to marry a girl he'd once called a whore.

Calliope swallowed hard, refusing to allow herself to show any weakness to him, despite her blazing cheeks.

"For instance," continued William slowly, "we could once again connect over our mutual love of books. Is your library here at Sumhall as well stocked as in Grandhampton Court?"

Calliope's throat was suddenly so parched it hurt. Her cheeks were ablaze.

"I didn't realize you were interested in books," said Preston. "Did you know that, Calliope?"

Calliope's back was drenched in sweat. The weight of Miss Furrington on her lap didn't feel reassuring anymore.

"No," she said. "I never knew Huntingham was interested in reading."

"Are you quite all right, darling?" asked Penelope quietly. "You look so pale."

He made her this paling, cowardly person she was not going to be. One word spoken by him at the most intimate and vulnerable moment of her life had broken her. Could he still have such power over her fourteen years later?

She wouldn't let him. She had control over her life, and she wouldn't allow him to rob her of it.

A little too abruptly, she removed a protesting Miss Furrington from her lap. Free of the little protector, she stood up, hating herself for being unable to confront William, and resorted to flight.

"Indeed, I am unwell, sister," Calliope said. "You must forgive me, Huntingham. I will be quite busy in the next weeks. In fact, I will probably leave London. I wish you every success with your search for a wife who, sadly, will not be me."

Feeling like she was a witch being chased away by the Holy Inquisition, and under the shuffle of Preston's and William's feet as they leapt up, she hurried out of the drawing room and up the stairs to her bedroom.

This was serious, she thought as she pumped her legs, climbing the seemingly endless stairs to the next floor. She couldn't tell Preston about William's behavior in the past as she couldn't face him thinking so poorly of her for reading such a book at a young age.

Her only option to avoid William and ensure he wouldn't blackmail her into marrying him was to find Spencer as soon as possible. Not only to protect her, but also to save Spencer from whatever mortal danger he may be facing.

And to locate him, she needed to go to Nathaniel at the Admiralty and ask him to help her find information on where Spencer could be and what could have happened to him.

And she needed to do that right away.

She stopped on the stairs and looked down. What better time than when she felt "unwell" and they would leave her alone to recover? She turned around and descended the stairs, sneaking out of the house before even Teanby, their butler, would notice.

2

As eight pairs of male eyes landed on Calliope, she wondered for the first time if, perhaps, she had made a mistake coming to the Admiralty alone. The low, male rumble of laughter and talk had gone silent when she'd opened the Conscription Office door.

All of them were quite dashing, dressed in dark navy uniforms with golden braids. Two sat at large mahogany desks covered with papers, inkwells, and heaps of ledgers. Six others gathered in a group in the aisle between two rows of desks, some standing, some leaning against the tabletops.

Calliope pressed out a confident smile, throwing a quick glance over the large room.

The walls were adorned with charts and flags and oil portraits of naval heroes and commanders, and the windows offered a view of the busy streets outside. The smell of ink and paper and male sweat filled Calliope's nostrils. Three large bookcases were crowded with leather tomes and nautical instruments like sextants, compasses, and telescopes. Several ship models stood on the shelves.

She must be the sole female in the huge building, where navy soldiers and officers lived in barracks, trained, ate, slept, and did other manly things. The thought made her stomach quiver with uneasiness.

Damnation. She'd been in such a hurry to get away from William and resolve the problem of his marriage intentions that she had been quite impulsive. She shouldn't have come alone, after all. An unmarried lady without a chaperone... If this came out, it would damage her reputation in the ton and harm her family's reputation, as well.

On the one hand, damaging her prospects could play well for her, as it would make William less inclined to pursue her. And she didn't care about her marriage prospects in any event —she would never rely on a man or trust someone enough to give them control over her life.

However, a poor reputation would mean exclusion from important social circles, and that would be highly inconvenient once she would open her investigative agency and would need easy access to exclusive information.

But however risky this was, coming here alone, she couldn't wait any longer to recover Spencer.

Boots heels clicked against marble floor as officers stood at attention, and the relaxed faces changed into polite social masks hiding the questions underneath.

"May I help you, my lady?" asked one of the officers. "Are you lost? Is your husband...or your chaperone...somewhere near?"

Her gaze dropped to the one man who wasn't paying her any attention, and her whole being melted, goddamn it, just as it had a few days ago at the Royal Navy ball when he'd danced a waltz with her, and she'd been in his strong, muscular embrace, inhaling his scent.

What a stark contrast from William.

Nathaniel Fitzgerald, Duke of Kelford, sat at a desk and kept scribbling with his pen over paper. His golden hair was gathered in a tail at the base of his head, just as it had been at the ball a few days ago, his broad shoulders like boulders as he wrote. His chiseled face made her wonder for a fleeting moment if he was not a Greek statue come to life.

Back at the ball, his eyes had been on her as they had danced...it was like being in the presence of a sun that had shone just for her. The timbre of his voice...the way he had talked to her...it was as though no one else existed for him.

But she knew better than to fall for those charms. He was a rake. Her brothers had warned her about him, and they were right. He probably talked like that with every woman, with that velvety, deep voice as smooth as the best French brandy.

"My lady?" asked the officer, and she reluctantly tore her eyes off Kelford.

Calliope squared her shoulders, looking straight into the officer's eyes. Perhaps William had shaken her, but she needed to remind herself she was more than a cowering little girl. She was fearless. She was about to start a business, and she was ready to turn over the world to find her brother.

She thought quickly. None of them, besides Kelford, knew who she was or even if she was married, or indeed, with a chaperone.

"I'm not lost," she said with her head high. "And my chaperone—"

She was just about to say her chaperone was going to join her when another officer, as tall as a column, leaned down to his friends and murmured, "Yet another one can't stay away from Kelford."

Her cheeks blazed. Of course Kelford was a charmer, and he'd never be interested in someone like her. She was probably just a lady to toy with, to see how quickly he could seduce a bluestocking. She'd rather spend her time with a good book than dancing quadrilles at balls, walking on Bond Street or in Hyde Park, trying to be seen and noticed.

At that, Kelford raised his head and their eyes met. A mixture of expressions flitted across his face. Pleasant surprise. Puzzlement. Then, finally, extreme displeasure.

He rose from his desk, tall and majestic, with his golden hair and the braids of his uniform a striking contrast against the dark navy of his coat.

"Lady Calliope," he said. "Is one of your brothers joining you?"

"I have a quite urgent matter to discuss. May I speak with you?"

The rest of the officers cackled and snickered like children.

Kelford threw a deadly glare at them. "Leave the lady alone and return to serving your country."

They stopped snickering and busied themselves with something at their desks. Nathaniel, no matter how dashing, no matter how gorgeous, may be the key to finding her brother and giving her freedom from William.

She walked deeper into the room, her small heels clacking against the marble as she navigated among the heavy desks, and towards him.

"I need your assistance, Kelford," she said as she stood before him, and oh dear lord, he smelled just like he had at the ball—something earthy and herbal and fresh. She had the strange urge to press her mouth to his skin to see if he'd taste just as delicious. "When we met, I wasn't aware you served in the Conscription Office—"

He stared down at her with his breathtaking turquoise eyes, an unusual mixture of green and blue, with a burst of gold around his pupils. Just like the sea on white Scottish beaches.

"Lady Calliope, you shouldn't be here." He stretched his arm to the door. "You should leave. If you please..."

She raised her chin. "My eldest brother, Spencer, the eleventh Duke of Grandhampton—we learned that he was most likely conscripted into the navy during one of the raids. It was September 3, 1812, and I need your help to discover which ship he may be on."

He frowned. "Forgive me, but wasn't he dead?"

"We all thought so, but we were incorrect. We now believe that he was press-ganged onto one of your ships."

Nathaniel chuckled. "My lady, you are confused. What you're proposing is inconceivable. A duke wouldn't be press-ganged."

"Do you authorize press-gangs?"

"I do."

There was something disturbing about a law that allowed anyone to be forced into a war regardless of station, but that was another matter altogether. Right now, she needed to concentrate on just one victim.

"And you're certain you haven't signed that authorization?" she inquired.

The chuckle around his lips deepened, and he looked her over in such a way that her corset felt tighter. "You little admiral," he murmured. "Demanding things you have no right to. But I sympathize with your brother's situation. If one of my sisters disappeared, I'd come storming any establishment."

The rake had sisters he'd do the same thing for. Who would have thought?

"But I will reply, and once I do, do you promise to leave? I care about your reputation, even if you do not. Coming unchaperoned to seek out a man like me may land you in *The Society* by tomorrow morning if you're not careful."

"I do not care about *The Society* or the papers. I care about my brother."

He tapped with his finger against the surface of the desk he stood next to, burning eyes steady on her. "Well, I don't remember signing that one."

She blinked. "That is your reply? You don't remember?"

He shrugged with one shoulder. "I don't remember every authorization I sign."

She suppressed a gasp. "How can you not remember signing a paper that defines the lives of six hundred men?"

The other officers threw curious glances at her and at Kelford.

Kelford narrowed his eyes at her. "How do you know it's six hundred?"

She straightened her back. "I read. So should you, sir. And especially, you should read what you sign."

His previously cautious expression turned into pure threat. But she wouldn't let him intimidate her.

"What else should one expect from a notorious rake than a lack of responsibility?" she continued.

He glared at her with the ferocity of a thousand suns. The other officers had all stopped and were openly staring now. The tall one let out a few stifled snickers.

"Lady Calliope," said Kelford, his voice low and intoxicating, "you should not be lecturing me about my reputation when your own is in grave danger. Why does neither of your brothers come and inquire after this information? Perhaps you should take your own advice and read a little more about a proper lady's behavior."

Despite herself, heat blasted across Calliope's cheeks. A familiar sensation of fiery humiliation licked through her.

Whore, William's voice rang in her head. Another man was

about to humiliate her, make her feel small and worthless, make her feel dirty.

But she'd be damned if this would be all it took to have her back down from finding her brother. Spencer's life was on the line.

"Kelford," she said, pushing down her embarrassment, "just look up that date. September 3, 1812."

"No." He crossed his arms over his mighty chest. "There's no reason for it. Your brother, who was duke then, couldn't have been press-ganged."

Anger rolled through her body like thunder. This was hopeless.

"This is not over," she said, throwing as deadly a glare as she could muster at Kelford. "Good day."

With that, she turned around and walked out of the office, Kelford's gaze burning holes in the back of her spencer. She took her pocket watch from her reticule. Another unladylike thing—having a pocket watch. She found it much more convenient than pendant watches ladies wore.

It was almost four in the afternoon. The Admiralty would close in about one hour. If Kelford wouldn't help her, she'd do it herself. After all, that would be the kind of investigative work she'd need to do for her clients once she'd opened her business.

She walked out of the Admiralty and got into the carriage she had hired to bring her here. She watched for an hour as officers left the building one by one or in groups. Finally, when a large group was leaving close to five o'clock, she got out of the carriage and, as nonchalantly as she could, walked back in. The two officers on guard didn't stop her.

Her low heels clacked against the smooth marble tiles as she climbed the great stairs up to the first floor. She saw a gentleman leave a room next to the Conscription Office and walk away in the opposite direction from her. Before the door closed, she rushed forward and stopped it, then sneaked in.

The room was blessedly empty. Through a slit between the planks of the wall, she watched the officers leave the Conscription Office, and then Kelford's tall figure. With an effortless, graceful masculine swagger, he walked away.

For a moment, she forgot her anger as she watched his broad back—no doubt, mountains of muscle rolled under that dark navy fabric, and she remembered the feel of his hard arms under her palms as they danced.

This is not the time to turn into a swooning debutante!

"Stubborn, arrogant man," she muttered.

He turned his head a little, and she felt her heart jump, afraid he'd heard her. But he couldn't have.

When he resumed walking, she sighed out a long breath of relief. After another five minutes, no one was coming or going from any offices on this floor, and Calliope opened the door as quietly as she could.

Stepping softly, she went to the Conscription Office. She cracked the door open and peered inside.

No one.

She slipped inside and looked around. There was Kelford's desk with stacks of ledgers, papers, and maps. She approached the desk and opened the first ledger. Letters...names... addresses...for last month. His handwriting was masculine. Precise. Beautiful. So much more readable than her own. She admired the small, pretty, ornamental tails of his letters *g* and *j*.

She flipped through the ledger. More names and addresses, but all were for this month and last month. And there were no ship names whatsoever. She sighed in frustration, picked up the heavy ledger, and put it aside.

A distant echoing knock of something against stone made her freeze and listen, her back growing damp with sweat.

Seconds ticked by, but no more sounds came. After a couple of minutes, she put down the second ledger and opened the third one. February...better, but still not right...

"What the devil are you doing here?" said a now-familiar, brandy-smooth voice, and when she looked up, the Duke of Kelford stood in the door frame, blocking any hope of escape.

3

THE INFURIATING female was gaping at Nathaniel from behind his desk, one of his ledgers open in front of her. Her beautiful eyes were wide, her delicious, plush lips parted. And a rosy blush crept over her high cheekbones, the same blush that he remembered from the night of the Royal Navy ball. When they had danced that waltz and she was all breathless in his arms.

He had been breathless, too, afraid to spook that creature of lush auburn hair and big, intelligent blue eyes.

Her fingers still lay on the pages of the ledger. "I—" she said. "I—"

"You sneaked in here after you promised to leave," he said, letting his voice roar as he marched towards her, maneuvering between the desks. "I knew you'd be trouble."

She shook her head, a single wavy auburn curl falling onto her flushed cheek, and straightened her back, her chin raised high. Every bit a duke's sister, proud and well-bred. His own three sisters should take her example, as there was no female in their lives who could teach them.

"What are you doing here?" Lady Calliope demanded

indignantly, as though this was her desk, and he was the intruder. "I thought you were gone."

He went into his drawer and took out a brown leather folder. "I forgot this."

It was a copy of his father's will. Nathaniel was meeting his solicitor in an hour at his home and had forgotten the final payment to Mr. Cadden, the money he'd borrowed from Admiral Robert Langden, an old friend of the family. The man who had sponsored Nathaniel's navy service when Nathaniel had needed him.

Lady Calliope's earlier words were too close to the truth. He wasn't as responsible as he should be, taking care of three younger sisters. Otherwise, he'd have done his duty and found a rich wife years ago.

The Kelford line was, perhaps, not as old as Grandhampton, but it was much, much richer. In fact, had Nathaniel had access to the inheritance his vengeful father had locked in that damned will, Nathaniel would now be the richest man in England. He would own tens of thousands of acres of land, including numerous counties in Wiltshire, Somerset, and London, and have thousands of tenants, including those renting farmland and houses in towns and villages.

The annual income of one hundred thousand pounds and estates worth five million pounds were out of reach thanks to his father's conditions and Nathaniel's refusal to meet them. With access to his fortune, he wouldn't have to come to the Admiralty and write papers all day. He wouldn't sink into gambling debts hoping the next win would finally set him free. He wouldn't need to watch his sisters sew their own clothes, patch and wear their mother's old dresses, and stare at the empty squares left on the walls from paintings he had sold long ago.

Lady Calliope stood a few inches from him, and he couldn't

look away. How could one female be the most impressive he'd ever met and the most annoying one at the same time?

She baffled him with her courage. What well-bred aristocratic lady would dream of sneaking into a building full of hundreds of men? Clearly, she was spirited and stubborn.

"You don't mind, then, if I look through this, do you?"

Like a little fox—the resemblance made even stronger by her gorgeous coloring—she picked up the ledger.

But he was faster. Catching her by the arm, he ripped the ledger away from her graspy fingers, pulling her close to him. Her sweet, small body hit his. She was so close, he could feel the warmth of her smooth skin, could smell her. A delicate, citrusy, and flowery scent...like bergamot, and something spicy, like ginger...and her. Just...indescribable, feminine, delicious. He ached to drink it in.

She was scandalously, scandalously close. He remembered how good it had felt to hold her in his arms as they'd swirled around the ballroom. How much he'd wanted to kiss her.

Not as much as he ached to kiss her now.

"No, madam," he murmured. "You may not have this. In fact, you must leave, and you mustn't come back. Otherwise, I will be forced to tell your brothers." Her eyes widened in concern, and he knew his guess was right. The little fox was here without their knowledge or consent.

She swallowed hard, and he watched her delicate neck move. He wondered how her skin would feel under his lips. Warm. Smooth. Like a petal.

They were alone. He could just lean down and taste her.

Why wasn't she protesting? She was enjoying it, as intrigued by him being near as he was by her. Her chest rose and fell quickly. Her full lips were parted. And that gorgeous blush tinged her cheeks. Her pupils were dilated. Oh, she was just as affected as he was.

"Don't tell my brothers," she said, her voice like honey. "They'd lock me up and not allow me to investigate. They'd put me on a tight leash."

"Tell me, Lady Calliope...do you like to be a naughty girl?"

His cock liked the thought of her spread naked under him, just for him.

She parted her lips, speechless. Perhaps she felt him harden against her as her eyes widened.

Only, unfortunately, it wasn't lust he saw now.

It was embarrassment. And fear.

She pushed him away and rushed back so fast, she slammed against the desk behind her. A spyglass rolled from the desk and fell onto the floor with the unmistakable sound of shattering glass. He watched her in astonishment as she glared at him like a cornered, hunted animal.

"Back off, sir," she said through gritted teeth.

He cursed under his breath. She was a virgin, no doubt. Of course she was confused and shocked by his body's reaction. He'd forgotten how delicate virgins were. He didn't take virgin lovers on principle. The women he took were experienced and very willing.

"Your rakish ways won't work with me," she said. "You do not behave like a gentleman. You won't affect me like you do all those other women."

With her head high, she marched towards the door, her heels clicking against the floor.

As he watched her depart, her body swaying under her thin white muslin dress, he shook his head. Part of him regretted her leaving his proximity. But it was better, anyway.

As soon as she was gone, he realized he needed to investigate what she had been looking for.

She'd said the third of September 1812. He could look up any orders he'd signed for that date. Putting the folder with his father's will down, he went to the bookshelf with the ledgers for the last year, found the one for September, and looked through the dates one by one. There was a page missing.

He looked at the door again. No, that couldn't be right.

He looked at the whole ledger again, one document at a time, hoping perhaps it was misplaced and out of order.

But after looking through twice, it was clear to him.

The page for September 3 was not there.

Had Lady Calliope taken it?

He'd call on her tomorrow and learn the truth. As he put the ledger back onto the shelf, he realized he'd very much look forward to seeing the little fox again—seeing that gorgeous blush on her cheeks, inhaling her scent.

He picked up the brown leather folder and walked towards the door. Her scent lingered in the room, and he shamelessly took a lungful of it, craving every last drop.

4

Half an hour later, Nathaniel dismounted and, with a sinking feeling in his gut, walked his horse out the back of Roxburgh Place. Today was his twenty-ninth birthday, and the final day that would tell him if the will could be overturned and he could finally provide his sisters with the lives they were always supposed to have.

Unlike many houses even in Mayfair, which were row houses, this beautiful mansion stood separately with its own mews, an entire carriage house, stables, and even a small workshop. Also unlike the homes of his neighbors, which were well maintained, almost pristine, Roxburgh Place was in desperate need of repair. The stonework of its classic architecture was crumbling. Window frames had white paint chipping off and falling away. Some of the glass panes were missing or broken, cracks running through like large spiderwebs. He could see the holes in the roof over the three-story building, where his housekeeper-cook-maid used buckets, basins, and pots, if there were any available, to catch dripping water any time it rained or snowed.

As Nathaniel closed the heavy gates, the joyous barking of his three dogs erupted from the mews. Large paws thumped against the ground, growing closer, and then three bodies jumped on him, slamming him into the gates behind him.

Hermes, the stallion he'd won in one of his attempts to salvage his financial situation, neighed and stepped back as the three dogs licked Nathaniel's face, stinking of hound.

"Hello, boys." He laughed, turning his head to the side in a futile attempt to avoid Argos's wet tongue. The black mastiff could almost reach his face, and was leaping higher to make up the distance. "I'm glad to see you, too, but...Argos, you're going to hurt yourself. And Orion and Cerberus, you two still haven't learned any manners, either, have you? Sit. Sit."

Reluctantly, the three dogs let go of him and put their behinds on the ground, watching him, ears upright, tails wriggling, dust rising in small clouds from the cobblestone mews that no servants had swept in months.

Cerberus, although named after the three-headed dog guarding the underworld, as his ability to scent was as good as three regular dogs combined, was the smallest one of the trio, a beagle with one brown ear split in half. Nathaniel had found him dirty, beaten, and shivering, hiding under a carriage on a rainy October day.

The final dog, Orion, was a white mutt—some mix of setter, spaniel, and hound, Nathaniel suspected. He was medium-sized, with a body made lean and agile by the demands of street life and a gorgeous bushy tail. His floppy ears framed a face that was disarmingly expressive, capable of shifting from mischief to longing within moments. When Nathaniel had been invited to the Harmony of Roses annual soirée last year, the dog had somehow wandered right into Lady Brewster's rose garden full of elegant ladies and gentlemen. He was shooed out of the garden with kicks and yells by the footmen, but something about seeing the poor beast being chased away like that had spoken to Nathaniel.

So he'd left the soirée and taken the mutt in.

Finally, Argos... He had a special bond with Argos. Two years ago, after Nathaniel had stumbled out of Portside where he'd fought a boxing match for money, and won, he sat leaning against the wall of the building, breathing through the pain from various bruises. He'd heard whining, and when he looked up, four thugs had been kicking and yelling at the black mastiff.

"You worthless piece of shit, you were supposed to win! You lost us all money! Why are you so huge when you can't win!" yelled one of them as he retrieved a wooden plank and hit the dog with all his might. The dog had yelped and fallen unconscious.

Nathaniel had taken him home and nursed him back to health.

These were the three protectors he trained and cared for so that they could guard his sisters while he was away.

It was hard to keep them fed, but he couldn't let go of the three beasts. He loved them with his whole heart. Hermes was another luxury he couldn't really afford, and his groom, Joshua, was also the butler, valet, and footman.

"Good boys," he said as he patted their heads. "Did the girls feed you?"

"Of course we fed them, brother," said Hazel as she climbed down the stairs from the servants' entrance at the back. Hazel, the eldest of his sisters, was seventeen, with Mama's lovely brown hair.

Bustling blond twins, Poppy and Violet, followed their sister. They both resembled him, with their hair like polished gold, the only inheritance they'd received from his wretched, vengeful papa. They were identical twins but were easily distinguished by Violet's spectacles.

"Where have you been, brother?" demanded Poppy. "Mr. Cadden has been waiting for you for one hour." She bounced up and down on her heels, with Cerberus bouncing up and down with her, as well.

He was glad Cadden hadn't left despite Nathaniel being so late because of his blue-eyed, document-stealing fox.

"And then we have your birthday cake!" declared Violet as she picked up a stick and threw it into the opposite corner of the courtyard. All three dogs sprinted after it. "We made it ourselves as Mrs. Nicholson said she didn't have time to do it as she was busy with dinner."

Hazel sighed. "She thrust a cookbook into my hands and told us to just bake the cake. But we didn't have all the ingredients, and I didn't know if the oven was too hot or not...so it's slightly burned."

Nathaniel's chest tightened. "Thank you, Hazel, I'm sure it's going to be delicious." Though Violet had said, "We made it," he knew the twins had probably hindered more than helped.

What he wanted to say was that she was Lady Hazel, the sister of a duke, and she shouldn't be cooking at all. She shouldn't be helping Mrs. Nicholson with washing, cooking, shopping, and housekeeping. All because of his papa's will, forcing Nathaniel to behave like Papa wanted him to even after he was long dead. Only a man like Papa could control the destiny of several people from beyond the grave.

And today he was nine and twenty, and had only one year to claim his rightful inheritance. He was out of time.

"Let me go and not keep Mr. Cadden waiting for me any longer," he said. "Hazel, could you please ask Joshua to take care of Hermes?"

"I wanted to be present at your meeting," said Hazel. "Perhaps he found a solution."

Violet's eyes sparkled. "And then we can finally come out!"

Nathaniel sighed deeply. "You aren't supposed to come out for a while, girls. You are only fifteen."

"Some come out at fifteen!" declared Poppy.

"But even if we don't, Hazel should!" said Violet.

Hazel rolled her eyes. "I, for one, do not want to."

Nor could she with manners like that. It was his fault, once again. With their mama deceased and no money to hire a proper governess. Not that he had even tried.

"I don't care about coming out," said Hazel. "I just don't want you to imprison some rich woman into a marriage she doesn't want. Like I wouldn't want to be imprisoned."

Nathaniel sighed. "Girls, please go and find Joshua. I have to see Mr. Cadden. He has waited long enough. I'll see you later for dinner."

He patted the dogs, who had returned with the stick, and climbed the crumbling stone stairs leading up to the servants' entrance into the mansion. He walked down the long stone hallway, the soles of his shoes echoing off the wooden floor. Several doors lined the corridor, and he saw Mrs. Nicholson through the open door to the kitchen as she stood with her back to him, stirring the stew. The small, latched door next to it was the pantry, and the wider archway opened into the laundry area. There was no hum of activity that underpinned the life of the grand house like Nathaniel remembered from when he had come to the kitchens for a snack as an adolescent.

The aroma of the simple stew reached him. They had been eating stew—and not much else—for years now, as Mrs. Nicholson was not a great cook. But she had done her best to keep them fed after he'd had to let the cook go. The rest of the rooms were quiet, though this part of the house was big enough to accommodate a full staff of at least thirty people.

Nathaniel went through the door leading to the family quarters. The lack of portraiture was evident, stark patches on the walls indicating where majestic oil paintings had once been.

He strode through the grand entrance to the vast chamber that had once hosted elegant dances and high society gatherings. The chandelier hanging high above his head was missing several crystal pendants, their loss casting erratic shadows across the worn floor. The room was completely empty; even the curtains were gone. He remembered how full it used to be when his mama had hosted events here, glittering with light reflected from crystals and mirrors, as well as diamonds, rubies, and sapphires on the guests.

When he entered the drawing room, Mr. Cadden had already stood up, picking up the stack of papers from the tea table. A man in his fifties, he had a balding head of gray hair, small spectacles, and a round belly.

This room felt bare, too, considering its large size. Only a two-seat sofa and a single high-back chair stood there. All three were threadbare, their patterns a ghost of their former vibrancy. On the windows, the absence of velvet drapes allowed the afternoon sunlight to illuminate the room, the dust particles dancing in the golden rays. The place where the pianoforte should have been stood empty. There was no coal in the grate in the fireplace. No table to play cards. No paintings to look at as ladies and gentlemen had tea or read to each other.

Nathaniel could still see how beautiful and dignified this house had been and should be. And he wanted to make it so again, for his sisters. He wanted to be able to dress them in the finest fashions, see them as well treated and as well fed and happy as princesses.

"Ah, Your Grace," Cadden said, a deep frown pulling down his jowly face. "I didn't think you'd come. I can't stay much longer, in any event."

"I apologize. Something urgent kept me." His own forgetfulness...and then the gorgeous, infuriating little vixen. "I have your payment." He went into the pocket of his uniform and retrieved the banknotes, laying them on the tea table in front of Cadden. "Please tell me you have come with good news."

Cadden gave him a deep sigh and looked at the papers in his hands. "I'm afraid not, sir."

Nathaniel's heart sank. "What? Not at all?"

Cadden sighed. "I know how much you wanted this."

Nathaniel's stomach dropped into his heels. "You said there was a loophole. You said we could deem my father's requirements upon his heir illegal."

Cadden nodded. "I did. But I failed. Your father's lawyers were very skilled. The will is ironclad."

Nathaniel cursed. Desperate rage rushed through him in a prickly, white-hot wave. He clenched his fists, itching for a vase or something to smash to hell.

All this money, all the nights when he'd fought in the ring for money, all the rich widows he'd prostituted himself for, all the bets he'd made in rough establishments had been for nothing.

"I could have married someone by now," Nathaniel rumbled. "I could have fathered an heir. All these years, Cadden, for nothing."

Cadden nodded. At least he had a decency to look sheepish when he had just basically destroyed Nathaniel's sisters' futures. "I understand how frustrating this must be for you, Your Grace. You gave me until your twenty-ninth birthday to resolve this legally and find a way to overturn the will. But please remember, I never guaranteed you that result. You simply must be married and have fathered an heir within one year."

Nathaniel slumped down onto the sofa, which gave a dangerous creak. He hid his head in his hands, his fingers digging into his long hair. Desperation clenched his whole being in a cold vise.

"The heir must be born within one year," said Nathaniel. "Which means, I only have three months to find a wife and get her pregnant. Or my sisters and I will be forced to sell this house, the last thing we have of value. My sisters don't deserve this. They will be destined to live like paupers for the rest of their lives."

It was like being a thirsty man next to a trough of water and not being able to take one sip.

The money was there.

He just couldn't touch it.

"It looks like your father achieved what he desired," said Cadden. "He forced you to marry and have a family. I must confess, I've always wondered why you went through such an effort to avoid marriage when it could solve everything. I'm married and have children. Most people are. Why would it be so bad for you, Your Grace?"

Nathaniel's mind raced to the day that had changed his whole life. The day his mother had died because of him. The day he had realized he couldn't protect people.

"It would not be bad for me, Cadden," he said somberly. "It would be bad for them."

5

Two days later…

"What the devil were you thinking, sister?"

Preston stormed into the drawing room of Sumhall. Grandmama looked up from her cards and followed him with her eyes, a single eyebrow raised. Miss Furrington, who lay in a furry ball right on the card table, lazily observing Calliope and Grandmama's game, raised her head, the tip of her tail twitching.

Uneasiness stirred in Calliope's gut. After she'd left the Admiralty, she'd thrown herself into research, finding old papers with the news from both fronts, and looking through all the books she could find in Sumhall's library on naval ships and warfare. But, although she now knew about the overall course of both wars and had more general knowledge about the navy, nothing had given her a single clue about where Spencer could be.

She wished she knew more about Spencer's claim that he

was being followed. But he'd only mentioned it to Richard in passing a short time before his disappearance, and there were no more details to follow up on.

The only way to make any progress was to go back to the Admiralty and find those ledgers.

"If it's about Huntingham," she said, "or any other lord you have in mind, I'm not interested in marriage."

Grandmama laid her cards on the table, picked up the teapot, and poured more tea into their cups, adding one for Preston. Miss Furrington sniffed the air and stared at the elegant milk jug, which Grandmama closed with a lid. "Preston, dear, I know you mean well, but I can't help but agree with Calliope. She did tell you."

Preston pinched the bridge of his nose. "That is not what I'm talking about. Although now you may *have* to marry Huntingham." Preston sighed and looked at Grandmama. "I didn't want to mention this in front of you."

Grandmama's face lost all humor. "Then you should most definitely do so."

"Calliope," Preston said as he came closer to her, "the truth is, you really should be looking for a husband. And Huntingham, whom you have known you since you were a girl, will be more inclined to dismiss the gossip about you."

"What gossip?" demanded Grandmama.

Calliope didn't care about gossip, but she had a suspicion what it might be.

Preston took the third chair at the table. "There's talk among navy officers that the Duke of Kelford may have ruined Calliope."

Grandmama gasped, and Calliope suppressed a curse. Preston had heard that after only two days? She hadn't thought it would spread so quickly. She'd hoped the officers would forget about her visit as soon as she left—surely, they had more important things to do than gossip. Apparently, she was wrong.

"I remember you danced with the man," said Grandmama. "But ruined?"

Preston glared at Calliope. "I know you're not ruined. You know better than that. The whole thing is ridiculous. They say you came to see him in the Admiralty alone. That can't be right, can it, Calliope? You wouldn't be so naive."

Calliope raised one eyebrow. "I wasn't naive. But yes, I was in the Admiralty because I was lost."

Preston shook his head with a low grumble. "You were lost? What are you talking about?"

She laid the cards on the table and shrugged one shoulder. "I was. And I was looking for directions."

Preston scoffed. "Who gets lost and goes to the Admiralty for directions?"

Calliope shrugged and fingered the cards lying on the table. "Whyever not? Who else would help out a lady than the officers?"

"Do you think I believe you?"

"Preston, please, stop growling or you will turn into a wolf."

Grandmama snickered.

Preston let out a long puff of air. Oh, he was livid, his dark eyes glistening like ripe cherries.

"Please, sister, this is not a sleuth novel. This is serious. I went to the Admiralty, too, to ask for the records of ship departures, so you do not have to lie about your reason for going there."

Calliope tensed, suddenly feeling quite silly. "Did you find out anything?"

"No. They wouldn't allow me to look at the records. But if I wasn't successful, neither would you be. I will ask for an introduction to Admiral Langden himself through my connections. So you shouldn't be worried about any of it at all. You should be going to balls and meeting other eligible bachelors, if the Marquess of Huntingham isn't to your liking."

Calliope was seething inside. "Balls? Meeting bachelors? You know me better than that, Preston."

"Sister," Preston said tightly, "I don't think there's a man on earth who's worthy of the tip of your little finger, but it is my duty to see to your future and your safety. Until now, your reputation has been pristine, and your fortune, as well as our family's standing, make you a desirable bride. You should be able to marry well."

Calliope felt so helpless. Was she not allowed to make decisions about her own life? She stared at Grandmama. "And what do you have to say about this?"

Grandmama sighed. "Dearest, I moved into Sumhall to make sure your reputation remained unblemished, but it appears as if you have sealed your own fate by going to the Admiralty unchaperoned. Perhaps seeing another man would have been fine, but Kelford..."

Preston nodded. "Anything...*anyone* he touches, he ruins."

Calliope's stomach was twisting, bile rising. "I don't care about my reputation. I truly don't want to marry. A chance to find happiness like both you and Richard is very small. I'm not interested in anyone—especially not in Huntingham—and only wish to follow my own course."

Grandmama nodded. "Following your own course is certainly better than being married to the wrong man. Thanks to your generous, deceased papa and Preston, you have an income to enjoy and can pursue your own ambitions. You don't just want to sit back and do nothing like most ladies of the ton."

Grandmama was certainly correct about that. And Calliope

saw inspiring examples of women creating their own destinies. Jane, her new sister-in-law, ran a school and gave lessons. Penelope was learning from great artists and planned to sell her own paintings. Calliope's mama had always taught her to be independent and to think for herself. And she knew exactly what she wanted.

"I want to start my own sleuth agency," Calliope said.

She met Preston's dark gaze with a challenge. Slowly, he shook his head. "I thought you'd grow out of those childish notions."

"I'm quite sincere. It makes sense, really. The Bow Street Runners don't have enough people to investigate crimes. Uncovering the truth and defending oneself in court falls to the victims or the accused and their solicitors if they can afford them. They are often unqualified and don't have time and resources. It's quite a clever business idea, actually. There's a need among the population and few with the skills or inclination to undertake the task."

Grandmama pursed her lips, hiding a smile. "You can't argue with that, Preston. Your own wife is a woman of independent ambitions, and you're the first one to support her. Jane is the same, and Richard never forbade her to run her school. He's providing funds to assist her."

"Exactly," said Calliope. "So why do you support Penelope and Jane and yet restrict me from pursuing my business idea?"

Preston ground his teeth. "For a simple reason, sister. Neither Penelope nor Jane intends to run after dangerous men who steal, kidnap, and, perhaps, even murder. Not to mention the damage to your reputation, which is exactly what happened two days ago. Pick another occupation, and I'll be the first one to cheer you on."

Calliope ignored his tired argument about her reputation. "It does not necessarily have to be dangerous. As a woman, I'll be less suspicious because no one expects a woman to be an investigator. I'll be careful. I'll hire other investigators, too. I'll do things cleverly rather than with force. Besides, Spencer and Richard have taught me boxing and fencing in case it comes to that."

Grandmama scoffed. "She'd do it better than most men."

Just as Preston opened his mouth, no doubt to contradict her, the door opened and their butler, Teanby, appeared. "The Duke of Kelford has come to call."

Sweet tickles ran through Calliope's body, and for a few moments she couldn't breathe. Preston blinked at Teanby as if stunned.

Grandmama gave out a chuckle and looked at Calliope. "Speaking of dangerous men and ruined reputations..."

"Tell him we're not at home," Preston said, then muttered something foul under his breath.

"Tell him he's welcome to come in," said Calliope.

Poor Teanby darted his eyes between her and Preston, and for the first time Calliope could recall, a few drops of sweat broke out on his stately, lined forehead.

"Tell the duke he's welcome to come in," said Grandmama with a calm smile.

Finally recognizing the authority of the woman who'd hired him as a footman so many years ago, Teanby nodded and, avoiding the duke's angry gaze, retreated.

"Grandmama!" said Preston.

Grandmama gave him a look that spoke of power. She had an uncanny ability to illicit both respect and obedience. If Calliope could have one exceptional skill at Grandmama's age, it would be this.

"You do not live here anymore, Preston," Grandmama said. "I do."

Calliope suppressed a chuckle. It was quite a sight to

behold one of the richest and most powerful dukes in England shut his mouth after a single look from his grandmother.

The door opened, and Kelford came in, all tall, muscular, and breathtaking in his dark navy uniform. His turquoise eyes landed on her, and the room blurred and darkened around him. She straightened her back, his very presence sucking all air from the room.

What could he want here? He'd told her he didn't want her anywhere near the Admiralty. He didn't want to help her.

"Good day," said Kelford.

Miss Furrington stared at him with the same wide eyes as Calliope herself, then stood, lazily jumped from the table, and walked towards him. As though he was an old acquaintance, she pressed against his ankles and wrapped her tail around one of his boots. Nathaniel stared at the cat with the most puzzled expression, then he sneezed.

"Pardon me," he said.

Grandmama's eyes twinkled, and she coughed slightly.

"Kelford," said Calliope through a parched mouth. "Please meet my grandmother, the Dowager Duchess of Grandhampton."

Kelford gave a polite nod, meeting Grandmama's eyes. The dowager cocked her head as she looked him over with a hint of female appreciation.

"Pleased to meet you, Lady Grandhampton," said Kelford.

"The pleasure is mine," said Grandmama.

"And, of course, you know my brother," Calliope said.

"Kelford," Preston said through gritted teeth. There was a clear threat in his dark gaze.

"Grandhampton." Kelford nodded.

Kelford came deeper into the drawing room, his chest and shoulders deliciously broad under his uniform. Miss Furrington followed him, and when he stopped, she wrapped the end of her tail around his other boot. He blinked at the cat in confusion, while Preston stared at it as if it was a traitor.

Kelford's gaze locked on Calliope. She begged him with her eyes not to tell them the reason she came to see him two days ago.

"I am quite surprised to see you here," said Preston. "But it may help to gain some clarity, anyway. You see, there's a rumor that I've heard going around polite circles, and if it turns out to be true..."

Kelford's eyes never left her. They held her in their gaze, and they had all the power. Two days ago, he had threatened to tell her brothers. And here he was. Had he come to act on that threat, to tell Preston she broke into the Admiralty and stayed after hours, and that they were, after all, alone?

Please, do not tell him...please don't...

For a very long time, Kelford said nothing, just stared at her.

"It is true," he said finally, reverting his gaze to Preston, "that we saw each other. Lady Calliope was lost. She lost her chaperone, and I helped her find a way."

"Calliope!" Preston practically growled.

"You see, just as I told you, brother. I do not know that area that well."

"Do you think I believe a single word? You? Were lost?" demanded Preston. "You're like a hound—you will find your way anywhere."

"We were never alone," said Kelford. "There were other officers. You have no reason to doubt her reputation."

"But the ton surely does!" said Preston. "What is the reason for your visit, anyway, Kelford?"

Kelford's Adam's apple bobbed as he swallowed, appearing to be at a momentary loss. "Lady Calliope forgot something," he said. "Her umbrella."

"Well?" Preston looked him up and down. "Where is it?"

Kelford looked around himself. "Forgive me, I broke it on the way here. I came to inquire, Lady Calliope, if I may buy you a new one and which is your favorite manufacturer."

That was a great reason. She had to give him credit.

Calliope's heart slammed hard. The way he looked at her made her feel as if her bones were melting. How could a man speak about an umbrella and yet cause her to overheat as though their drawing room was suddenly ablaze? She appreciated that he was in her corner and hadn't betrayed her. He'd kept her secret.

"She can buy her own umbrella," spat Preston.

Grandmama stood up with a mysterious expression on her face. "She can, but I had planned to go shopping on Bond Street, anyway. Calliope, Kelford, would the two of you like to accompany me? Then, sir, you could buy my granddaughter a new umbrella."

When Preston opened his mouth to protest, Grandmama raised a single elegant dark eyebrow. The look that Calliope knew from her childhood—the one that had always managed to stop whatever mischief she and her siblings were up to.

That glare froze Preston and briefly brought out the expression of a naughty boy who was caught.

And all he could say was "As you wish, Grandmama."

6

Nathaniel walked by Lady Calliope's side, meandering among elegantly dressed ladies and gentlemen strolling along Bond Street and filling the air with lively chatter. The dowager walked behind them, at the right distance for a chaperone—close enough to show that she was part of their trio, but not close enough to eavesdrop. Horse-drawn carriages maneuvered past each other, the clip-clop of hooves echoing on the cobblestones.

Luxurious shops displaying the finest wares lined both sides of Bond Street, offering everything from bespoke clothing and hats to exquisite jewelry, high-quality timepieces, and ornate silverware. The rich scent of exotic teas and spices wafted from specialty grocers, while the sweet aroma of French pastries and confections enticed passersby from the windows of exclusive patisseries.

Nathaniel noticed Calliope's gaze linger on the latest publications on offer at a bookshop they passed. She could afford it; any whim she had on this street, she could allow herself. He didn't remember the last time he'd gone shopping here.

And with his last hope of overturning the will dead, his only chance of accessing his fortune and providing for his sisters was to find a wife and to impregnate her as soon as possible. God in heavens, how he hated his father for this.

Anything of luxury, like the dresses his sisters would need to make a proper appearance in the best ballrooms of London, would sink him deeper and deeper into debt.

"We shouldn't miss an accessories shop." Calliope chuckled. "What would I do without that umbrella you broke?"

He chuckled back, warmth spilling through his whole body. Just her presence, just walking next to her did that to him. What a pleasant change from the last two days of dark desperation.

"Your brother wouldn't forgive that umbrella to me."

Calliope threw a careful glance over her shoulder at Grandmama. "So, what is the real reason you called, sir?"

He leaned closer to her, lowering his voice. "To ask you to give back the page you stole. Otherwise, I assure you, I'll get you in enough trouble that your brother won't allow you to see the light of day without his presence."

Calliope frowned. "Page? What page?"

"Please, Lady Calliope. I understand your need to come up with excuses before your grandmama and your brother, but let's not play games between us."

"Kelford, I assure you I didn't steal anything." She looked into his eyes without wavering. "I only looked through two ledgers, and both were for the wrong months, anyway. When I picked up the third one, you came in."

A large gentleman and three ladies walked towards them. The gentleman wasn't looking where he was going and was heading straight for Calliope. The street was so busy, there was no room to avoid being trampled. Nathaniel stepped to his side to shield Calliope from collision and take most of the gentleman's strike on himself. The impact knocked the breath out of him.

"Pardon me!" said the gentleman, but his attention was diverted by something one of his companions said, and he quickly passed by.

"Thank you," said Calliope with a smile that made his heart ache.

They kept walking, and Nathaniel's gaze returned to her. Could he trust her? Was it possible she was telling the truth? The ledger for September had lain where Nathaniel had expected it to lie.

"But that means, if you didn't take it," he said thoughtfully, "someone else did. The page was torn out."

Calliope's eyes sparkled. "See, there's more to it," she blurted. "Someone else must be involved in this whole thing. Before he disappeared, Spencer mentioned someone had followed him..."

Suddenly, Nathaniel very, very much disliked the idea of Lady Calliope being involved in anything where someone had followed a duke and was involved in his alleged death or press-ganging. He had no idea what her eldest brother could have done and what kind of people he could have angered to cause such actions, but whatever it was, Lady Calliope had no business getting mixed up in all this.

"Please, Kelford," she said as she looked up at him, her blue eyes so big and bright, breathtaking against her auburn hair. "Please, help me find out if Spencer really was press-ganged and how and where he may be now."

He swallowed hard. It was almost impossible to say no to that gorgeous face. "Your brothers should be helping you. Why are you so determined to take it on?"

"Because they wouldn't do it as well as I could. Preston already tried but was refused."

"So were you."

She gave him a mischievous smile that made her look like a fox once again. "And yet, here you are."

A growl was born low in his throat but got swallowed by the noise of the street around them. She liked to play with him, and goddamn him to hell, he loved the game. How could this petite beauty be both a scholarly bluestocking and a seductive temptress? Her gazes could be flirtatious, yet she could turn cool and assertive in an instant, never backing away from a challenge. She'd jeopardized her reputation to save her brother. Was it selflessness or sheer madness?

For the last two days and nights, he couldn't stop thinking about her. Every waking moment, he remembered her face and her scent, the warmth of her body as he held her in his arms at the ball and in the office.

He'd never been obsessed with a woman.

And yet, his mind kept coming back to her. He'd even fantasized about her as he'd taken his bath and pleasured himself. Imagined those plush, pink lips on his skin. He wanted more of her. More time with her, all the troubles she may bring him be damned.

"I can help, Lady Calliope," he said, his voice rasping. "But this seems to be a dangerous business you're determined to involve yourself in. If one of my own sisters was so reckless, I'd lock her down and wouldn't let her out of my sight for her own safety. Therefore, I will only help if your brothers do get involved and you step back."

Calliope scoffed. "I can protect myself, sir. Spencer taught me boxing."

Boxing... Something about seeing Calliope, like a warrior woman, with her fists ready to strike, shot another wave of hot desire through him.

"Are you not afraid you'd ruin your reputation? You've

already put it in danger by going to see me alone. Any more of this, and you won't be able to find a husband at all."

"Not you, too. Preston is already trying to force me into marrying, but it's the last thing I want. Unfortunately, my brothers are unlikely to leave me alone. Preston won't back down until he sees me wed."

A woman passed by them, laughing hard, and as her eyes met Nathaniel's, she went silent. It was Lady Seraphina Strefford, one of his previous lovers—a widow he'd done his best to cheer up. She had rewarded him with a jewel that he was able to sell. That had gotten him and his sisters through the next five months. He hoped she did not think poorly of him now. As a widow, she had much more freedom than a young, unmarried lady like the one at his side, whose brothers were determined to find her a husband.

He understood the pressure of external forces governing one's marital decisions. He needed a wife, and now. If he lost his fortune, his sisters would also lose their significant dowries. What a cruel thing his father had done. In his rage and disappointment in Nathaniel, he'd actually punished his own daughters more than he'd punished the son he had hated so much.

And now, not a single mama would allow her unmarried daughter to step near him. His rakish reputation was bad enough, but most mamas were willing to overlook such things when a rake possessed a fortune and had a title.

He had a title, but it was useless with his fortune being tied into an impossible will. He was in a vicious circle. He needed to marry to access his fortune, but he couldn't marry without a fortune. And even if he told a prospective match about the will, not every woman would want a gamble. She may never be able to get pregnant, in which case, all would be lost.

He felt his shoulders sag a little. Then, like a bolt from the blue, a solution so glaringly obvious yet audacious unfurled in his mind. His gaze fixed on Calliope's perturbed expression as she recounted her brothers' persistent meddling. The ton avoided him because of his reputation and lack of wealth... But Lady Calliope cared for neither. Perhaps she was the singular exception in the entirety of England. She wasn't actively husband-hunting, yet circumstances demanded she find one.

If he could propose an arrangement beneficial to both, would she consider it?

And it had nothing to do with the delicious thought of spending every day in her company...of bedding her on their wedding night...and so many other nights. After all, he'd have to try to get her with child as soon as possible.

"Lady Calliope," he said slowly. "I will help you find out what happened to your brother. I know most people in the Admiralty, and those I don't know, I'll find."

"Really?" Calliope bloomed, looking at him with the broadest grin. "You would do that? I knew you weren't as cold-hearted as you tried to appear."

He chuckled. "I'm afraid I am exactly as I appear. I have one condition. Well, two."

She frowned. "What conditions?" she asked, her voice cooling.

"You see, I find myself in need of a wife. And not just a wife, but an heir, too. And, as your brothers are hounding you to find a husband, I imagine we can help each other with that. In exchange for your hand in marriage and your ability to birth my heir, I will not stop until I help you find your brother."

He would need to bed her...a lot. Every night. Multiple times. Kissing her and touching her and making her quiver and squirm from pleasure in his arms... Good God, his loins tightened and swelled in the middle of Bond Street.

So much so that he didn't notice at first that Calliope had

stopped walking and was frozen in place, gaping at him. He walked two steps back towards her, and passersby glared at her because of her sudden stop. She was drawing attention to herself, quite improperly so for a young lady.

"What do you say, Lady Calliope?" he asked as he covertly grasped her elbow to get her moving.

When she resumed her stroll, her eyes were big and darting quickly between his own, her mouth open. Clearly, she was in shock. He imagined it took a lot to shock this feisty little fox.

His breath caught as he waited.

"Heavens..." she muttered. "I never imagined my first marriage proposal would be this..."

"What have you imagined?" he asked. "I realize this sounds like a business proposal. Because it is. I do not need a woman to love. I need a wife who's able to give me a child within one year. And what I offer isn't love, either. It is help that you require to find your brother."

She chuckled, her cheeks reddening. "I understand that. My answer, however, is no."

He hadn't expected her to say yes right away and smiled to himself. He could turn a no into a yes. He'd done it countless times.

"I just do not want a husband," she replied. "I have my own plans, and a husband would surely forbid me doing them, just as my brothers do."

"I am not most husbands, Lady Calliope. Whatever you wish to do, I am sure we can come to an agreement."

"You don't know what you're talking about."

"Perhaps I don't. But I do know your brothers won't leave you alone until you find someone."

She sighed heavily and muttered, "Yes, someone like the Marquess of Huntingham."

Her voice trembled at the name, something about it making a protective part in Nathaniel bristle up.

"Who?" he asked.

"The Marquess of Huntingham. Preston thought he may be a good match."

Something possessive came over Nathaniel. The very thought of another man courting her made his hands curl into fists. "And is he?"

She gave a small scoff. "No."

"So maybe I am."

She stepped aside closer to him to avoid stomping on a small dog darting under her feet. As a gentleman tugged the dog's leash to him, she stepped away from him again. "My brothers do not hold a high opinion of you, Your Grace."

"I am aware. Most of the ton does not. However, once you give me an heir, I will leave you alone. You will have my permission to do whatever it is that you want. Within reason, of course."

She narrowed her eyes at him, attentive. "What is within reason for you?"

"I will not tolerate lovers," he said coldly.

"You will not need to worry about that. It seems there's something about me men find disagreeable."

Disagreeable? Who would find her disagreeable? She may be the most fascinating female he'd ever met in his life.

He could think of only one thing he didn't care for... When she lectured him about responsibility. But even with that, she was annoyingly right.

"But I would not betray my husband," she said. "I take the promises I make very seriously."

He knew she would. She was loyal and kind, or she wouldn't have risked everything to search for her brother.

"Does that mean you're reconsidering my proposal?" he asked.

Calliope looked over her shoulder at Grandmama, who walked ten steps behind them. Grandmama caught her gaze and raised her eyebrow questioningly. If only Grandmama could imagine that Kelford had just proposed to her and was trying to convince her to say yes.

What would she say? And why was Grandmama even helping her at all? Why hadn't she forbidden her to see Kelford just like Preston had? As one of the most influential ladies in London, she knew everything that went on in the ton and knew Kelford was bad news.

Kelford had asked if she was reconsidering...and was she?

The thought of him being her husband both filled her with dread and covered her body with sweet tingles.

Grandmama had once told her in confidence not to marry without love. She knew what it was like. Though, with time, she had learned to love her husband.

Calliope herself had grown up raised by two parents who were incredibly happy. That was, happy enough to produce four children.

But was it only the thought of William as her husband—a thought that filled Calliope with prickly disgust and cold dread—that made standing at the altar with Kelford seem quite appealing?

Of course, she didn't know if Kelford would be the same as William. If he would think her a whore, a woman with disgusting habits. But, from what she knew about rakes, between her and Kelford, it would be he who was much more experienced.

If their genders were reversed, Nathaniel would be condemned as a whore while Calliope would be merely applauded for reading arousing literature and enjoying herself doing it.

"Are you reconsidering?" asked Kelford again, still awaiting her reply.

His face bore no signs of emotion, but his eyes were twinkling, his pupils large and dark. He looked at her as though he didn't see anyone else in the world.

She supposed she was thinking it over. If he didn't object to her investigative agency, having a husband would actually be an advantage. She wouldn't need to worry about her brothers. She wouldn't have to watch her every step guarding her maiden's reputation. She wouldn't need to live with Grandmama anymore... As much as she loved Grandmama and Miss Furrington, it meant needing to take her as chaperone practically everywhere. So inconvenient when one had to sneak into the Admiralty or other places forbidden for ladies.

So, perhaps, there was something about his proposal that made sense.

It was only that thought of having babies with him that filled her with unease. Not the idea of having children per se; she liked children and had always enjoyed the idea of being a mother.

It was the act of conceiving a child that filled her with dread. The memory of that painful pinch on her neck at the very moment when she felt pleasure like bathing in honey, thinking of William...

Logically, she knew the act could be pleasurable. The book said so.

But there was nothing logical in her body's revulsion and fear at the thought of being open and vulnerable like that with a man. The thought of being weak and giving up control.

However her body reacted to the thought of the act itself, she knew that if she had to choose between William and Nathaniel, her choice was clear.

She'd marry almost anyone but William. She'd be safe from his attentions, his advances. She'd never have to see him again. She'd be free from his threats and his blackmail, too.

She'd just have to endure the sex.

And once she gave Nathaniel an heir, she could start her agency.

"You will allow me to do anything I want after I give you the heir?" she confirmed. "Do you promise?"

"Within reason."

"Yes, that is what I meant. And reason being no lovers."

"Yes."

"And you will help me in any way possible to find out what happened to Spencer?"

"Yes. And I will shoot Huntingham from the balcony to make sure he doesn't bother you again."

That made her chuckle, and she bit her lip to stop herself from grinning. "Thank you, but there's no need. If anyone would shoot my suitors, it will be me."

Even though she didn't want to admit it, having a child and a husband were secretly delicious ideas. She did crave the love she'd seen between her parents, the love she'd hoped to have before William King had destroyed that part of her long ago.

She nodded. That was good enough. He still didn't know about the sleuth agency, and he may still thunder when he would eventually find out. But she'd get his promise in writing in their marriage contract.

Her heart slammed hard. Was she really about to agree to get married?

But there was one thing she needed him to promise, too.

"If I'm not to have lovers, neither will you."

He chuckled. "I have a suspicion that once I have my hands on you, that promise will be easy to keep, Lady Calliope."

A warm thrill ran through her. She stumbled over an uneven stone in the sidewalk and Kelford caught her hand and steadied her.

Still, despite just what he'd said, he would likely not be very interested in his role as a husband. Which suited her perfectly.

For Spencer, she thought. This was for Spencer.

She felt like she stood on the edge of a cliff, staring into the dark abyss, about to jump.

"Then, Your Grace, I will marry you."

7

"Calliope, how lovely to see you!" exclaimed Penelope as Calliope entered the sitting room of Newdale Place the next day.

She looked lovely with her glowing face, blushing cheekbones, and shiny eyes. Pregnancy suited her.

With a welcoming smile, Preston jumped to his feet from a blue sofa that echoed the warm pastel-blue walls. Calliope found the drawing room of Preston and Penelope's new place so inviting, with artwork of sunlit, blooming gardens and spring landscapes, most of which Penelope had painted herself. Three large windows let in plenty of daylight. Penelope had carefully picked modern furniture for the room, but several ancestral vases and other art pieces had been brought from Chalworth, the traditional ducal residence of Grandhampton. Chalworth was being repaired after a devastating fire, but it would likely never be the same.

"Lovely to see you, sister," said Preston warmly, his sharp gaze scanning her quickly. "Are you well?"

Oh, Preston's face would lose that smile in a minute, Calliope thought. Nathaniel was just arriving.

It was heartwarming to see her brother and his new wife so happy together. From a man with hard edges who was too quick to bristle and reject people, Preston had turned into a warm, smiling man, and Calliope loved the change.

Calliope was so nervous. She still couldn't believe she'd agreed to get married so spontaneously when for years she'd claimed she wouldn't marry. And now, very willingly, she was going to have a husband.

It was for Spencer, she told herself again. For Spencer.

And she'd be free from William.

"Yes, all is well," she said, forcing out a smile. "I wanted to see you. How are you feeling, Penelope?"

"I'm feeling fine," said Penelope as she gestured for Calliope to take a seat on the sofa across from hers while Preston took his place by Penelope's side. "Preston is worried oil paint fumes may be bad for the baby, but I'm being careful."

Calliope chuckled nervously and glanced at the door. She saw Kelford ride up on a horse and stop behind her carriage. And, heavens, he looked so striking... She'd seen more than a few female heads turn in his wake, both at the ball and during their stroll on Bond Street.

They may turn, but he would be hers...

Something pleasant squeezed in her chest at the thought. Even though he'd never love her, he would still be hers. She would never love him, either, of course. All her feelings towards him were nothing but infatuation...lust, perhaps.

He should reach the drawing room at any moment. She threw a glance at Preston, who was happily ignorant about the visitor and poured tea into a cup for her.

What would he say? What if he refused Nathaniel? And

what would they do then? As the head of the family, Preston was the one to accept or decline any proposals she received. Could she dare marry Kelford even if Preston refused to approve it?

The door to the drawing room opened, and Porter, Preston's butler, entered. "Duke of Kelford."

Just as Calliope had feared, Preston's face fell, and his arm froze with the teacup in his hand. He glared at Calliope. "What is he doing here?"

"May I ask the duke to come in?" asked Porter.

Penelope widened her eyes at Calliope, and Calliope threw her a pleading glance.

"Of course you may, Porter," said Penelope.

Penelope was a good friend. Porter nodded and disappeared behind the door.

"Penelope!" declared Preston. "He shouldn't breathe near Calliope or you, let alone come to pay a visit two days in a row."

"What will happen with such a protective brother as you by your sister's side?" Penelope asked warmly and patted Preston's thigh.

Kelford walked in, and Calliope's breath left her body. Their eyes locked with meaning, and she couldn't feel herself anymore. He'd come here for her. He'd come to ask for her hand in marriage.

It felt...strangely pleasant, heated and tingly, and like she was about to fly up to the ceiling.

Preston slowly stood, his dark eyes intense on Nathaniel.

"Lady Grandhampton." Nathaniel nodded to Penelope. "Grandhampton. Lady Calliope."

"Kelford." Preston nodded. "I thought I was clear yesterday—"

"Preston, where are your manners?" asked Penelope with a slight gasp. "Would you like tea, Kelford?"

“I would.” Kelford nodded. “Thank you. However, before we do, I’d like to ask you, Grandhampton, to talk in private.”

The room held its breath for a moment.

“What about?” asked Preston coldly, shattering the silence.

“About Lady Calliope.”

Preston’s nostrils flared, and his upper lip curled. He threw a furious glare at Calliope. “I do not know what you’re playing at, sister, but I do not like it.”

Then he nodded to Kelford and gestured to the door with his arm. When both men left, Calliope let out a long breath, her stomach in knots. Penelope stood up and came to sit on the sofa next to Calliope. She took Calliope’s hand in hers and squeezed it.

“Whatever it is about, it will be all right. But may I ask if you know what the duke wants with Preston?”

With her heart slamming in her chest, Calliope’s cold palm squeezed Penelope’s warm one back.

“He wants to ask for my hand in marriage,” said Calliope.

Penelope gasped. “Oh, dearest!”

Calliope nodded. She should be indifferent about the outcome of that talk.

If Preston said no, she’d have to seek another way to gather information about Spencer. Perhaps she’d even need to give up her idea to do it by herself and actually involve her brothers.

Would Preston’s introduction to the admiral help with anything at all?

“And do you want Preston to say yes?” asked Penelope.

Calliope swallowed. “I really, really do.”

Because it was better than being married to William.

And it wasn’t just because Kelford would open many doors for her.

It was because the idea of being married to him made

pleasant flutters move in her body. Flutters she kept trying—and failing—to ignore.

~

The decisive thump of Preston's study door echoed crisply behind Nathaniel. As he proceeded deeper into the room, he saw high bookshelves lining the walls, their mahogany surfaces gleaming with reflected daylight. The spines of law texts, military treatises, and Latin classics filled the shelves, their leathery scent mingling with the aroma of fresh wood and beeswax polish.

Daylight streamed in through tall, paned windows, casting long fingers of light onto a large intricately carved desk on which stood only an inkwell, a quill, and a set of brass scales, their facets winking in the sun.

Near the fireplace was a pair of leather-upholstered wingback chairs, their surfaces smooth and plump. The chairs faced each other, a square side table sitting between them.

Preston walked to the desk. "Did she find the new umbrella agreeable?"

Nathaniel turned to Preston. "Yes. Lady Calliope said she did."

"What else is there to talk about regarding my sister, then?"

Nathaniel's stomach churned. He knew Preston wasn't an easy man to impress or befriend. Especially when he was so protective of his sister. Which Nathaniel understood all too well—he'd kill any man who'd look at his sisters in the wrong way.

But he needed Preston to be on his side. He needed him to agree.

Nathaniel walked three steps closer. “With your papa deceased, I have come to you as the leader of your house.”

Preston’s face fell with understanding. He straightened up, his expression threatening. “Oh no,” he muttered.

Nathaniel swallowed hard and braced himself. There was no way back. He needed to ask this. He had to marry Calliope and conceive an heir, or his fortune would forever be lost, and he would never be able to provide his sisters with good dowries and ensure their futures.

This was for Hazel, Poppy, and Violet.

“I’m asking your permission for your sister’s hand in marriage,” said Nathaniel.

Preston launched at him, teeth bared, shoving Nathaniel against the wall. The glasses clunked on the sideboard standing nearby, and paintings knocked loudly against the wood- paneled wall—a small one fell and knocked Nathaniel’s head. Pain burst through his skull.

“You scoundrel,” roared Preston into his face. “You did it, didn’t you? Seduced her? Dishonored her?”

Nathaniel gathered all his willpower to remain calm and to suppress his instinct to fight back. “No. I assure you. Lady Calliope is innocent.”

Preston’s black eyes were wild. “I don’t believe you. I demand satisfaction with a duel.”

“There’s no need for that, Grandhampton. Nothing happened. I find her most agreeable and want to marry her.”

“Do not jest with me. The whole of London knows you’re a rake. Your poor finances are notorious. That is why you’re serving in the navy, even though you’re a duke. You’re a fortune hunter, are you not?”

Nathaniel’s blood boiled. All were true, and all sounded like insults. He needed to calm Preston down. “No. I am not. I have a fortune to my name, which will exceed Lady Calliope’s or even yours. It's just locked in a will. My father wants me to produce a legitimate heir or heiress by my thirtieth birthday. So I will have my own fortune once I accomplish that. I do not require any of Calliope's money if that's your worry. We can have that in the marriage contract."

"You want to use her to get your money. Do not try to fool me."

"That is just one of the reasons, Grandhampton. I am in need of a wife, and I cannot think of a better woman than your sister."

Preston studied him, his expression still murderous. Then he shoved him one last time and let go, walking away from Nathaniel to the other side of the room.

"How have you even gotten to know each other?"

Nathaniel straightened the lapels of his military coat. "We met at the Royal Navy ball. You know that. I could not get Lady Calliope out of my head."

That was entirely true. Lady Calliope had occupied his thoughts ever since.

"One week is not enough for you to have concluded she's the one for you."

"I could see her qualities within five minutes in her company. Anyone with eyes would."

Preston scoffed and glared at Nathaniel, who glared right back. "I will not give you my permission."

"Grandhampton, I assure you—"

"Unless she wants you," he said strictly, but there was an undertone of softness in his voice. "Unless I know there's a chance for her happiness in this match."

Nathaniel swallowed. The glimmer of hope was too small and fragile, but it was there. "There is. I think highly of Lady Calliope and have every intention to ensure her happiness."

Preston marched to the door and stormed out of it. In the

distance, Nathaniel heard him asking for Penelope and Calliope to come with him.

When Lady Calliope and the duchess came in, Nathaniel's gaze locked with Calliope's. She eyed him and her brother carefully and with concern.

"What were you thinking about, sister? You refuse Huntingham, a perfectly respectable gentleman with a sizeable fortune, and instead you wish to marry the most notorious rake in London who has not a penny to his name? Do you seriously think a man like that deserves you and will make you happy?"

Preston was right. Nathaniel wouldn't approve if Hazel were to pick a man like him one day.

And yet, his breath caught as he awaited Calliope's response.

Calliope squared her shoulders and looked at her brother with calm authority. "I appreciate your concern, Preston. Kelford is the right man for me, and I have every belief he will make me happy." Her eyes, the color of the sea, locked with Nathaniel's and something light and wonderful spread through his whole body. "This match is what I want, and I wish for you, brother, to agree to it."

Preston grimaced as he looked at his wife. The duchess came to him and touched his hand. "If your concern is Calliope's happiness, you need to think about our story, yours and mine. We never thought we'd be happy in the beginning, but look at us now."

Preston seemed to melt a little, softness touching his hard eyes. What was their story? Nathaniel wondered.

Finally, Preston turned to his sister. "Calliope," he said calmly and slowly, "is this really what you want?"

Calliope nodded curtly, her back and neck as straight as a bow. "It is."

Preston sighed deeply and met Nathaniel's gaze. "Then, under two conditions, I give you my permission. First, you may not touch Calliope's money. She will have a sizeable dowry, but I will make sure the contract states it stays under her control completely."

Nathaniel nodded. "Fair enough. As I said, I am not after her money."

"Good. Two, if you betray her or make a single minute of her life unhappy, I will find you, and I will make you sorry."

With relief lightening his whole body, Nathaniel nodded. "I would do the same to the men who'd dare to marry my sisters."

8

THE NEXT DAY, Calliope descended the stairs of Sumhall into a bright morning. Grosvenor Street was lined with elegant Georgian town houses, their red brick facades accented with white Portland stone, and their sash windows gleamed as they caught the sun's light.

The street itself was bustling with activity as tradesmen and servants began their daily tasks. Coal merchants delivered their wares to the kitchens of the grand homes, their horses' hooves clopping rhythmically against the cobblestones. A milkmaid in a neat white apron balanced a pail of fresh milk on her shoulder. In the well-tended gardens behind the town houses, the air was full with the scent of roses and lavender. Leaves rustled and birds sang.

Fashionably dressed ladies and gentlemen emerged from their homes, perhaps to embark on a leisurely stroll in Hyde Park or attend a morning social event. The ladies were dressed in their finest muslin gowns. Their bonnets, adorned with silk ribbons and fresh flowers, fluttered in the soft breeze. The gentlemen were resplendent in their tailored waistcoats, well-cut breeches, and shining Hessian boots.

But all that splendor and beauty of the summer morning didn't compare to how her stomach squeezed in excitement at the sight of the simple gig in front of the house and the dashing gentleman in his navy uniform waiting for her.

Now that Calliope and Nathaniel were engaged, they were allowed to appear alone in public, even though they still needed to ride in an open gig to ensure propriety. This meant they could go to the Admiralty together.

As she descended the stairs, he hopped down from the driver's seat. The gig had seen better days, with black paint chipping off the shiny doors and cracked wood peering through. The Kelford coat of arms was in need of a good layer of gilt paint. As Nathaniel stood before her, tall and handsome, her heart pounded hard in her chest. He was so breathtaking in his uniform. All tall and broad-shouldered. Long blond hair. Turquoise eyes. Golden skin...

The devil himself couldn't look more handsome.

"Lady Calliope," he said with a wicked grin. "Still no umbrella, I see."

She hid her smile while biting her lip. "I guess it's hard to find something that didn't exist in the first place."

"Hm," he said as he looked her over with male appreciation. "I do think you need to wear more things that are invisible."

Her face lit up to the roots of her hair, and a wave of heat rushed through her. She stood speechless, unable to find a single word of reply. There was a heat in his gaze, but she knew better than to think he really wanted her. Most likely, this was some sort of a jest, some reference to her sexuality that she didn't understand.

Embarrassment chained her from head to toe. How could

she ever share his bed and try to conceive his heir when the only thing she knew of men was how embarrassing they considered her? How filthy it was for a young girl to explore and think about what went on between a man and a woman in bed?

And that she was wrong to enjoy that prospect at all?

"Pardon me," said a voice next to her, and she turned around.

The wind cutting her heated cheeks like razors, she looked at a young courier standing before her with a rectangular box.

"Is this Sumhall Place?" he asked.

"It is," Calliope replied.

"There's a delivery for Lady Calliope Seaton. I should get this to the butler."

"I'm Lady Calliope," she said, glad of a distraction, trying to calm her ragged breath. "You may give this to me."

It was, of course, unheard of for unmarried ladies to get their own correspondence without a chaperone or a butler having made sure it was safe first. But she was already here. And she didn't think highly of that rule, anyway.

The courier glanced at her, then at Nathaniel.

"You may give it to the lady," said Nathaniel with authority in his voice, and an awareness ran through Calliope.

The young man nodded and handed it to Calliope. When he left, she opened the lid of the box and gasped from a horrid stench that came from within. There was a dry bouquet of flowers with the stems rotting. Next to them lay a note.

"Heavens," she said, through the stench. "It must have stayed rotting in the water for days."

Nathaniel took the box from her hands. "Do not touch it."

With her gloved hands, she reached out and tried to take the box back, but he evaded her.

"Kelford, you're overreacting!" she said with an outraged chuckle. "There's a note addressed to me, and I must see it!"

"It's dangerous, Calliope." A pleasant sort of jolt went through her at how he forgot her formal address and called her just by her given name. "I will open it."

Setting the warmth in her chest aside, she glared at him. "No. It's for me, and you have no right."

She put her gloved hand into the box and tried to snatch the note when Nathaniel quickly moved it aside and once again out of her reach. He grasped the note and put the box onto the driver's seat of his gig.

"Nathaniel!" she cried out.

And only then realized that, just like him, she hadn't used his official name, the one by which she should address him.

Swiftly, he opened the note and read it, paling. Calliope craned her neck.

In a sharp, masculine hand, it said, *Lady Calliope. You must stop digging, for your own good.*

Unease washed over Calliope in a sleek, cold wave. "Does it say who it is from?"

Nathaniel snatched the card away. "No. And if you think I will let you keep investigating, you're sorely mistaken."

She glowered. "What? Your help in this investigation was the whole reason for this. For us." She gestured between them.

"I do not care. Clearly, as I suspected, there's someone who doesn't want your brother to be found, and they know you're digging. You must stop. I'm not taking you to the Admiralty anymore. You're to stay away."

Outrage hit her like a slap, and she took two steps to the gig and laid her hands on the handles and her foot on the step. "No. That is not an option. We agreed. You cannot forbid me anything."

"Calliope!"

She climbed onto the driver's seat and took the reins. "I will not let a silly note and a bunch of dry flowers stop me from saving my brother's life!"

"Calliope." He looked around. "You must get down from that gig this minute. Your investigation is over."

Important-looking ladies and gentlemen who passed by cast curious glances at them.

"Get in," she said. "The investigation is just beginning."

It was actually quite endearing that he was so afraid for her. But she wasn't the wallflower he thought she was.

Nathaniel stood with his expression murderous, his fists clenching and unclenching, his turquoise eyes blazing. "I am starting to regret being engaged to you."

She knew he was angry, but that hurt and sent a stab of embarrassment through her. "I'm not too happy about it, either."

He took one step closer and put his hand on the handle. "Do you even understand what they can do to you?" There was something so deep and broken in his voice that she blinked, staring at him. "They could kill you and I—"

His voice cracked, and something in his face collapsed as he looked down. He breathed for a moment, then visibly collected himself and met her gaze again. "People like that kill women, men, anyone who stands in their way. And I may not be there to protect you."

Calliope blinked, worry churning in her gut. "Look, Nathaniel, I know you're a navy officer, and protective instincts are in your nature, but I assure you, I know what I'm doing. You're not giving me enough credit. Our priority should be to act swiftly and locate Spencer."

He stared at her for a long time, then finally nodded. "All right. But under one condition."

"Another condition?"

He climbed up next to her. "We have to expedite the wedding."

She raised her eyebrows. "How much faster can we marry? It's already in three weeks!"

"First, I need an heir and time is not on my side." He looked her over in such a way that heat washed through her. "And second, I can protect you better. Someone wants to stop you from investigating."

"But they won't."

"That's why I must be at your side. As a husband, that is exactly what I'll be able to do. Protect you day and night."

She whipped the reins, and the horse walked forward.

As the floor of the gig moved under her feet, she sighed. "All right. But you're the one who has to talk to my brother."

9

WALKING through the hallway of the Admiralty with Calliope by his side, Nathaniel kept clenching and unclenching his fists. Yet again, a woman in his life was in danger—perhaps mortal danger. And she was stubborn and disobedient...and, just like his mama, Calliope wouldn't let him protect her.

It was hard to walk, as though his legs were made of pure lead. Nervous energy ran through his body like prickly tingles.

"Are you feeling well?" asked Calliope.

He glared at her. How could she look so confident, so serene when someone had just threatened her?

"Am I feeling well?" he demanded, his voice louder than he'd like, echoing against marble floors.

An officer turned the corner of the hallway and nodded to him in greeting, throwing a curious glance at Calliope before passing through one of the many mahogany doors to either side. Nathaniel continued with a lower voice, which took him some effort. "That was a real threat, Calliope. Someone will harm you if you don't stop. I'm concerned for your safety."

"I'm concerned for my brother's safety."

"How do you not understand? Someone wanted your brother gone. Someone no doubt powerful. Perhaps deadly. Your brother must have stepped on their toes, and now you're about to do the same. They could do the same things to you."

She cocked her eyebrow, her face unconcerned. "Let them try."

What was he doing? After what had happened to his mama, he was marrying a woman who didn't care if she was in danger. His arms felt heavy, hands aching to grab her and lock her up somewhere away from danger.

But he had to be civilized.

Around the farther corner of the corridor, two male silhouettes appeared, walking towards them, deep in conversation. Nathaniel could hear the rumble of their voices echoing off the walls of the corridor. He recognized the deep voice and the upright posture of one of the men: Admiral Sir Robert Langden. In his fifties, the admiral was of medium height but with a muscular build and a slightly rounded stomach. Even when he was strict, he always had an underlying expression of kindness in his eyes, with the wrinkles of a smile around the corners. He listened to the other man carefully, his arms held against the small of his back as they walked. As they approached, Nathaniel could see the admiral's navy uniform with golden epaulets bearing intricately embroidered stars.

Calliope, however, gave out a small gasp and a curse he hadn't expected from her. She grasped him by the fabric of his coat and tugged him behind a column.

"Shh!" She laid one finger on her lips, glaring at him with wide eyes.

"What is it?" he whispered.

"Do be quiet," she mouthed. "It's Preston!"

Nathaniel released a quick breath. Of course. Her brother would be continuing the search himself.

He nodded. Footsteps sounded closer to them and so did the voices.

"...so if you would allow me to look through the records of sailors or officers that departed during September, I would be much obliged," droned Preston's baritone.

"Of course," said Langden, "I wish I could grant you anything you need. I cannot, however, allow you to see everything as we are in two wars, sir, and certain information must remain secret. We cannot be too careful."

"I understand. I am happy to have one of your officers supervise me as I look through them."

Nathaniel could see them passing by the column now. Calliope, whose breasts were pressed against him, stilled and didn't breathe. Neither did he—but not because of the admiral and her brother.

Because her scent was so lovely and the warm touch of her body so seductive. And they were hidden in the darkness... If he just lowered his head, he could kiss her.

"I'm afraid I cannot allow that, either, sir. I can, however, have someone look for your brother's name and report if they see something worth reporting."

Their voices trailed off as the two of them passed Nathaniel and Calliope and then disappeared from Nathaniel's vision, probably taking the corridor leading to the other wing.

When Nathaniel couldn't hear their footsteps or voices any longer, Calliope sighed out a long breath of relief.

"Aren't you happy you have me?" Nathaniel asked, still relishing the feel of her so close to him. "The admiral will not provide much information even to your brother."

Calliope gave him back a little smile that made his stomach bubble with some sort of joy.

"Yes, I am very lucky to have you," she said from under hooded eyes. "And I'm paying a high price for the privilege of your help. Now, come quick. Let's do what we came here to do before Preston sees me."

Their destination, the Naval Transport Board, maintained lists of ships and their captains, as well as information about their cargo and destination. They also kept track of departure and arrival dates for ships and their crews.

Nathaniel and Calliope entered a large formal space with tall windows, high ceilings, and elaborate moldings. The walls were adorned with portraits of naval heroes, maps, and other nautical artwork. Clerks and officers sat at polished mahogany desks, talked, or searched through the records of the books placed on the tall bookshelves. The sounds of quills scratching on paper and voices calling out instructions or talking filled the space.

Looking around the room, Nathaniel located a thick man in his forties wearing glasses. He leaned over his desk, dipping his pen into the inkwell and then writing something.

"Come with me," he said to Calliope and walked to the corner of the large room where Officer Hughes sat. Hughes looked up as they approached, his eyes narrowing as they landed on Nathaniel. His eyebrows furrowed, and his lips pressed tightly together.

Nathaniel knew Hughes, although not very well. It must have been three years ago when, on a drunken night, Hughes had shared with him that he was courting a woman he hoped to make his wife, but she wasn't responding as well as he'd hoped. Nathaniel had given him advice on how to change that. His courtship had become a success, and now Hughes was a happily married man with a two-year-old daughter.

However, when sober, Hughes, just like Calliope, disapproved of Nathaniel's rakish lifestyle. Besides, he was a man known for his meticulousness and hated being interrupted.

But Hughes owed Nathaniel a favor.

"May I help you, Your Grace?" Hughes asked.

He glanced at Calliope and his frown deepened.

"Let me introduce my fiancée," said Nathaniel. "This is Lady Calliope Seaton. Lady Calliope, this is Officer Hughes."

"Lady Calliope." Hughes nodded. "Pleased to meet you."

"The pleasure is mine, sir," said Calliope.

"Hughes, I require your assistance," said Nathaniel. "I need to know which ships were docked in London on September 3, 1812, and when they sailed off."

Hughes looked at him over the rim of his spectacles. "Why?"

"I'm afraid I may have misplaced a document assigning navy officers to the ships, and this information will help me find it."

"Right," said Hughes, as though that was exactly what he'd expected of Nathaniel. "The admiral must be quite displeased with you." He stood up, walked to the bookshelf behind him, and searched through the large leather books in neat rows. "You never bothered about a document you misplaced in your life."

Nathaniel's jaw tightened, and he balled his fists at his sides, willing himself not to lash out. Part of him wanted to be pleasing to Calliope, even though he had no reason to. He glanced at her, and she met his gaze with an amused expression, her eyebrows raised.

"No, not until now," said Nathaniel.

"Which date did you say?" asked Hughes.

"September 3, 1812," said Calliope.

Hughes removed a large leather-bound tome. "I am not certain why your fiancée needs to be present to locate a document..." he mumbled and set it on the desk in front of them.

"Here you are."

Calliope's eyes practically burned as she laid her hands on

it. "May I?"

Hughes frowned with an expression as though he was about to refuse her. "I'm afraid it's not for laypeople—"

Nathaniel interrupted him. "How are your wife and daughter doing, Hughes? Are they well?"

Hughes paled and swallowed. "They are. Thank you."

"Hughes has quite a story of how he courted the young woman, do you not, Hughes? Being much younger than you, she almost refused you, or am I mistaken?"

Calliope watched the two of them with a suspicious frown. "You're quite right, Kelford," said Hughes with a suddenly pleasant expression. "But this is the Admiralty, not—"

"It's so fascinating to think that had it not been for her change of heart when you gave her that book of Shakespeare's love sonnets, she may be married to someone else now and your daughter wouldn't have been born... Do you ever feel thankful someone gave you that idea and encouraged you to try again and again?"

Hughes swallowed and nodded. "Quite right, Kelford. That someone was indeed quite helpful, and I will forever be thankful. I see you found a good future wife, too. Clearly, she will keep you organized. Please do look at it, Lady Calliope."

Nathaniel gave him a satisfied nod. "Excellent, thank you. Do you, perhaps, need to confirm something with Peterson over there?"

He tipped his chin to the other corner of the room where several clerks and officers sat at desks with their backs to them and wrote or talked quietly.

"Indeed I do. Nothing will happen to important navy records with an officer present," said Hughes with a drop of sweat forming at his forehead. "I'll leave you to it."

As he left, Calliope looked at Nathaniel with an amused smile. "I can only imagine what that was about, but I see that

I'd never be able to access this without you. You did a nice thing for him back then, did you not?"

Nathaniel cocked his head in agreement.

She smiled. "Glad to know being a rake can lead to something good, after all..."

Something cracked and warmed in his heart at seeing her beautiful smile and sparkling eyes directed his way.

She opened the book, and Nathaniel watched over her shoulder as she flipped through pages of tables with dates, ships, and lists of names.

"Here it is," she said, her finger pointed at the date.

"'Departed on September 3, 1812,'" Calliope read.

Below was the list of the ships and Calliope's finger slowly moved down. "Five navy ships were docked in London: *Titan*, *Concord*, *Minotaur*, *Hector*, and *Aeneas*. But nothing else." She looked at Nathaniel. "Is there information in here about where they eventually sailed and when?"

He nodded and reached over her shoulder, suddenly very aware of her gorgeous back and her buttocks being almost pressed against his front. He sucked in a breath, trying to ignore the warmth of her and how heat rushed through his entire body.

He flipped through three more pages.

"Here," he said and took a step away from her.

Heavens, conceiving a baby with this woman would be the easiest task ever. He didn't know how he would ever be able to keep his hands away from her.

"Ah, here's *Minotaur* and *Titan*," she muttered, "sailed to France two days later. But *Concord*, *Hector*, and *Aeneas* shipped to America the very next day!"

"It could be any of the five," he said. "What are the names of the captains?"

"White for *Minotaur*, Lawson for *Titan*, Dean for *Concord*,

Ross for *Hector*, and Barker for *Aeneas*. One of those captains might have Spencer on their ship. Is there a list of sailors?"

"The most accurate list of sailors is kept in the captain's log," said Nathaniel. "But it may also be in the Navy Board as they keep personnel records for payment. We might find something there. I know just the man to talk to."

The man to talk to was Officer Bartholomew. He had no leverage on Bartholomew, though, who was notorious for his strict discipline and tough character.

Hughes came back. "Have you found what you were looking for?"

"Quite," said Nathaniel. "Thanks, Hughes. My warm greetings to your family."

As they walked out of the room, Nathaniel's inner vision filled with the memory of a moonlit night in the woods, his mother's body lying on dark grass, blood flowing from the bullet hole in her chest. Their rich carriage stood nearby, horses snorting softly, three-year-old Hazel's pale face peering from the carriage window. Poppy and Violet were inside, still babies.

He imagined Calliope like that. Dead and cold, blood oozing.

Because he wouldn't be able to protect her, like he couldn't protect his mother.

He knew he needed to act fast and act alone. The sooner he knew Calliope was out of danger, the better he would sleep at night.

But as he glanced at her determined profile walking at his side, the sense of unease grew stronger in his bones. How would he be able to keep her out of danger when she was so determined to jump right into it?

Perhaps he'd bought more than he bargained for with this woman.

10

Three days later...

"I pronounce that they be man and wife together, in the name of the Father, and of the Son, and of the Holy Ghost. Amen."

The Bishop of London's words had Nathaniel's stomach squeezing in a mixture of anticipation, excitement, and anger. With the bishop being the Seatons' family friend, the special license had been arranged in three days.

His chest felt too tight for his heart, which jumped around like a wild thing. As the salon of Sumhall erupted in cheers and claps behind him and Calliope, he turned to her.

God knew how much he despised the idea of having a wife. Over the years, he'd gone to desperate measures to avoid succumbing to his father's will and binding himself to someone.

And especially not to father a child.

But here she stood, his wife.

Beautiful and fierce, with her big blue eyes framed with

long eyelashes, a pretty blush on her cheeks, and her auburn hair swept up, yellow irises framing her curly chignon. She wore a gown of an intense yellow color, as though the sun itself shone upon him. They were a striking combination, her in glowing yellow and him in his dark navy uniform, as though he were absorbing all the light that came from her.

Someone so delicate, so precious was now his responsibility. How could he ensure this woman and their future child would be safe? And he still needed to make sure of the same for his sisters.

Cold dread rolled down his spine as he and Calliope turned to their guests, facing the Seatons, their friends the Duke of Loxchester and his wife, and his three sisters. Even the damned cat was there in the dowager's arms. Everyone clapped as he and Calliope walked down the aisle, between the guests.

As yellow petals showered over them, the most delightful laughter came from Calliope's throat.

He must be losing his mind, but his heart did something, a warm lurch of some kind, and he felt a strange buzz as though full of bees. He grasped her hand, and they walked through the passageway that their families and friends created together. A shock of something wonderful shot through their fingers, just as when he'd held her as they'd danced at the ball. And as he held her in his arms just a few days ago in the Admiralty, so close he could kiss her.

They passed through into the dining room, where light spilled through tall windows, dressed with heavy brocade curtains—a rich shade of burgundy trimmed with intricate golden embroidery. Walls in a warm Mediterranean terra-cotta color were adorned with gilt-framed landscapes depicting the rolling Spanish countryside. Ornate candelabra cast a warm glow, illuminating the beautifully arranged table settings.

Soft music was played by a small chamber orchestra, and

laughter and lively conversation filled the air as the guests went to their seats.

The guests and the Bishop of London gathered around the large dining table draped with pristine white linens, each setting boasting fine china, polished silver cutlery, and sparkling crystal glassware. An impressive centerpiece combined a floral arrangement featuring yellow irises with elegantly crafted silver and gold decorations.

"Let me guess." Nathaniel chuckled. "Do you like yellow irises?"

Calliope shrugged one shoulder. "Your observational skills are unprecedented."

He cocked one eyebrow in question. "Aren't they a little too simplistic for a duke's sister...and now wife?"

"I beg your pardon! My mother loved them as they signify hope and wisdom. She always said she needed both, being a duke's wife in England." She looked at a large portrait of a very handsome and muscular dark-haired man. "We can use all of the hope we can get at the moment."

Nathaniel recognized Spencer, the former Duke of Grandhampton. He'd seen him in Portside boxing, as well as at drunken soirées usually attended by rakes.

"Besides," she said, "I love the vibrant color, and I think they're very pretty."

As the guests gathered around the table, the footmen came to help everyone sit. The old butler came to Calliope and with tears in his eyes said, "On behalf of the whole staff downstairs, madam, may I offer our best wishes for your health and happiness."

Calliope smiled warmly. "Thank you, Teanby." Then she looked around at the footmen, who cast warm glances upon her. "Thank you, everyone."

They all took their seats at the table, which held seemingly endless platters of perfectly presented food: cold cuts of meat and cheese, bread, poached salmon with hollandaise sauce, asparagus vinaigrette, and slices of succulent roast beef accompanied by a tangy horseradish cream. The wedding cake stood on the sideboard, ready to be served. It was an intricately decorated fruitcake with white sugar flowers and icing. Nathaniel didn't particularly enjoy fruitcake as he found the combination of dried fruits, nuts, and spices, and the layer of marzipan and white fondant too intense. But after years of eating stew at practically every supper, he was not about to be picky.

While the footmen served the first course, Nathaniel became aware of more than one heavy set of eyes on him. Grandhampton, who sat on the other side of Calliope, glared at him, while his wife, Penelope, chatted happily with the Bishop of London, an elderly man with a round head and a powdered wig.

Calliope's brother Richard and his new wife, Jane, had arrived from the country, and his was the second pair of heavy eyes that kept Nathaniel in their glaring focus. The third was from the Duke of Loxchester, Sebastian, the best friend of Preston, and a close friend of the family.

The dowager duchess, regal and stately, sat next to his sisters and talked to them with a pleasant expression. Nathaniel's heart melted as he watched Hazel's turquoise eyes glimmer with excitement and awe as she gazed upon everything and everyone around her. Despite the rebellious and distant front that she put on every day—no doubt trying to show she did not care about anything—he knew that deep down she missed a female presence in her life. She had no one to look up to, no one to listen to. The same was true for Poppy and Violet.

"What a splendid house," said Violet as she picked up the

fork for the main course to select a piece of cheese. "Do you have a library here, Calliope?"

Nathaniel didn't care if anyone present thought them ill-bred; he'd put anyone in their place if they dared to point out the holes in his sisters' etiquette.

Calliope beamed at Violet across the table. "We do, indeed. Do you like reading?"

Violet made a gesture over her nose as though she was pushing her spectacles up. She hadn't put them on this morning, eager to make a good impression on her new relatives. Poppy and Violet stared at Calliope as though she were a goddess that had descended from the heavens and not merely a woman. Hazel, however, eyed her with skepticism.

"I do!" declared Violet.

"Well then, you have a lot in common with your new sister-in-law," said Lady Jane. "And with me!"

Nathaniel remembered how, on the day he'd met Calliope at the Royal Navy ball, a scandal had erupted around Miss Jane Grant, as she'd been called then. Her half brother, the infamous Thorne Blackmore, had stormed Carlton House with his band of men to break up Jane and Richard's engagement and to take her home. Nathaniel thought both Thorne and Richard were quite daring, the former angering the prince regent, the most powerful man in England, the latter angering Thorne, the most dangerous criminal lord of London's underworld.

"I, for one, don't," said Poppy, holding her nose higher than she should. "I prefer adventures."

"Well, you have that in common with Calliope, too," said the dowager with a soft smile. "Our Calliope may seem like a wallflower, but that is just one of the covers she likes to use."

Nathaniel cursed inwardly. Yes, Calliope was brave and smart and didn't back down from her goal. And he'd be hard-pressed to keep her safe.

"What all three of you need," said the dowager, "is someone to help you when you come out. With your brother's permission, I would be pleased to take you all under my wing."

The twins' delighted sighs and gasps were like knives through his heart, a reminder of how he had failed them in his duty to take care of them and give them the best future. Hazel, however, said nothing; he saw how hard she was trying to keep a straight face, but her burning eyes gave her away.

"Kelford, we must have a conversation now that you're my brother..." said Richard. "Which was a big surprise, by the way, sister," he said to Calliope, "when I warned you to stay away from him."

"So did I," said Preston.

"Both of you," said Calliope. "It's done. Please don't stir the pot. Preston, you gave your blessing. Richard, all you can do is be supportive of my new husband."

"I just wonder about your intentions," said Richard as he laid his fork and knife down. "Just to clarify, you signed the marriage contract where you won't touch Calliope's significant dowry."

Nathaniel straightened his back, putting his fork and knife down, as well. "Indeed."

"But your papa was considered to be the richest man in England," Richard said. "Was he not, Grandmama? Richer than the royal family. Richer than the devil himself. Those were the rumors I heard."

"That is what I heard many years ago, too, yes," said the dowager carefully. "But I am not the one to ask. Surely the current Duke of Kelford can enlighten you."

"What my brother is trying to ask is why did your father lock his fortune away from you, Kelford?" asked Preston bluntly. "Why did the richest duke in England make his own son the poorest one?"

Nathaniel's body went rigid and cold as the chatter in the room shuddered to a halt, and he felt the attention of every guest on him. The only sound was the music, and even the musicians threw odd glances at him.

But the opinions that mattered to him most were his sisters'. They knew nothing of the true reason the relationship between himself and his father had completely fallen apart. Being too little at the time, they didn't even remember they had witnessed the same horror he had. No matter how much Calliope's brothers wanted him to explain, he wouldn't subject his sisters to the awful truth.

How the highwaymen had stopped their carriage late at night. How he had heard his family's guards descend from the back of the carriage and fight. How he could have left the safety of the carriage and grabbed a pistol and done something...

Instead, shaking from fear, he had sat inside with little Hazel pressed against him. On the opposite seat, his mother had cradled sleeping one-year-old Poppy and Violet, her rocking movements fast and her eyes wide.

As though feeling his distress, the white cat rose from her place on one of the chairs along the wall between footmen, jumped down, and walked towards him. As before, she hugged his boot with her tail. His nose and eyes itched. Surely it must be a reaction to the cat's hair, not the emotion that tried to break through.

"My father didn't think I was a worthy heir," said Nathaniel.

This was true. Father had always had high expectations of him, and Nathaniel constantly thought he disappointed him. But after that night, Father had simply despised Nathaniel... and rightly so. Nathaniel hadn't managed to save his mother, the duchess.

"My father thought I was disobedient, irresponsible, and rebellious. He thought I had no place becoming a duke." Nathaniel swallowed hard. "I believe this will was his revenge and the means to teach me a lesson, to change me from a worthless cad into a family man."

Hazel's hand shook so hard, her knife rattled loudly against the plate, and she hastily put it down with a loud clank. Both Poppy and Violet stared at him with wide, sad eyes. He had said too much. They remembered Papa well—he had passed when Nathaniel was twenty-one and the twins were seven and Hazel nine.

"I had dropped out of Oxford," said Nathaniel. "Or rather, I was politely asked to not show up there again. I drank brandy for breakfast since I was sixteen."

And I am the reason my beloved mama is dead...

He swallowed the thought like bile.

"And so my papa thought the only way to make me a responsible man was to take away everything unless I married and produced an heir... Unfortunately, by having punished me, he has also punished my sisters. But if an heir or heiress is born before I reach the age of thirty, all our vast inheritance will be restored."

Silence still hung over the room. Nathaniel felt the shift in the air. The sharp eyes of Preston, Richard, and the Duke of Loxchester softened.

"I know a thing or two about harsh fathers," said the Duke of Loxchester.

"I sympathize, Kelford," said Preston. "I understand what it's like to never feel good enough to be born into the nobility."

"Or not living up to one's potential," said Richard.

Something warmed up right in the center of Nathaniel's chest. He hadn't expected these three men to understand him. But he supposed he had spent so many years in isolation, punishing himself for that night, that he didn't really have friends to talk to.

"However, I warn you not to use my sister as a brood mare," said Preston. "She is so much more. She is truly remarkable."

Nathaniel chuckled. "Believe me, Grandhampton, I am well aware."

Calliope would be either the best thing that happened to him or the worst.

His wife leaned close to him, her eyes shining. "I am sorry to hear your father was so cruel."

A sweet lightness pierced Nathaniel's middle. But he didn't deserve it. They all thought now he was the martyr, the victim. He wasn't. He was the one to blame. "He had his reasons," he said, throat tight.

The dowager nodded. "I do remember your papa and mama. He was an important man, but not an easy one by any means. He was very close to King George while the king was well."

"I wish Spencer were here," murmured Calliope, who was looking at the portrait again, completely shredding his heart.

Everyone followed her gaze, and silence fell over the room once more.

"I know he would have wanted to see me get married," Calliope continued. "Would have wanted to meet you," she said to Nathaniel, and he swallowed, his throat dry.

He should have helped her without asking her to marry him in exchange. Clearly this family was hurting for the beloved brother who was missing.

"What is the situation with the wars?" asked Penelope, her eyes on Nathaniel. "What have you heard, Your Grace? Do you have any inkling where Spencer could be?"

Nathaniel nodded. "If he was sent to the war with Bonaparte, he might be in the Baltics now or in the Mediterranean. Last we heard, the British Royal Navy conducted operations to disrupt French trade and supply lines in the Baltics. In the Mediterranean, we are maintaining control of the sea routes, to support the armies fighting in Spain, and preventing French supply ships from reaching their destinations."

"So that is good, then," breathed Calliope. "If he's there, it looks like we're winning, so he might be returning home soon!"

"And what if he's in America?" asked Preston.

Nathaniel let out a long sigh. The American war had started last year, prompted by the dominance of the Royal Navy, the apparent conscription of American sailors to man British ships, and trade restrictions. The first thing the young country had done was try to invade Canada, but those attempts hadn't brought them success. With so many men currently fighting Napoleon, Britain was in dire need of men for the war in America. And so they had started a series of press-ganging operations.

"If he's in America," Nathaniel said, "I'm afraid things are more dire. Fort George on the Niagara Peninsula, which had provided crucial naval support, was lost to the Americans recently. If he was in that battle, I do not envy him."

"Can you help?" asked Preston, his voice cracking. "You are a member of the family now, and a navy man on the inside. Spencer is now your brother, too. Can you do anything to find him?"

Nathaniel's eyes prickled, and he nodded. He should have done it in the first place just because he was a decent human, not for his selfish reasons.

Besides, Calliope had been right. Knowing he was just doing his duty as an officer, he hadn't given a thought to what he was signing: orders to tear men away from their loved ones and send them to fight without their consent. Seeing this family—so affected, so worried, so disturbed by their brother's disappearance—made his own stomach churn in sorrow and disgust. The Seatons were a powerful, rich family. What about the poor who had been press-ganged without a second thought? What about their families?

"Of course I will," he promised. And this wasn't just a promise for Spencer. If he ever regained his fortune and was in a position of power, he should do something about regular press-gangs, too.

"Thank you," said Richard.

"And I thank you," said Preston.

He felt her warm hand on his under the table. As conversation swung to other topics, he met Calliope's eyes.

"And I thank you, too," she said, and he felt like his heart was soaring in his chest as he looked into her big beautiful eyes. "Did you learn anything from Officer Bartholomew?"

"I'm afraid not, Calliope. He wasn't there when I went to call on him."

She frowned, and her warm hand left his. "He wasn't there? In three days?"

"I could only call once," he said, annoyance prickly on his neck. "I had a wedding to prepare for in three days."

"That is more important than the wedding," Calliope whisper-shouted at him through her gritted teeth. "And what did you really have to do for the wedding besides show up?"

"You are going to move into my house," he retorted. "And it has to be to your liking, has it not?"

"Oh yes," ventured Violet excitedly. "We did do a good clean, although there was not much to clean... But the dogs will be happy to have a new mommy!"

Calliope's face paled. "The dogs?"

“Aren’t you taking Miss Furrington with you?” asked the dowager, leaning towards them.

“Who’s Miss Furrington?” asked Poppy.

But even though Calliope hadn’t told him what the white beast’s name was, he knew it must be the cat.

“My cat,” said the dowager. “You should have someone familiar in the new house, dearest, especially since you’ve always been Miss Furrington’s favorite.” Her pale eyes fixed on Nathaniel. “At least, until now.”

11

"Welcome to Roxburgh," said Nathaniel, supporting Calliope's hand as she climbed down from the carriage later that day.

A gasp escaped her throat. It was a grand property indeed. Calliope could imagine how fine carriages must have once lined up, bringing elegant ladies and gentlemen to a ball.

Yet now, the mansion, as well as the grounds, were in a pitiful state.

The walls around the property were crumbling in a few spots, with the odd missing brick and speckled with bird droppings. The gravel driveway had weeds growing through it, and the garden resembled an overgrown forest.

The house itself was majestic, with gorgeous stonework around large windows though some of those stones were crumbling, too. One of the two stone lions flanking the grand entry stairs looked like it was missing a tooth and the other one an ear. And the double doors had chipping paint, the knocker hanging from a single nail. Above the door, the Kelford coat of arms had rain-damaged wood peering through the faded paint.

"I know this place!" Calliope exclaimed, unable to take her eyes off the facade. "I've passed by this building countless times. This is such a great location in Mayfair, and detached houses are so rare and valuable in London."

She didn't say that she'd always thought what a pity it was that no one took the time and effort to repair such a gorgeous place.

Nathaniel helped his sisters to climb down from the carriage after her.

"It is rare and valuable. It's the only property from my papa's vast fortune that we are allowed to use," said Nathaniel quietly as he came closer to Calliope while Hazel, Poppy, and Violet hurried towards the grand stairs. "But not because it's detached or big or has a fashionable Mayfair address. It's because it's the only home my sisters know. And I've been fighting tooth and nail to keep it for them."

Calliope's heart squeezed for him. What he'd told everyone at their wedding had crushed her heart, that his papa had punished him so cruelly by withholding the means to their survival. She wondered what Nathaniel had to do to keep it...

"Why didn't you marry in all those years, Nathaniel?" she asked carefully. "Eight years is plenty of time to have fathered an heir."

The ache in his turquoise eyes broke her heart all over again. "For the first few years I simply didn't think much of it, I admit. Then when I knew I was slowly running out of time, I hired a solicitor to find a legal way for me to claim my inheritance. But a few days ago, I was informed there is no hope. That my father won, and I had to obey him. Even from beyond his grave, he got what he wanted." He looked at the girls, who were already at the top of the stairs.

"Come on, sister!" cried Poppy, the cheerful twin. "Come in! We must show you your new house!"

"I just hope this won't be a disappointment," Nathaniel said.

Calliope nodded, picked up the cage with Miss Furrington from the carriage, and walked after Nathaniel to enter Roxburgh Place. Miss Furrington watched everything with wide, dilated eyes, her ears perked and flicking around as different sounds reached her, her whiskers erect.

Abigail, Calliope's maid, who had traveled on the back of the carriage, approached her with a light piece of luggage in her hands.

"Shall I take Miss Furrington, my lady?" Abigail asked, throwing uncertain glances at Roxburgh Place.

"No, I can take her, thank you, Abigail. Well, here we are, our new home... I'm glad I have you with me. Let's go."

Her home for the rest of Calliope's life. Calliope swallowed what felt like a stone in her throat as she walked towards the house, her stomach in knots. What had she gotten herself into?

As she entered, a vast but empty entry hall met her. Patches of bare plaster peeked through the chipped and worn-out dark red paint.

Underfoot, the marble floor had a faint, intricate pattern that wove its way across the stone like a fading memory. The worn spots were evidence of the countless ladies and gentlemen who had walked and danced over these floors during grand soirées and balls.

A sweeping staircase showed signs of wear, the hand-carved balustrades in need of polish. On either side of the staircase, ornately carved niches stood empty, their intended occupants—probably statues and vases—long gone, leaving behind only vague outlines on the dusty shelves.

In the middle of the ceiling, a worn circular mark on the white wood suggested the previous existence of a huge chandelier. A lonely sconce now clung to the wall, its glass cover cracked and sooty.

There were no paintings, no sideboards, no statues, no vases with flowers, no chairs, and no tables where one could sit and calmly put on a bonnet.

There were, however, two servants who stood looking at Calliope with wide eyes.

Nathaniel looked at the woman in her fifties with a sturdy frame and gray hair tied in a knot behind her head. She looked at Calliope with sharp small brown eyes, two deep wrinkles around her mouth curving downward. "Let me introduce my wife, Calliope, the new Duchess of Kelford. This is Mrs. Nicholson, our housekeeper, cook, and lady's maid."

For such a large house, this woman was doing all that alone? No wonder she had a bitter expression.

Nathaniel looked at the blond man, who couldn't be older than twenty-one. Tall and with a big nose and large hands, he was dressed like a footman but had blotches of dirt on his clothes as well as seams and square patches. "And this is Joshua Martin, our butler, footman, and groom."

"All at once?" gasped Abigail behind Calliope.

Everyone stared at her, and she closed her mouth, looking down, her cheeks reddening. "Beg your pardon."

"Between Mrs. Nicholson and us three, we manage," said Hazel with a sharp edge in her voice.

Calliope smiled politely. "I'm sure you do."

Unease washed through her. Only two servants managed this giant house that could be a respectable royal residence...

Yes, this was quite different from what she was used to: a proper butler, housekeeper, well-trained footmen, carefully selected maids, and a small army of the lowest rank of servants

—scullery maids and hall boys. Not to mention that their kitchens always had the best cook they could find and several undercooks.

But, it seemed, this was all Nathaniel could afford without the income from his inheritance.

Well, she and Abigail would just have to make do with this. And, thankfully, Calliope had her own dowry and income she could do with as she pleased. So, perhaps, she could help.

"Pleased to meet you both." She beamed. "Mrs. Nicholson... Joshua...forgive me, is it Martin?"

Normally, the butler was addressed by his last name, but since this man did several jobs, she wasn't sure.

"Joshua is fine, my lady," the young man said with a huge, disarming smile, showing his crooked yellow teeth. "I'm more of a footman than a butler, but I can't complain. With my experience, I'd never have been a butler had His Grace not given me a chance."

Calliope nodded and smiled warmly. She imagined there weren't many butlers who would want to take on the jobs of a footman and a groom at the same time, and that for, no doubt, less than modest wages. She couldn't imagine Nathaniel being able to pay much.

"Joshua it is," she said.

"Please, follow me," Nathaniel said, his face tense.

The rest of the house was the same as the entrance hall. The grandeur of this place was breathtaking, and yet the state of it was sad. The interior was clearly old but clean. In some rooms, paper hangings peeled in places. The sparse furniture that remained was dated, perhaps fifty or so years old. The shaded silhouettes of now-absent chests of drawers, paintings, and sideboards haunted the walls like strange ghosts.

Calliope opened Miss Furrington's cage and held her in her arms, her body warm and fluffy. They went up the stairs and saw two long, wide hallways with many doors to bedchambers. Even higher up the stairs, on the second floor, was more of the same. Miss Furrington watched everything with large eyes.

In her mind, Calliope had already started making a list of urgent repairs, followed by a list of beautiful things she'd like to see. The more she saw, the more she itched to lay her hands on this place, order paint, new floors, paper hangings, new furniture and draping. She would ask Penelope to do the paintings—she had such a pretty style... Paintings of flowers would be gorgeous in the bedrooms and hallways. Landscapes and seascapes downstairs in the reception rooms, the study, and the library. And, of course, family portraits.

"Let's go out the back," suggested Hazel. "There are also household buildings."

Nathaniel tensed. "Hazel, I am sure Calliope never saw the household buildings in her home as the daughter and sister of a duke. Why should she as a duchess?"

Hazel stared coldly at her brother. "The girls and I are a duke's daughters and sisters, and yet we go there multiple times per day."

Calliope's throat clenched tightly. "I'd love very much to see the mews."

"There's not much to see," said Violet sadly as they walked down the creaking stairs. Calliope made an internal note to get Mrs. Nicholson to hire someone to repair them.

"Roxburgh is beautiful," she said. "It certainly has great bones. Just look at the size of the rooms. The windows are gorgeous, and the ceilings are so high."

The twins beamed back at her. Hazel pursed her lips in a thin line.

Nathaniel winced as they walked through the servants'

door under the grand stairs. “Please, there’s no need to say things you do not mean, Calliope.”

The servants’ quarters were so quiet and as dated as the rest of the place, but they smelled clean, and there was not a spot of dust.

“No, no, Nathaniel,” she said enthusiastically. “I do mean it. You may see chipped paint, creaky stairs, and holes in the walls. I see potential. I see how glorious it can be. I see the gorgeous light that will flood these rooms once the windows are replaced or cleaned. I see how much space there was in the drawing room to put a pianoforte for the girls and a large table for games and how beautiful the fireplace moldings will be decorated with branches of holly for Christmas. I see how grand the dining room will be with crystal chandeliers hanging over a large table to receive friends and family.”

They reached the end of the hallway and what must be the door to the backyard, but something was wrong. The more she talked the more the frown on Nathaniel’s gorgeous face deepened, the sharper the angles of his square jaw became. And his turquoise eyes turned stormy, a dark navy blue.

“And who, pray tell, will pay for all that potential?” He spat the last word out like a curse.

Calliope laid her hand on the door handle. “I will. This is my home now, and I have my dowry. Also, your sisters will need new gowns, and I’ll be happy to—”

“No,” Nathaniel barked out. “I will not have a penny from you.”

The words hit her like a slap, Calliope jerking briefly. “Nathaniel, clearly that’s what your house needs. What your sisters need. Let me help.”

“Brother, this is Calliope’s home, too, now,” Poppy said.

“I will not accept charity. Your brothers didn’t want me to touch your money, and I will not.”

Charity? The disdain in his voice wrenched Calliope's insides.

With that, Nathaniel opened the door and stepped outside.

"Nathaniel!" Calliope said, walking out after him.

She had taken only a few steps across the landing when loud barking burst through the air, and three beasts ran towards her across the cobblestones several feet below, growling, barking, flashing their sharp white teeth. One of them was so tremendous, it looked like a short-haired bear on long legs. One was a little beagle, though it was barking just as fiercely. The third, probably a mutt, looked the most vicious. Sharp pain sliced Calliope's arm and breast. White fur flashed against her face as a panicked, loud yowl burst through the air and the cat flew from her arms.

Terror raced through her like a war chariot, and Calliope gasped and mindlessly hurried backward on the landing. She'd never liked dogs, and these three had murder in their eyes, clearly ready to tear her apart...and her poor cat.

Closer and closer they came, almost at the stairs now, closer to her throat with those giant jaws and sharp fangs, especially that humongous one.

She took a few more quick steps, and her back bumped against something hard—the railing—then there was a wooden crack, and she was falling backward.

She flailed her arms, trying to grab on to something, but finding only empty air.

She could already anticipate the long fall, the way her bones would twist, her skull cracking against the cobblestones.

But the impact never came. Two strong arms wrapped around her, and she was yanked back to the surface in Nathaniel's solid embrace. His scent enveloped her—a delicious blend of his skin and his clean clothes and his cologne. She clutched at the material of his coat like he was her lifeline.

His eyes were on hers, and she was sinking, sinking. She couldn't catch another breath, her chest feeling too tight, her heart drumming. Why was she not afraid? Why was she not pushing him away, eager to let go of him and put as much distance between them as possible?

Instead, she felt quite safe, quite protected, despite the dogs still barking.

"Thank you..." she murmured.

"Sit!" cried Violet, and the barking stopped. "You scared the poor cat and your poor new mistress."

Without breaking eye contact with her, Nathaniel nodded, then gently let go of her.

To Calliope's surprise, all three beasts sat at the bottom of the stairs calmly, looking between Hazel, Calliope, the girls, and Nathaniel. The smallest one looked up at the house. Poor Miss Furrington sat on the triangular portico, her tail slicing through the air, her terrified eyes on the dogs.

"Brother, but you must admit that we do need some repairs now," demanded Violet, looking pointedly at the broken wooden railing so weatherworn it looked quite fragile. "Calliope almost broke her neck."

Nathaniel's gaze hardened as he stared at the sharp edges of the railing. "Indeed. I will repair this myself. There is some wood in the shed. I will fix everything else in the house once my inheritance is returned to me..." His hot gaze dropped to her stomach, and Calliope's insides clenched in delicious anticipation and cold dread.

And then something she hadn't thought about became very, very clear.

Tonight was their wedding night, and he was eager to impregnate her.

12

London was dark beyond the window when Calliope followed Nathaniel into his bedchamber after dinner.

Her skin prickled as she watched the muscles of his broad shoulders move under his navy coat as he lit tallow candles in the candelabra standing on the round table. The door slowly swung shut behind her, and he turned to her, his angled features so handsome in the golden candlelight, her heart could break.

His high cheekbones looked even sharper in this light, his gorgeous eyes surrounded by long, curly eyelashes like clear pools. His strong, straight nose, full, wide lips and angular jawline were all such perfection one could paint countless masterpieces inspired by him. A high cravat was wrapped around his long, thick neck that swept down into the broad, manly shoulders with muscles like boulders. Did he have real flesh under his clothing or artfully carved marble?

Calliope's throat was dry, her lips parched. His gaze was dark and piercing, as though he was attempting to get under her skin, to uncover her soul and all her secrets.

"May I offer you some wine?" he asked.

She'd already had two glasses at dinner, and usually that was all she allowed herself. But her feet were weak, and she didn't like how she couldn't stop clutching her hands and picking at her cuticles. Anything to relieve that tight knot at the base of her stomach.

"Please," she said.

While he poured the wine, her gaze darted to the large bed standing on the other side of the room. Grandiose in its design, the bed had intricately carved posts that ascended towards a richly detailed canopy. The canopy's faded blue silk curtains and the counterpane of the same color whispered of bygone eras, their once-vibrant patterns now mere shadows. The bed seemed as though it might have been crafted during the days of his father or even his grandfather, an heirloom passed down with the house.

In addition to the bed, there were two night tables with a few stacked books, which made Calliope curious. A small door in the opposite wall probably led to his dressing room. There was a fireplace with cracked paint and an old black grate, which was now cold and empty.

Besides that, there was nothing in the room.

Like all of the other rooms, this one's pitiful state was apparent, but Calliope could see its former grandeur so clearly. She'd have the paneled walls painted in turquoise, but a darker, duskier tone than Nathaniel's eyes. And she'd put golden drapes and a golden counterpane on that glorious bed, and many pillows. She'd refresh the tired wooden floor, and get a large, plush carpet so that stepping on it with one's bare feet would be a pleasure.

What paintings would he like? Trying to remember if he ever mentioned the sort of things he was interested in, she narrowed her eyes at Nathaniel, who approached her with a small carved-crystal glass holding red port wine. His fingers brushed lightly against hers as he passed her the glass, sending a jolt of awareness straight through her knees.

"What are your interests?" she asked breathlessly.

He chuckled slightly. "Right now? I have only one interest. You."

His eyes were dark with meaning over the rim of the glass as he drank. She took a sip, too, not really tasting it. She should be more confident, so much braver than she was at this moment. Everyone was settled after dinner. The girls had gone to their rooms. After the terror of meeting the three dogs, and being rescued by Nathaniel, Miss Furrington hid under the bed in Calliope's new room connected to Nathaniel's through the larger door to her left. Calliope had left the cat with a little ping of jealousy. Shaken by the beasts, by her near fall, by this new house, and by her new family and new husband, Calliope didn't want to face her wedding night...

Not now...

Probably not ever.

And that strange, burning excitement that seethed at the very pit of Calliope's stomach surely wasn't anticipation of what was to come. She knew exactly how good it could feel to lie with a man—if books could be believed. *Villains and Velvet* was a collection of nine short stories where well-bred damsels were seduced by all kinds of rogues, scoundrels, and rakes while on swashbuckling adventures, being chased by pirates, vagabonds, and highwaymen.

Nathaniel could have easily stepped out of that book, with that large, muscular body and that voice as deep and as seductive as sin.

Heavens...and what if the night with him would be just as good as in *Villains and Velvet*? Just as good as she'd felt when she'd read those stories—before William had found her. Just as good as she'd felt when she'd touched herself right there?

Could he make her feel like that, too?

Her heart slammed so fast against her ribs, she couldn't breathe. She took the last sip of her wine—gosh, it tasted like sweet vinegar—and put the glass back on the table.

"I meant, what sort of paintings do you like?" she asked. "Your walls are bare."

Nathaniel's jaw muscles worked, and he put his empty glass on the table, too. "Let's not talk about my bare walls, dearest." He turned to her and took a large step, standing so close she could smell him. "Let's talk about something I'd like to see bare...you."

Her throat contracted. Goodness, he was just like the hero from one of those stories! Heat flushed through her, making her all achy and longing for something...

Was it heat or embarrassment? William King's shadow lurked in the depths of her psyche like a silent guard, dark and powerful.

She saw it in Nathaniel's eyes. It would happen between them. If she didn't stop him.

In a cold slap of panic, she whirled around and walked to the first thing she saw...the books.

She grabbed one of them mindlessly. The book was titled *Things as They Are* by William Godwin. A book about political injustice. She threw a curious glance at Nathaniel and flipped through it. His dark gaze followed her every step. It was like a warm, heavy caress on her body.

How could she be like this? Want this, ache for it, and fear it at the same time. "Did you like this one?" she asked. "Given you condemn innocent men to serve at war against their will, I didn't think you would be interested in books like this."

He slowly walked to her and stood five steps away, leaning against the poster of the bed. "Like what, Calliope?"

"This book is about how powerful institutions can destroy a person's life with no regard to their circumstances. Isn't that what the system of press-gangs is doing to people? Tearing them out of their lives, dropping them into a war with no consent? Isn't that what that system did to my brother?"

There was a tiny flinch on his face, a flinch of regret. Of sorrow. Calliope's heart lurched.

"I had to do many things to keep the roof above my sisters' heads," he said. "Things I'm not proud of. Reading books like that reminds me that I'm still human. Gives me hope it all could be different one day. By marrying me, you gave me such hope."

And just when she was looking for more ways to dislike him, to reject him, to keep him at a distance, he said things like that... Things that made her knees weak and stole her breath away. Maybe he really wouldn't be like William. Maybe she just needed to chase that shadow away and let Nathaniel in. Let him teach her. Change her.

After all, William King was no longer a threat. He couldn't marry her anymore.

"I can quite understand that, Nathaniel," she said with a slight smile. "In fact, I read it twice."

She put the book down and picked up the next one in the stack.

And dropped it like it was red-hot. On the cheap paper cover was the all-too-familiar print with a blooming rose underneath... *Villains and Velvet* by Lucien Montpellier.

She froze, burning with shame and embarrassment just like fourteen years ago when William had found her with that exact book. How could this be? She hadn't seen the book in years, yet the very memory of it was both arousing and shameful.

"What is it, love?" he asked, his eyes glinting in amusement... "Does that book interest you? Feel free to borrow it. It's a much more entertaining read than Godwin."

Amusement! Was he laughing at her just like William? Her reaction must seem childish to him. Prudish. He was much more experienced, so perhaps her naïveté was amusing.

What would he say if he knew his supposedly well-bred wife had read literature like this while still a young girl? That she'd liked what she read? That she'd enjoyed herself?

The shadow in her psyche grew stronger, darker.

Whore...

"No," she said, walking away from his nightstand like it was a nest full of snakes. "That won't be necessary."

When she walked past him, he caught her hand and turned her, gently bringing her to him. "What is it? You're quite distraught."

She couldn't look away from him. Her heart beat so fast against her ribs, but not with excitement and anticipation like before. Even though there was no trace of his former amusement, she couldn't shake the shadow that that book and that smirk on his face had brought to life.

"I'm fine," she said.

He studied her with a frown. "Are you concerned about what is going to happen between us?"

Concerned? She was ready to flee to another country.

She hated William. God, how she hated him. He had tainted her with one word, with one look, with one movement of his fingers for the rest of her life.

She could tell it all to Nathaniel. The kindness in his eyes, his genuine concern told her he might understand. Might not judge her, after all. A wife and a husband should be open with each other, love each other, respect each other—like her parents had.

Only, a man like Nathaniel would never understand someone like her. They were too different, like cats and dogs. Like bright yellow irises and the deep blue sea. He was a rake. She was a bluestocking.

That was who she should remain for him. Well-bred, smart, independent.

Not vulnerable and weak. Not a woman with a dirty secret.

When she said nothing, he gently brushed his knuckles down her cheek and looked at her lips like they were a delicious meal he ached to taste.

"I know you must be," he said. "Your first time. I promise you, you'll love it."

She'd love it… Oh, how she wanted to believe him.

"I wanted you from the moment I saw you," he murmured as he drew her closer to him, wrapping his strong, hard arms around her. "From that damned Royal Navy ball when you were so breathtaking, your intelligent eyes cutting into me like a knife through butter. And I loved it."

She couldn't muster a word. What could one say when one was completely mesmerized?

"And now, you're finally mine," he whispered and lowered his mouth to hers.

The moment his lips brushed against hers was like the sun colliding with the earth. The floor shifted under her feet as heat went through her with bone-melting power. She closed her eyes, softening into the exquisite feel of his lips, inhaling his manly musk—the scent of herbs and that cologne that was fresh like the wind flapping in the sail of a ship at sea.

The scent alone was enough to have her fingers clutch the fabric of his coat and tug him closer. She heard him inhale deeply and press into her, his arms strong around her. He brushed his tongue against her lower lip, and she shivered from sheer delight. Heavens, this was nothing like in the book—it was so, so much better.

A real kiss.

She opened her mouth and let him in. Oh Lord, the sensual, decadent touch sent a jolt of heat right into the apex of her thighs, sending a delicious shiver through her. He brushed against her tongue again and again, and she echoed his actions. Their lips mingled and played and came together, and she never wanted it to end.

He released one arm from behind her waist and cupped her jaw, his palm large, calloused, and warm, urging a rush of tingles through her skin.

As his lips and tongue explored her, his hand went down her neck, bringing that warmth down her body until...

Until his fingers found the exact spot on the right side of her neck, at the dip between her neck and her collarbone where William had so painfully pinched her. Branded her forever.

Nathaniel's touch was nothing but a gentle caress.

But it was that spot.

The memory flashed through her, tearing her away from the beautiful sensations like a slap. Inexplicable terror flooded her. The shame, the embarrassment of that day pushed away the warmth, the desire, making her want to curl into a ball.

Her eyes flew open, and she pushed Nathaniel as hard as she could, backing away from him.

He staggered, almost falling onto the bed, his eyes wide and confused, his mouth open. "Calliope?" he asked, blinking.

She clutched at her neck in a mindless gesture of protection. "I can't."

He took a step towards her, and she took one back. "Did I do something?"

Her mind raced. This was their wedding night. He had every right to bed her. How could she explain this sudden rejection?

A boy pinched me and called me a whore when he saw me pleasuring myself while reading a book.

How could she ever tell him that? Or anyone at all? Not a soul knew except for her, William, and Spencer.

Spencer...right. She could mention Spencer!

"I will not let you bed me," she said, panting hard, "until we make progress with my brother. You promised to find Officer Bartholomew, who could tell us more. You failed to fulfill that promise. I will not let you into my bed until you do."

The change in his face broke her heart. From confused and regretful, a cold realization smoothed his expression.

"Right," he said, straightening his neck, his eyes gleaming like glass. "Because I'm nothing to you but a means to an end."

She swallowed hard. "Just like I'm nothing to you but a womb to impregnate. The last chance for you to get back your fortune. Because looking at all this, it is obvious how much you need it."

She regretted the words the moment they left her mouth. She hated herself for saying them. His head jerked back in an expression of hurt. He didn't say anything, then slowly shook his head.

"You don't want me in your bed? You want to progress in your search?" He nodded slowly. "As you wish, madam. I will deliver. Because you're right. And thank you for reminding me. You're nothing to me but a woman to birth my heir. And I am nothing to you but a blue coat to give you access to the navy. I hope you find your cold bed comforting."

With that, he crossed the room and marched out.

Calliope stood alone, listening to his retreating footsteps.

She was left with nothing but William's dark shadow.

She'd been so wrong. Even though she was not married to the hateful man, he was still present deep inside. Would she never be rid of him?

13

The fist came at Nathaniel's stomach and the whole left side of his torso exploded with pain.

Good.

Anything to distract him from the fact that his gorgeous new wife didn't think he was worthy to bed her unless he delivered the information she sought.

The crowd in Portside erupted in bloodthirsty cheers around him.

"Noble Knuckles!" he heard a small part of the crowd cheering for him. "Noble Knuckles!" He grimaced at the embarrassing nickname, though he truly appreciated the support.

All bets were on his opponent tonight—a huge Scotsman a whole head taller than Nathaniel—a MacDonald from Islay with striking black hair and brown eyes.

"MacDonald!" the majority of the club cried. "MacDonald!"

Noble Knuckles was a distant call in the sea of voices cheering for the Scotsman.

Nathaniel welcomed the challenge. Not only would it allow him to win a larger-than-normal sum, but there also couldn't be a more worthy opponent to beat the thoughts of Calliope out of his mind. To replace his burning desire for her with pure pain.

The wooden planks sank slightly as he moved his bare feet, evading MacDonald. Both men were shirtless, and MacDonald was built like a mountain, with biceps as large and hard as casks of whisky, and chest muscles like boulders. Those arms could do much damage, as Nathaniel had just felt with that incredibly powerful blow. His head spun, and the vision of the Scot swam before him slightly.

Surely not the effect of the brandy he'd drunk after he'd stormed out of his own bedroom.

The Scot's hard eyes were on him like those of a wolf hunting prey. Nathaniel saw an opportunity and made a jab with his fist, but the Scot pulled back, and Nathaniel's fist grazed the side of the Scot's face.

A mistake.

MacDonald drove his fist into Nathaniel's ribs, and something cracked and exploded in Nathaniel's insides.

He gasped for breath, and staggered back as MacDonald's other fist came closer, aiming to start pummeling him in the torso.

No doubt seeing Nathaniel's error, the crowd erupted into excited cheers and shouts, with angry men waving their fists fervently. All bets were on the Scotsman, but if Nathaniel emerged victorious, he'd return home with a hefty purse. That money would be more than sufficient to repair the railing Calliope had fallen through, and to settle the overdue payments for Mrs. Nicholson and Joshua.

Circling with his back to the ring's ropes, Nathaniel sucked in air, breathing through the pain in his side. Damn it to hell, but the man was strong. If Nathaniel didn't go home with a broken rib, he'd be surprised.

Home… He could be in bed with his new wife, plunging into her no doubt sweet, tight depths, making her come over and over and over.

He could have changed her mind. Something had spooked her, and it wasn't a sudden thought of her brother.

He could have turned her rejection into a yes if he'd really wanted to. He knew how.

Because he was never in love with any of his conquests.

Neither was he with Calliope.

So why did it hurt so much when she rejected him? What was he running away from?

Perhaps it was because none of his lovers had seen the raw humiliation that was the true state of Roxburgh Place.

But his wife had. She'd invaded his home with her rich clothes, with her comments of how she was going to fix everything. With her plans to improve it. Reminding him of all the wrongs he'd done his sisters by not providing them with a proper income and home.

And also…

Heavens, he wanted her to think well of him. He wanted her not to look at him with pity because of his finances and disappointment because of the lack of his responsibility. Not to look at him with fear, like he was going to hurt her—he would never.

He wanted her to want to be in his home. To be with him.

To look at him like she'd looked at him at the Royal Navy ball when they were nothing to each other but a man and a woman who waltzed.

Why he should want her beyond what he had told her back on Bond Street, he didn't know. A womb, she had said. Well, that was what she should be to him. He had told her there wouldn't be love. There wouldn't be romance or happiness.

So why did he find that disappointing now? He was a fool, that was why.

MacDonald followed him as he backed away to gather his strength.

But then Nathaniel saw an opening. MacDonald was also hurting. There, he kept his left arm lower, and it looked a little limp. Perhaps that was why he had hit Nathaniel so hard with his right arm; he needed to finish the battle before Nathaniel would have a chance to fight back.

Nathaniel wasn't the biggest boxer like this beast, but he certainly was fast, and he knew how to estimate an opponent's condition.

He made a false lunge to his left, as if he was about to dart away from the ropes, to trick MacDonald and get him on his unprotected side.

Pushing down his pain and taking back his rage at Calliope, at himself, and at his father, Nathaniel called all the strength and power he had in him. With a quick jab, he plunged his fist into the man's ribs.

MacDonald barely managed to cover the place with his elbow, and part of Nathaniel's effort was gone in vain. But the man was disoriented, and he turned to Nathaniel enough for him to send his next hit into MacDonald's bad arm.

The Scot grunted in pain, giving Nathaniel enough advantage to pull his arm all the way back and hit the man right in the jaw. There was a slight crack and a sound like a slap, and his head turned sharply to the side, saliva flying from his lips.

The crowd booed.

Nathaniel saw the man's eyes rolling back as he shook his head, swaying, struggling to stay on his feet. But Nathaniel needed the money. He needed this victory. Something to give him hope.

Stretching his other arm all the way back, he hit the Scot in the cheekbone, the impact reverberating in his bone marrow. The man crashed like a felled tree, sending tremors through the floor.

Nathaniel woke up the next morning in his own bed. He hadn't removed his clothes last night, nor had he wanted to bother Joshua to prepare his bath, so he stank quite badly after the sweaty match.

He was already quite late, he knew, glancing at his pocket watch as he stood next to his bed in the bright daylight pouring from the bare windows. The bed he should have awoken in with Calliope. The bed where he should have brought her her first breakfast as his duchess.

The duchess of the poorest duke in England.

He needed to take that bath now, actually. He'd just go down to find Joshua. Then, once he was clean and properly dressed, he'd go to the Admiralty and speak to Bartholomew. He walked out of his room, brushing his tangled hair over his aching head.

As he approached the dining room, he could hear the chatter of his sisters and the clanking of cutlery against plates. "...here you go," he heard Calliope's voice. "You work so hard, I think it's fair to give you a raise."

He turned the corner and saw Calliope giving banknotes to Mrs. Nicholson and Joshua, both of whom eyed her with such adoration Calliope may as well be a goddess.

Rage hit Nathaniel through his whole body like churning butter. "What are you doing?"

They all glanced at him, and silence fell over the room.

Calliope, however, turned to him with her gorgeous face calm and her chin up, her long neck perfectly straight. Her eyes slowly glanced over him, and one eyebrow cocked as her mouth curved downwards.

"Good morning, husband," she said. "I see you just came home from...wherever you've been."

He could just see himself from her eyes. He'd walked out of their wedding night and spent it somewhere else. His hair was disheveled, his clothes untidy and crumpled, his face unshaven...and that reek of sweat and vanilla and brandy. He could smell it on himself, and he was disgusted.

"You did not answer my question," he said. "Mrs. Nicholson, Joshua, what is that?"

"Forgive me, Your Grace," said Mrs. Nicholson with no trace of regret in her voice. "These are our wages that were owed to us for the past three months."

Damnation! The guilt and rage mixing within him were as dangerous as gunpowder. "I am sorry for that, Mrs. Nicholson and Joshua." He went into the pocket of his coat and retrieved the crumpled pounds. "Here. I am perfectly capable of paying my own staff, Calliope. Please, return my wife the wages and take these."

He shoved the money into Mrs. Nicholson's and Joshua's hands.

"This is too much, Your Grace," said Joshua.

Calliope's face was hard on him. His sisters gaped at him. Heavens, he must be quite a sight.

"Nonsense. Joshua, please prepare a bath for me right away."

"Very good, Your Grace."

But a bath would take at least an hour to prepare. Could he wait that long?

"Actually, no," he said. "No. Go and saddle Hermes. I'm riding right out."

Joshua carefully looked him over. "Perhaps you would prefer a sponge bath, Your Grace? It won't take long—the water is already hot for the tea."

"Hermes, please." He stared into Calliope's gorgeous eyes that blazed at him with anger. "A bath can wait. My wife has assigned me an urgent task that cannot."

The young lad retrieved Calliope's money and gently placed the notes on the dining table. Mrs. Nicholson did the same. Then they both left the room with their thanks.

Calliope's blue gaze turned as dark as the ocean during a storm. "That is right, it cannot wait. Especially given that my husband gave me an oath of fidelity."

Her voice trembled and staggered on the last word.

Nathaniel cursed under his breath and glanced at his sisters, who watched them both, disappointment in him apparent in their eyes.

He took Calliope by the elbow and led her out of the room.

"You refuse my money and my help," Calliope muttered angrily. "You left me last night and didn't sleep at home until the early hours of the morning. You come back with scratches and reeking like some sort of vanilla perfume. Where have you been?"

He stood with her in the drawing room, glaring at her. "Where I have been has nothing to do with you. You made it clear you will not let me bed you, so why do you care if I bed someone else?"

"Because you stood before a man of God and you gave me your vow," she spat.

He glared at her, feeling his bruised chest heaving in need of air. "There were no other women, Calliope. Nor will there be."

She kept staring at him. “Then where have you been?”

He couldn’t tell her. He didn’t even tell his sisters how he earned coin in a way that was so ridiculous and completely humiliating for a peer. How low could he fall?

No, he wouldn’t tell Calliope. She’d never look at him the same way again.

“Like I said, there are things I have to do to provide for my sisters. For you.”

She chuckled. “You don’t need to provide for me. I can provide for you. Let me help.”

Let her help? Or rather, sink deeper into his humiliation. “Your brother made sure I am not allowed to touch your dowry.”

“You will not be breaking that agreement if I give it freely, and not just to you. To your sisters. To my new family.”

His chest tightened with an impulse to agree, to let her in. To lean on her. He had been alone for so long in this, it was hard to imagine a life where he wouldn’t need to do it anymore.

But no. The only thing he had left was his pride.

“I am going to get that information to you today,” he said, more coldly than he’d like. “And once I do, I will bed you.”

Her eyes widened.

“Hermes is ready, Your Grace,” said Joshua, appearing in the doorway.

“Thank you,” he said and turned back to Calliope.

“Are you going to the Admiralty?” she asked.

“Yes. I am.”

She marched to the door. “I’ll come with you.”

Not this again. It was still dangerous for her. “No. You’re to stay here.”

“But Nathaniel—”

He turned and strode out the door.

Twenty minutes later, he dismounted, only to see a well-dressed lady with auburn hair under her bonnet descend from a carriage with the Grandhampton coat of arms.

His wife.

14

GOD ALMIGHTY.

Striding across the expansive square in front of the Admiralty, he glared at Calliope hurrying towards the entrance from the opposite corner, matching his pace and determination. All the while, his fists rhythmically clenched and unclenched.

"Calliope," he rasped when she was less than twenty feet away from him. "I told you to stay at home."

"And I told you I want information," she retorted, her green skirts tangling and highlighting the form of her long, sculpted legs. Legs he could have had wrapped around his waist last might. "Clearly, you're unable to move fast enough to get what we need. So I'll follow the ancient wisdom. If you want something to be done well, do it yourself."

They came together ten feet from the stairs leading up to the Admiralty, glaring at each other. Her auburn locks were playing in the wind. He could see the ovals of her breasts moving up and down as she breathed hard.

"If you think you'll take one step inside," he spat, "you're sorely mistaken."

He turned and walked towards the building, then climbed the stairs, taking two steps at a time.

"If you think I'll stay out," she cried after him as her heels clicked against the stones, "it's *you* who are mistaken."

He walked to one of the two officers standing guard, both of whom stared at Calliope and him with wide eyes.

"Do not let her in, either of you," he barked. "Under no circumstances is she allowed in."

"Yes, sir." Both of them saluted him.

He walked into the darkness of the building and turned, watching with satisfaction how the two men stepped in front of Calliope, who stood shooting daggers at him.

"Nathaniel!" she yelled. "It's not a game. My brother's life is at stake!"

"I know that," he retorted. "He's missing, and you must stay out of this investigation or...or you may go missing, too. I will take care of everything."

He then addressed the two officers again: "Do not let her in."

Leaving her seething, he turned and passed through the wide hallway, his boots clicking against the polished marble floor. He was supposed to stay home today, for two weeks actually, for his honeymoon.

A honeymoon that would not be happening without him finding the information his wife needed.

He climbed the stairs to the first floor, then turned to the hallway leading to the Navy Board. He found the Navy Pay Office.

The room was big enough to fit six massive wooden desks and the clerks who sat hunched over them. Polished oak-paneled walls gleamed beneath the flicker of oil lamps. Rows of heavy leather-bound ledgers were arranged methodically in large bookcases, their worn spines etched with years and ship names in precise gilt letters.

The room smelled of ink, paper, and musty, old wood. The scratching of quills against paper was punctuated by the occasional knocks of abacus beads and muted murmurs as the clerks did their calculations and discussed their entries.

One of them was Bartholomew.

Nathaniel walked up to him. He was a well-built man in his forties with harsh eyes. He looked up from his papers.

"Kelford." He frowned. "Are you not supposed to be on leave for your honeymoon?"

"I am. There's an urgent matter."

"What can I do for you?"

"I wondered if you have the lists of sailors for certain ships that sailed from London last year."

"Oh." Bartholomew put down his pen and stood up. "Certainly."

He walked towards the bookshelf with the ledgers. "Is there some mishap with conscriptions?"

This was going far easier than Nathaniel could ever hope. "Yes, I just need to check on which ship one particular sailor is serving."

"Of course." Bartholomew stopped next to the rows of ledgers and laid one hand on the edge of the shelf. "What ships?"

"Five of them—*Minotaur*, *Titan*, *Concord*, *Hector*, and *Aeneas*."

Bartholomew froze and threw a strange, inquisitive look at Nathaniel. "On which date?"

"September 3, 1812," said Nathaniel carefully, not liking Bartholomew's reaction at all.

Bartholomew opened and closed his mouth.

"Is there something amiss?" Nathaniel asked.

"No. Of course not," the man said. "Let me see where the ledgers are for the payments to the sailors and officers aboard those ships."

He turned back to the row of ledgers and started looking through the books. He found one and pulled it out, then the door behind them opened with a loud bang and heels clacked against the floor.

Nathaniel and Bartholomew turned around. Calliope charged into the office, fuming.

Bartholomew let go of the ledger and stared at her with confusion and surprise.

"Calliope," Nathaniel snarled when she stood next to him. "How did you get in here?"

Calliope raised one brow. "Please. Your officers are much too gallant. What must they do when a young lady faints from heat in front of them? They must bring her inside into the shade, of course. And while one of them went to fetch a doctor, the other one went to fetch water. I'm sure they'll be quite surprised to find the bench in the lobby empty upon their return."

Nathaniel shook his head.

"Nathaniel, please find your manners and introduce me."

Nathaniel's stomach was churning. He could not fathom this woman, but he could not simply ignore her, either, as much as he might wish to at this moment.

"Bartholomew, allow me to introduce my wife, the Duchess of Kelford."

Bartholomew's expression cleared in understanding. He gathered a polite smile on his face. "Pleased to meet you, madam."

"The pleasure is mine," said Calliope with a charming smile.

What a stubborn, sly woman. Why could she not just listen to him and keep herself out of danger's path?

"So." She looked eagerly at the row of ledgers. "Did you find the lists of sailors?"

Bartholomew's face fell. He gave Nathaniel a hard stare.

"I'm afraid there was a mistake, Kelford. As much as I enjoyed meeting your new wife, I cannot in my good conscience allow military information to be shared with civilians. Especially not women."

Calliope's enthusiasm evaporated. "Officer Bartholomew, I assure you—"

"Please." Bartholomew waved his hand towards the door.

"But—" Nathaniel started.

"Kelford, I am warning you," said Bartholomew. "My duty is to my country and my king. My word is final."

Feeling the sense of a lost battle, Nathaniel nodded somberly. "Come along, Calliope. You heard the man."

"But, Nathaniel..."

He gently took her by the elbow and tugged her after him.

"Good day, Bartholomew," he added as he and Calliope walked out of the room.

When the door closed behind him, he turned to her, her big eyes on him with regret. "He almost gave me those lists before you came in!" he grated out through clenched teeth, forcing his voice down. "I told you to stay away. Will you listen to me for once in your life? Do you see how you are actually doing more harm than good?"

She straightened her neck. "Is Bartholomew's family rich?"

Nathaniel shook his head. "Excuse me?"

"What is his social status?"

"What does that have to do—"

"Just answer my question, please."

"No, he is not. His papa is a small boat builder somewhere up north."

She wore a triumphant look. "See, that's what I thought. And yet, he has a big golden ring with a very real-looking ruby on his finger. Did you notice? And why did his hand shake so when he touched the ledger?"

Nathaniel frowned for a moment. He didn't remember Bartholomew coming to riches recently. "What does that have to do with anything?"

"I'm not sure yet," she said thoughtfully. "But now that I'm out of the room, go in there and get those lists."

He softened and shook his head. "You didn't listen to me before, Calliope, but listen to me now. We must let him calm down. I'll ask him again, but not today. He's a man of strict rules, and he was right about not giving information to civilians."

Calliope opened her mouth to protest, then nodded. "Very well. But you must do it tomorrow."

"Thank you. Let us return home. I do need a bath, and I will think of other steps we may take to find your brother."

15

"Perhaps that one?" asked Poppy excitedly, pointing at a hat shop as Calliope and the girls strolled down Bond Street the next day.

The sound of hooves on cobblestones melded with the murmur of animated conversations as well-dressed gentlemen and ladies navigated the throng. Underfoot, the smooth stones felt oddly comforting, worn down by countless footsteps over the years.

Modistes showcased the latest fashions behind gleaming windowpanes, the delicate fabrics teasing the eye with splashes of vibrant colors and intricate patterns. The soft melody of a violinist seeking alms reached Calliope's ears, competing with the low hum of nearby conversations. Every so often, the sweet scent of fresh bouquets from a florist's stand broke through the more pervasive aroma of horse and leather.

Argos, Nathaniel's giant black dog, tugged at the leash in Hazel's hand, his nose quivering at the myriad scents—from the remnants of meat pies to the apparently enticing smell of other dogs. Every few steps, Argos would bark at a particularly flashy carriage or growl at another hound, his whole body a bundle of curious energy.

Remembering her first encounter with the canine, Calliope smirked. The name Argos, famously known as Odysseus's loyal companion, seemed a bit too grand for such a mischievous creature, especially considering their less-than-auspicious introduction in the mews.

Calliope, just like her cat, was quite careful around the dog and wasn't thrilled about taking him with them, but she understood the poor animal needed some air.

And how fun it was that, for the first time in her life, Calliope, as a married woman, could chaperone someone rather than being chaperoned. And, never having had sisters, she loved showing the girls around. Despite her general lack of interest in the social life of the ton, she was excited to help Hazel come out for her first Season. And the twins would surely come out in the next couple of years, as well.

All three girls were a delight to be with. They looked at all the shops and establishments with such wide eyes and enthusiasm that Calliope's heart melted. They'd never had a mother to take them shopping, poor things.

As they stood in front of the hat shop, Poppy practically pressed herself against the window. "Ohh, that bonnet is so pretty, look!"

It was a pretty one, indeed. White, with adorable little roses of colors ranging from blush to peach to pink.

"Let's go and get that one for you, then," said Calliope.

The squeal poor Poppy gave made several people turn their heads, and Argos woofed questioningly.

"Calm down," murmured Hazel.

"I prefer a book, anyway," said Violet with a sideways glance at the bonnet, which was full of envy.

"I'll get one for each of you," said Calliope. "And some fitting ribbons, too."

The smiles that bloomed on the girls' faces broke her heart.

As Calliope opened the door of the shop and let the girls and Argos pass first, she threw a mindless glance at the street behind them. There was someone standing at the corner of the building watching her.

She frowned, blinking. No, that couldn't be right. So that he didn't notice her watching him, she pretended to drop something on the pavement and knelt, keeping the man in her side vision. He was dressed like a working-class man, perhaps a carriage driver or a milkman. Sturdy, patched brown breeches hugged his muscular legs, while a faded, ill-fitting waistcoat clung to his broad chest. His shirt was speckled with the dust and grime of a day's work. A worn cap shaded his keen eyes, which darted around as if always alert to his surroundings.

But then he detached himself from the wall of the building, turned around, and disappeared behind the corner.

She must be imagining things, Calliope decided as she straightened back up. Nothing else was out of the ordinary on the street. People continued walking and talking, passing in and out of the doors of the shops.

When she entered the shop, the girls stood sheepishly waiting for her. She asked the milliner's assistant to allow the girls to try the bonnets they liked.

While Poppy put on the white bonnet and Violet a light blue one with lace, Hazel stood with a grim face and didn't move.

Calliope quickly scanned the street through the window to see if the man had returned. "Why don't you try one, too, Hazel?" she asked.

Hazel's eyes darted to a yellow bonnet, but she stubbornly lifted her chin. "Because I have everything I need. Besides, Nathaniel won't like you buying them bonnets."

"Nathaniel doesn't know what it's like in our places," said Violet.

"He does, actually," said Hazel. "Why do you think he comes back home with cuts and bruises?"

Calliope went to Violet, who stood in front of a small mirror struggling with the bonnet. Calliope corrected the position of the bonnet on her head, and it fit perfectly. She tied a bow under her chin. "Why does he, Hazel?"

Violet looked at Calliope from under her lashes. "I heard Joshua tell Mrs. Nicholson that's how he earns money."

"What? What does that mean?"

Violet shrugged. "That's all we know."

Calliope looked at Hazel, who avoided her gaze, darted towards the yellow bonnet, and busied herself with touching the ribbons, the lace, and the ornaments.

"Hazel?" Calliope asked again, approaching her. "What do you know?"

"I'm sure I don't know anything," said Hazel, her cheeks reddening but her neck still straight.

"He doesn't say anything to us," said Poppy sadly. "All I know is he's doing more for us than he wants to admit. He got the dogs to protect us, although from what, I don't know. He goes to the balls he doesn't want to. He doesn't come home for days. And when he does, he reeks of perfume and appears so exhausted he seems in need of a week's rest. But then he can pay Mrs. Nicholson and Joshua and tells them to order meat and sugar and finally good tea. Sometimes he can buy us new books."

"Poppy!" Hazel gasped.

"She should know, Hazel," said Violet. "She's his wife. Our new sister."

"Those are always our favorite days, Calliope." Poppy said as she turned this way and that, looking at herself in the mirror. "Because that's when Violet can read us new stories."

Calliope's heart did that lurch again. Nathaniel bore the weight of the whole world on his shoulders, and yet she'd called him irresponsible. Guilt gnawed at her as she thought about the hurt she'd seen in his eyes. Calliope's eyes blurred with tears, and she swallowed a sudden knot in her throat.

She wished he could accept that he didn't need to bear that weight all alone. That she was there to help.

"You know what," she said with a smile. "Let us get all those bonnets and go to a bookshop. And you can pick any books you like. And then we'll go to Sumhall and raid the library. What do you say?"

The twins giggled and nodded. Violet clapped her hands together. Hazel bit her lip but nodded reluctantly. She couldn't fool Calliope. Even though she refused a bonnet, her eyes glimmered at the mention of books.

And Calliope would still buy her the yellow bonnet.

After Calliope paid and the shop assistant packed the bonnets into three round boxes, they left, Argos loyally trotting by Hazel's side. They were chatting and giggling as they walked towards Calliope's favorite bookstore, which was just six shops down the street. Calliope glanced up and down the street to see if the man who had followed them was there...

And froze just for a moment as her glance grazed the man's figure. He was leaning against a carriage, looking straight at her.

Fear burst through her, but she pasted the smile back onto her face, looking away, trying to make sure he didn't think she'd noticed him. Walking down the street with the girls, she thought about what she could do now to protect herself and Nathaniel's sisters. It was good, she supposed, that they had Argos. The beast looked dangerous enough to spook some villains—hopefully, including that one.

They could scream for help; there were many people around, enough that the man, perhaps, wouldn't try anything.

But Calliope had to know what he intended.

As they walked, chatting about what books the girls wanted to read, Calliope covertly looked over her shoulder. The man was nowhere to be seen, only well-dressed ladies and gentlemen. She felt safe enough now. The bookstore she had in mind was situated in a narrow side street, and she and the girls turned there. It was much quieter. The brick walls of the buildings flanked both sides with paned windows decorated with red and pink geraniums, and there, about fifty feet away, was the sign of the bookstore.

"There it is," said Calliope.

They had stridden a few paces farther when she heard footsteps behind them. She turned.

Ten feet behind her, the man from earlier followed them, staring right at her. A cold wave of fear crashed over her as she turned to look straight ahead again.

"Hazel," she said as she leaned towards the girl, "in a moment, I want you to run down the street, calling for help. Reach the bookstore as fast as you can."

Hazel's eyes widened. "Why?"

Calliope swallowed. "I think there's someone about to rob us."

Hazel's face lost all color. "Rob? Right here, next to Bond Street?"

Perhaps the man wanted to do much worse things than rob, but Calliope couldn't say that to Hazel.

She looked over her shoulder again. The man was only five feet behind.

“Yes, dear, I’m afraid so,” Calliope replied.

She turned her head slightly and saw with her side vision that he was now only three feet behind.

“Now.”

Calliope stopped and turned completely around, facing the man, who widened his eyes, then threw his arm out towards her. With a small but powerful movement Spencer had taught her, one she had practiced with him countless times, she hit the man straight in the nose.

There was a crack of bone against her knuckle and a lightning bolt of pain through her hand. The man grunted.

She thought she’d hear the girls running away, yelling for help. Instead, there was a tremendous growl, and Argos flashed by Calliope in a huge leap of muscle and fur, his giant jaws clashing.

“Get him, Argos!” yelled Hazel.

The man had barely managed to recover from Calliope’s hit when Argos’s jaws came together on his ankle, and he yelled with such power that Calliope’s ears hurt. Still yelling, the man got out a knife and started to mindlessly stab at Argos. Calliope’s blood ran cold for the dog.

“Calliope!” called a tall, muscular figure at the entrance into the alleyway. “Girls!”

Calliope recognized the voice...Nathaniel. Her stomach flipped from the sudden joy of his presence and worry for him.

More people were coming into the alleyway. The man kept stabbing the air around the dog, but Argos had now let him go and was growling and barking at him, standing in a protective position.

As Nathaniel and the people behind him came closer, the

man dashed in the opposite direction. Argos and Nathaniel raced past Calliope in pursuit.

"Are you all right?" asked Hazel as she came to Calliope. "How are your knuckles?"

Violet took Calliope's hand in hers and removed her glove, staring at the reddened flesh with wonder. "You must be the most extraordinary woman ever."

16

"Calliope, how could you do this?"

Nathaniel paced the drawing room, his footsteps knocking against the bare wooden floor in a wild rhythm. He just couldn't get the image of the man stabbing at his dog, his wife, and his sisters out of his mind.

He'd returned earlier today from the Admiralty, holding the list of sailors on all five vessels, feeling completely triumphant. But the house was empty, and he'd asked Mrs. Nicholson where Calliope and his sisters were, only to find out she'd taken them shopping. Wanting to finally buy something for them himself, he'd followed them to Bond Street, only to see them turning that corner with a strange man on their heels. He remembered the utter horror as he'd imagined what the man could do.

The memories of his mother and that terrible night when he couldn't protect her clamped him in a cold, sharp vise.

He'd hurried after them, thankfully reaching them in time. But after the man ran away, Nathaniel and Argos hadn't been able to find him. The poor dog had gotten two cuts, though not deep. Nathaniel had cleaned and treated the wounds.

But that could have been one of his sisters...or his wife.

"How could I?" Calliope demanded. "I didn't ask that man to follow us."

"Yes, brother," said Violet, who had Miss Furrington on her lap. The little beast was curled in a ball and purring loudly, her nose hidden in her tail. "Calliope didn't ask for a burglar to follow us."

Nathaniel brushed both of his hands through his hair, some locks falling from the tie at the back of his head.

"Yes, he was a burglar," said Poppy. "He saw the boxes with our new pretty bonnets and thought we'd be easy targets."

Nathaniel shook his head in quiet fury. He saw some logic in that, but the image of the dead flowers sent to Calliope asking her to stop digging hadn't left his mind.

"Well," said Calliope quietly, looking at her feet. "He actually wasn't a burglar."

"What?" Nathaniel barked.

"What?" the girls echoed.

Nathaniel absolutely hated the glint of excitement and intrigue in their eyes. Why weren't they afraid like he was? How could they not know what men like that could do to women? That it wasn't a game to play. That they could lie in pools of blood, with their chests and hearts unmoving.

Forever gone.

"He wasn't a burglar," said Calliope.

"How do you know?" asked Hazel. "I thought he followed us to the alley with his knife to steal your purse."

"Well, no regular burglar would do that during the daylight on the busiest street in London. He was dressed like a working man, which was clearly camouflage. A true thug desperate enough to rob ladies next to a busy street would be dressed much worse. And then his knife... It was too sharp, too new. I think he didn't want money."

Her blue eyes met with his, and he saw exactly what she was thinking. It was someone connected to those flowers. Someone connected to Spencer's disappearance.

"It was because you didn't stay away!" he roared. "I told you to stay away from your damned investigation and you didn't. And now you endangered my sisters, my dog—and you endangered yourself! All of you"—he moved his arm in a large circle indicating all four females—"are forbidden from taking a single step out of this house. A single step!"

Calliope almost shrank visibly from the power of his voice.

"What investigation?" asked Poppy in a small, but terribly curious voice.

Ignoring her, Calliope raised her eyebrow and straightened her back. "Perhaps. In fact, I think you're right. But, as you also could see, I could defend us. I had a plan. I know boxing. I would have dealt with him."

"She really did have him, brother," said Violet proudly. "We were perfectly safe with her."

The growl that tore from Nathaniel's throat surprised even him. With a force he should not have applied, he clutched his hand around Calliope's elbow and dragged her from the drawing room up the stairs onto the first floor and into the first door he could find.

"You are the most infuriating female I've ever met!" he declared. "Do you see the danger you are? Not just you, but my girls? Can you now please stay away from all this and let me deal with it—if not for your own sake, then for my sisters'?"

Calliope crossed her arms over her chest. "I definitely agree about keeping your sisters away, but I will not be stopped, Nathaniel. And if anything, you should stay away from Bartholomew, as well. He really didn't want you and me to see that ledger. And that ring..." She shook her head. "Something is very wrong about him."

He scoffed. "If there was something very wrong, he wouldn't have given me the ledger."

Ah, the joy of seeing that shock on her face was almost as good as a climax. "He did?" she asked. "Well, where is it?"

He stared at her. "I will give it to you."

Suddenly, he noticed three vases with yellow irises stood in the room. Three paintings with Mediterranean seascapes hung on the walls. "Is this your bedchamber?" he murmured.

"Yes," she said, suddenly sheepish.

It was beautiful. The walls still needed fresh paint, but somehow, she'd gotten new curtains hung in a mossy green, the color of autumn. And the rug on the floor was woven with red and orange and yellows. He could see how pretty this room would be once Calliope finished with it.

He could imagine how grand this whole house could look from her touch, from her very presence.

He stared at the bed. They were alone. He had the papers. He remembered the taste of her lips last night when he'd kissed her, the wonderful feel of her small body in his arms.

"I will bring you the ledger," he said, taking one step closer to her. "Do you remember that you said you would let me bed you once I do that?"

Her face flushed so deep a red he could light a fire from it.

"Yes," she whispered.

He stepped so close he could smell her...delicious. Flowers and something herbal and sweet and hers. He picked up a strand of hair that fell from the array of curls she had framing her face and returned it to its place. "Yes, you remember, or yes, I can bed you?"

He watched with satisfaction as her perfect pink lips parted and reddened.

"Yes, I remember," she said.

"And yes, I may come to your bed?" he asked.

She swallowed and nodded.

A groan was born in the depths of his throat, but he suppressed it.

"Good," he said. "I already looked through the ledger and didn't find anything resembling Spencer's name, but you surely want to look at it yourself."

She nodded again.

He cupped her face. "Do not be afraid, Calliope. I'll make sure you enjoy every moment of it."

She breathed quickly in and out and said nothing.

He left her proximity and turned around at the door. "I was just very afraid for you and the girls. You already received a threat. Today was the next step to execute it. I simply want to protect you, but you make it very difficult."

17

Later that night, Calliope stood by the window in her bedchamber with Miss Furrington sitting on the windowsill next to the ledger Calliope had been studying for the past few hours. The cat watched the dogs, her pupils so dilated they almost covered her green irises.

Nathaniel was down in the mews. She couldn't hear him through the glass, but it seemed he was training the dogs. The three of them sat, staring up at him, looking all happy and sweet. Then he would say something and make a gesture, and they would rise, their ears standing at attention.

Calliope's chest warmed. Why did her heart do some strange sort of lurch every time she looked at him, every time she was in his presence? Perhaps it was something about him that made him look so lonely. She knew she had misjudged him early on, at that ball. She'd thought of him as nothing but a rake.

But the more she knew of him, the more she liked. The more she wanted to be in his company, look at him, talk to him...

Touch him.

That kiss he'd given her... The touch of his hands, of his body against her, they did something incredible and electric to her, sent beautiful currents of life flowing through her.

She touched the ledger he had brought from the Naval Board. He had done his part to meet the agreement between them. How much longer could she postpone the inevitable? Sooner or later, he would bed her, and she would, hopefully, get pregnant.

He'd come to her tonight, that was what he'd promised. The thought of resuming what they had started caused both a tight knot in her belly and a gorgeous exhilaration in her blood.

He turned, presenting his side to her. As he methodically picked up three sticks, tossing each into the farthest part of the yard, the slight downward tilt of his lips, the subtle furrowing of his brow, and the distant, hollow look in his eyes made her windpipe constrict tightly.

Her fear melted as the urge to talk to him won over, and she walked out of her bedroom and climbed down the stairs towards him.

As she opened the door, the dogs growled, turning to look at her, and she froze.

Nathaniel glanced at her, his expression warming. "Sit," he commanded the three beasts. "This is your new mistress. Argos, you protected her today. Good boy. You should do it every time she needs your help."

Argos stopped growling and looked at Calliope with wet eyes, his tail starting to wag.

"Um," said Calliope, still not moving. "Are you still busy with them?"

"No," said Nathaniel as he patted their heads. He didn't have on a waistcoat or a coat, only his white shirt, the ties at his collar undone and the sleeves rolled up to show his gorgeous, muscular forearms covered with soft-looking blond hair. A pleasant agitation settled in the pit of Calliope's stomach. "We're finished, aren't we, lads?" His gaze softened even more as he looked her over. "Don't be afraid, Calliope," he said with a tenderness that had her stomach clench deliciously. "They won't touch you. Come here."

She swallowed. "I'm not sure they want me to. I smell of a cat."

"Are you afraid of dogs?"

She sighed. "I'm certainly afraid of dogs with giant jaws that growl and bark and look at me like I'm food. I much prefer cats."

Amusement sparkled in his eyes. "Cats," he scoffed slightly. "They're useless animals."

Calliope gasped. "Excuse me? Useless? They're great companions." She put up one finger. "They're great hunters and catch vermin." Another finger. "They're cute." Another finger. "And when they sleep with you, they warm up the bed."

His eyes grew darker. "You don't need a cat to warm your bed when you have a husband."

She was unable to look away from him, completely kept captive in his gaze.

And at a loss for words, she suppressed her fear of the beasts and walked down the stairs and towards them, her heart drumming strongly against her ribs. They looked at her, and Argos bowed his head to sniff at her hand. Although the giant dog had gone with her and the girls earlier that day, she'd managed to always keep a few feet away from him. Calliope stood a step away from them now, her knees a little wobbly, her hand shivering.

"Good boys," said Nathaniel. "This is your new mistress. My wife."

He glanced at her then, their gazes locking, and something in her chest tightened at the words.

"Here." He picked up a plate of old, hard pieces of bread. "Give them a treat."

Calliope picked up a dry piece of bread with trembling fingers. Argos's jaws looked especially dangerous next to her hand.

"Don't be afraid, love," he said. "They're good boys. They just need to know you're in their pack, someone they need to protect."

Love... Oh, how good the word sounded on his lips.

He was a rake, she reminded herself. He didn't really mean those words. She shouldn't assume otherwise.

She nodded. He was right, of course. And she trusted him. She stretched her hand out towards Argos. He licked his jaws, whined slightly, and his giant tail began wagging from side to side as he looked into the palm of her hand. The other two watched her with great interest, too, shifting closer.

"Here, Argos," she said. "For you. Thank you for saving us today."

Argos whined and licked the bread off her palm, his tongue wet and warm. The shiver of fear that went through her was replaced with a thrill of joy as the dog crunched happily on the bread. Calliope giggled as she looked into Nathaniel's satisfied face.

"Well done, Calliope," he said. "See, not so scary."

She nodded. "Do you want some, too?" she asked the other two, who looked at her now with adoration. She placed a piece of bread in each palm and stretched them out for the beasts. "Here you go."

They gave thin little whines of excitement, and both grabbed their treats from her palms, their warm breath brushing against her skin.

She straightened and watched the dogs crunch on the bread, something warm and delightful spreading through her. They didn't look at her with animosity anymore, nor did they growl or bark. On the contrary, they looked at the plate in her hands with great anticipation.

"Can I give them more?" she asked Nathaniel.

He crossed his arms over his chest, his long, muscular legs standing wide apart, a calm, satisfied half smile on his lips.

"You can," he said. "I'd say Argos especially earned it. Had these two been with you, they would, too."

As Calliope fed them more treats, enjoying herself, smiling as she watched them crunch on the bread, she thought she may ask Nathaniel if she could borrow one of them once she opened her agency. She wondered why she hadn't thought of that before. She could see about training them to follow smells and therefore help her in her jobs that required searching, not to mention guarding her or her future employees.

"Good boys," she said as they ate the last pieces, and patted them on their heads, just like Nathaniel did. "Thank you for chasing away that man today, Nathaniel," she said without looking at him, but she felt his hot gaze on her. "And for the ledger."

"You're welcome," he said softly. "Did you find anything?"

"No mention of Spencer, as you said." She finally looked at him, meeting his eyes. That turquoise gaze sent a delicious shiver right through her core. "But the lists of the sailors and their wages from those five ships are all on different paper."

He frowned, his relaxed pose gaining tension. "Different paper?"

She nodded. "The paper the rest of the ledger is written on is slightly yellow. A little older. The paper on which those lists are written is whiter. Clearly newer and produced by a different manufacturer. There were also traces of glue."

Nathaniel's jaws opened and closed slightly as he stared into space with his brows drawn together. "Are you certain?"

"Quite certain," she said. "Someone doesn't want the real lists to be found. And that someone may be your friend Bartholomew."

Nathaniel jerked his head to the side once, the muscles on his forearms playing under his skin.

"But that means," said Calliope, "we still don't know which of the five ships Spencer was dragged onto. And I don't know what else we can do in the Admiralty to find that out. I think we've come to a dead end there. So I believe the next step is to go to Portside and ask around."

He untangled his arms and stood facing her, his eyes dark with warning. "Do not tell me you want to go there yourself."

"That is exactly what I want to do," she declared.

"You must stay at home. I told you to stay put."

"You have no say in this. It's my brother."

"Calliope!" he said, his voice ringing with barely contained anger. "I will go and ask around. A man just tried to attack you today!"

"And if the person who sent him thinks that will scare me, they're mistaken!"

"You're quite impossible!" he roared. "I will lock you in the house if I must!"

She gasped. "You will not! What are you doing here, anyway? Aren't you supposed to be out somewhere with courtesans drinking and such...or wherever you spent the other night?"

He was quite menacing now. Standing tall, gorgeous, and yet she was aware as never before how much taller and stronger than her he was.

"I told you, I haven't seen any courtesans. Nor will I. I gave my vow."

She nodded briefly, breathing hard. "Where were you, then?"

He sighed and bowed his head as though submitting to some decision. "I was in Portside. From time to time, I participate in boxing matches."

Calliope couldn't breathe. "So that was what the girls heard about?"

His face lost all expression. "They know?"

"Yes, from Joshua. Though Violet didn't understand what she heard exactly."

"Damnation," he cursed. "Please don't tell them. Of course, my wages in the Admiralty aren't enough to cover the expenses. That's what I've been doing for years."

The sun dipped behind the rooftops, casting the London sky in hues of amber and rose, the edges of the clouds glowing in gold. The wind became chilly and swept around Calliope, covering her skin in goose bumps.

"You're cold," he said. "Come, let's get you inside."

Calliope nodded and patted the dogs on their heads again. "Good night, doggies."

As they walked inside and climbed the stairs, his words from earlier came to mind... *You don't need a cat to warm your bed when you have a husband.*

"Are you hurt?" she asked as they climbed the creaking stairs onto the first floor. "From the boxing match."

"I'm fine," he said.

"You didn't look fine. Please, don't do that again," she said as they stood before the door to her bedchamber.

Nathaniel opened it and entered without any thought to answer her.

"Nathaniel!"

"I will do it again if I must, Calliope," he said. "I have tried gambling, betting on horse races, but it only drew me deeper into financial ruin. Boxing is something I have control over. I am good at it. I win."

Calliope's throat clenched. Spencer had disappeared during one such boxing match. And the sport itself could lead to terrible injuries. What if something happened to Nathaniel?

"Nathaniel, it's dangerous, you could get seriously hurt."

He came closer to her. She became very much aware of his proximity, the scent of male musk and his cologne, a combination so intoxicating she wanted to smear it all over her body.

He cupped her face. "Would you prefer me to go back to a wealthy duchess lover who used to shower me with gifts?"

She felt the blood drain from her face.

He chuckled softly with an edge of self-deprecation in his expression. "Oh yes, Calliope, that is how low I fell to provide for my sisters. My father was wrong. I wasn't completely worthless. This pretty face and my gentleman's charms weren't for nothing."

She swallowed. "Nathaniel—"

"You asked if I went to courtesans? I was a courtesan myself, darling. What else would you call someone who pleased wealthy, powerful women in bed for the gifts they could bestow upon me?"

He was quite ashamed of that. She could see it in his eyes. Her heart ached with empathy for him. "You will never have to do that again. You have me now."

His eyes blazed with heat as he slowly took in her face, her neck, her whole body, as though studying a completely new territory. "Quite right, darling. I have you. I have not seen anyone else from the moment my eyes fell upon you."

With that, he took her face in both hands and kissed her.

As his lips touched hers, heat swept through her, chasing away the goose bumps.

The kiss...the heavenly, beautiful kiss. His lips brushed and teased hers, coming together in delicious strokes, pulling apart, then returning. It was as though he was drinking from her, and yet the more he drank the thirstier he got. Her head was spinning, her body going limp and so, so warm. Every breath she took brought her more of his incredible scent.

She could do nothing but wrap her arms around his neck, pulling herself closer to him. She was burning, and he was her only salvation.

Her breasts became heavy and achy, and she felt a delicious clenching inside. Maybe this would be fine. He wouldn't laugh at her. He had told her he'd wanted her since the moment he saw her...

He'd probably said that to those duchesses he'd bedded, too, but this would be fine. He knew what he was doing.

"What is it, love?" he asked as he leaned back, breaking the kiss, his eyes dark. "I feel you tense. Are you still cold?"

She swallowed. "I'm not cold. I'm quite warm."

"Do you want me to stop?" he asked, looking her over.

She tried to contain her breath. "I don't know."

"If you ever want me to stop, just say the word and I will." He swallowed hard. He looked almost pained. "But I pray to the heavens you don't."

Then he was back to her lips, making her quite breathless again. His arms wrapped around her, bringing her to him like an iron vise. He picked her up, hooking one arm down under her knees and one under her back. Calliope gasped from surprise and from the feeling of weightlessness. It was a sweet pleasure, to feel small and fragile in the arms of this beautiful man.

He laid her on the bed and returned to kissing her. His lips went down her neck, and when he was close to that damned spot William had pinched, she stilled. But as though having sensed that, he didn't touch it, but continued, making his way down to the ovals of her breasts protruding from the top of her bodice. His kisses left delightful, burning sensations of desire.

She squirmed when he lifted one breast from her corset with a satisfied murmur. Calliope sucked in air.

"Nathaniel!" she panted.

How could she be so terrified and yet aroused at the same time?

"What a beautiful breast, darling," he murmured, and then, just like in one of those books, he leaned his face towards her and licked.

Calliope cried out as delicious fire rushed through her.

"Do you like this?" he asked, but without waiting for her answer, he lowered his head and took her nipple in his mouth completely, sucking it. The tugging sent pulses of desire through her, darting right into the apex of her thighs. She was all hot and achy there, and she brought her thighs together, trying to satisfy that ache.

"Oh, you do like this," he said as he stopped his heavenly torture of her breast and looked at her thighs. Then he looked up with hooded eyes and a half smile.

She swallowed, breathing hard. Was he smiling because he was enjoying himself...because he liked her...or because somehow she was embarrassing herself?

"Don't you?" he asked.

She didn't see any laughter, so she nodded.

"So do I," he murmured as his hand traveled down her leg and stopped at the gathering of her skirts at her knees. Then it moved under her skirts, and his fingers were on her stocking-covered leg. She froze, the feel of his large, heavy, warm palm spreading pleasure through her skin. And then very, very slowly, he moved his hand up her thigh.

With every inch it went higher, the throbbing inside her grew, and ached, and all she wanted was for him to reach his destination, that wonderful place where she knew herself there was so much pleasure.

How would it be to have a man's hand touch her there...? Would it feel as good as when he touched her anywhere else? Just like she had wondered what William's hand would feel like on her... The shadow of William King appeared at the edges of her psyche, but she forced it down.

Her legs fell open for him, and her reward was his satisfied murmur.

And then his hand was on her there, and she gasped as pleasure spilled through her like honey. He moved his finger around her folds.

"You're so wonderfully wet for me, darling," Nathaniel whispered.

Of course you're wet.

Whore...

She jerked and sat up, pushing Nathaniel's hand away.

"What it is?" He sat up, too, a worried gaze on her. "Did I hurt you?"

Whore...

How could she be so stupid? The shadow was there, everywhere, torturing her present in every inch of her skin. She would never get rid of William King, no matter how many years passed and no matter that she wasn't married to him.

Tears burned her eyes, and she hid her face in her hands.

"Calliope..." said Nathaniel, his voice alarmed. "What happened?"

She wanted to pull herself together and say something clever, something that would allow her to keep her pride and her dignity. Or even tell him what she was so afraid of. Tell him what plagued her. He hadn't done a thing yet to make her doubt he would understand.

And yet, she couldn't. Opening herself up meant showing him who she really was.

A dirty whore, a girl who had always been wicked and dirty, and read and enjoyed things she wasn't supposed to.

So she had nothing. All words were swallowed by her tears. Sobs of grief poured through her. She had a rake in her bed who was ready to pleasure her and showed no signs of judging her, and yet she couldn't let him do what was normal for a husband and wife to do...

Strong arms wrapped around her, and she was surrounded by his warm body, weeping on his hard chest.

"Shush, darling," he murmured. "Nothing is worth your tears."

If only he knew...

18

"Poppy, darling, I mean it with all my love, do not laugh so loudly," said the Dowager Duchess of Grandhampton with a sweet but strict smile.

It was the next afternoon, and Calliope, the girls, and Nathaniel had come to visit Penelope and Preston, as well as Grandmama and Richard and Jane, who had decided to stay in London after their honeymoon got interrupted to attend Calliope and Nathaniel's wedding.

The sitting room of Newdale was quite pleasant and lively. Penelope was talking with Hazel about a painting that hung above the fireplace, while Poppy was entertaining everyone with the story of their pursuit. In her typical manner, she was speaking at the top of her lungs and with much animation. Violet threw looks full of longing at a book which lay five feet away on the card table—she had heard the story an untold number of times and had been present for the event, of course.

Richard and Jane listened, their eyes darting between Calliope and Nathaniel. The girls had been instructed to tell everyone it was a thief who was after their money, even though Calliope had told them yesterday she didn't think he was.

Nathaniel sat next to Calliope on the sofa, perfectly quiet and austere, his knee so close to her own she could feel the warmth of his body through the layers of her petticoats and her gown. From time to time, his gaze warmed her skin, and when she met his eyes, they lingered on her for a long time. Something had shifted between them last night, after she had so embarrassingly let him touch her, then rejected him, and then cried in his arms half the night, only to fall asleep surrounded by him.

Who this man was, she wasn't sure. All she knew was that he wasn't just the officer and the rake she had thought he was.

He may be one of the best men she had ever met.

She felt safe with him. She felt accepted. Understood. She felt...happy. And even with his attempt to restrict her and confine her to her house, part of her knew he meant well—even though she loathed restrictions.

Despite his misgivings and his barking and his exterior of an irresponsible man, he cared about her.

And that was a man she could easily love. Too easily.

"Forgive me," said Poppy, correcting herself and wiping her adorable, excited look from her face, arranging her grimace in the same manner as Grandmama. Calliope thought it was a pity to hide Poppy's natural enthusiasm under the calm and collected mask of a well-bred duke's sister, but she had undergone the same education, which the girls lacked with no mother and no governess to teach them manners. "And so the man took out a knife—"

"A knife?" asked Jane.

Jane looked so lovely, Calliope couldn't stop a grin from

spreading across her lips every time she looked at her new sister-in-law. Jane wasn't a timid wallflower, dressing in the grays and browns that she'd been before marrying Richard. Instead, she wore dusky pinks and blues that favored her coloring. Her spectacles weren't the simple unassuming round frames she'd worn before, but had quite a daring, unusual design with slanted outer edges that created a striking feline impression. And the glowing love that was evident every time Richard looked at his wife melted Calliope's heart.

Both of her brothers had found happiness and love, but she'd never thought she would. Until last night when, for the first time, she'd felt she may be wrong about that.

While Poppy talked and everyone asked her questions, Calliope's gaze kept returning to Nathaniel, who, it seemed, kept returning his gaze to her, too. She couldn't get enough of his eyes, his handsome face. Something warm settled on her lower back.

And then moved down...

His hand!

She opened her mouth in shock, staring at everyone else in the room, wondering if anyone noticed he was touching her. She turned to him, widened her eyes, and mouthed, "Nathaniel!"

Devils played in his brilliant turquoise eyes, their corners wrinkled in a barely noticeable smile, and he slowly licked his lips. She followed the trajectory of the edge of his tongue, and her body began burning. And then his hand moved even lower, and her breath was stolen from her chest as he cupped her bottom...

She gasped and looked away as she felt the heat of his palm spread through her skin, through her flesh, and right into her sex.

"Are you all right, Calliope?" asked Jane with a frown.

Goodness gracious, this man would bring her to her destruction! Heat flushed through her. She should feel humiliated, embarrassed—what if anyone noticed something?

Instead, Nathaniel leaned closer to look at her, as though to see if she was well, and a satisfied grin lit up his face.

"Are you all right, darling?" he asked, then leaned even closer, as though to inspect her face. "Heavens, you're so beautiful when you're flushed," he murmured just for her. "And what a gorgeous bottom."

In addition to her shock, she felt...exhilarated. Desired. Appreciated.

Part of her loved this game. Even though she couldn't let it continue for long.

She bit her lower lip to stop her grin. "I'm quite all right, thank you," she said and stood up. "Just a little warm."

She turned away from him, or she would redden even more, no doubt, and they would make a scene, providing a bad example of social manners to his sisters. The goal was, after all, to hone their manners and prepare them for their first Season next year.

She stood up, feeling Nathaniel's warm gaze following her every movement. "Where is Preston?" she asked. "I haven't seen my brother yet."

"He has a visitor," said Penelope. "But perhaps he already left."

"I will go and see," said Calliope. This would give her a chance to ask if he had found out anything new about Spencer.

"Would you like me to come with you?" asked Nathaniel.

With her side vision, Calliope could see the excited and surprised look Jane and Penelope exchanged with each other. The heat in Nathaniel voice couldn't have escaped anyone.

"Please, stay, Kelford," said Grandmama. "Your wife is perfectly capable of finding her brother without your help. And do tell us about the latest news of the wars."

Nathaniel cocked his head in reluctant agreement. "As you wish, Lady Grandhampton," he said, his eyes still on Calliope.

Hiding her smile, Calliope walked out, closed the door behind herself, and leaned with her back against it, needing a little time to compose herself. What was Nathaniel doing to her? Despite her tears, he still wanted her. He'd made that quite obvious just now. There was a promise in his eyes and in his touch, a promise she wanted him to keep.

Could there truly be hope for them? Would it not just be a marriage where she got what she needed and so did he? Could there be more, perhaps even a glimpse of the true happiness she'd seen between her parents?

Could she really slay the shadow of William if only she opened up to Nathaniel?

Just as she tore herself away from the door, her eyes fell on William himself.

Shock slapped her, and she stood completely still, her feet as heavy as lead. He'd just walked around the corner, eyes blazing with anger under his polite social mask.

As he saw her, his face must have straightened in the same expression of surprise as she wore.

"Lady Calliope," he said coldly. "Or, shall I say, Your Grace."

He gave her a pointedly deep bow, then straightened up tall and dark, standing in the shadows of the hallway.

Calliope straightened her back as fear clenched her insides. What was he doing here? He did not have any power over her anymore, she told herself. She was married. William couldn't do anything.

"Lord Huntingham," she said. "I was just going to find my brother."

"Hm," he said as he slowly walked to her, his disgusted gaze moving over her body, making her want to shrink and disappear. How could there have been a moment in her life when she had been infatuated with him? Thinking he was the most wonderful boy in the whole world? "I've just seen your brother."

"Right," she said as she tensed all over.

He stood two steps away now, close enough to reach out to pinch her. Silly thought, no doubt, but the place over her collarbone hurt.

"I came to ask for your hand in marriage," he said. "Imagine my surprise when I learned that you already married someone else."

He said it like it was a personal insult, like she had betrayed him. His upper lip crawled up, baring a row of white teeth in an expression of contempt.

"Indeed, I am married," she said. "I am afraid you are too late."

His nostrils flared as he leaned closer to her, his handsome features transforming into something snakelike.

"Well, you lost your chance to marry the only respectable man who would want someone like you."

Calliope inhaled sharply, feeling herself shrivel into something small and insignificant.

"Remember, I know who you really are, you dirty little *whore*."

There it was, that word, like a slap.

"I saw you," he continued. "I know you. I would have taken you as you are."

A small particle of his spit landed on her neck and the skin right above her collarbone. Calliope began shaking, any words she wished to say stuck in her mouth. She should tell him what she thought of him. How wrong he was. He didn't know her at all. But that place he had pinched her hurt and burned.

"But it's better this way," he continued. "I must admit, you've entered my private fantasies in the darkest moments of my life, and I prayed to God to forgive my soul. I would have made you a better Christian. An obedient wife. But it's for the better. Sinful whores like you deserve to be married to such dirty rakes as Kelford."

Tears of humiliation blurred her vision and burned her eyes. She prayed the floor would open under her feet and she'd disappear. One trembling hand clutched at her stomach in a futile attempt to protect herself.

The door opened and a tall figure came to stand near her. "Step away from my wife," said Nathaniel calmly.

"Kelford," said William unevenly.

Through her blurring vision, Calliope saw a large dark navy figure with golden spots move sharply against another tall figure in black. There was the sound of a push and shuffling feet and then the rattle of a vase, and something heavy fell on the floor with crack. Calliope wiped her eyes with the backs of her shaking hands. Nathaniel shoved William against the wall. Shattered shards of a vase, flowers, and a painting with a cracked frame lay on the floor.

"I heard you, you scoundrel," hissed Nathaniel into William's face as he held him by the collar. "Apologize to my wife right now, or I will demand satisfaction."

The sound of many footsteps came from the sitting room, and the hallway filled with people. Preston, who appeared from the hallway leading to his study, rushed to stand by Nathaniel.

"Kelford, calm yourself! This is my visitor—my guest!"

"Your guest just insulted your sister in the worst manner."

Preston shot a worried look at Calliope, and the next

moment he stood by her side, his arm wrapped around her shoulders protectively. “Sister, what is it? I’ve never seen you distraught like this. Is this true?”

William’s terrified gaze was on Calliope, pleading with her to lie for him. But she’d had enough.

“You must apologize, Huntingham,” she said coldly, staring into the man’s eyes, her voice cracked and strange. “You know what you said.”

When William tried to free himself from Nathaniel’s huge hand, Nathaniel pulled his arm back and hit the man in the face. There was the sound of flesh hitting flesh and the crack of a head hitting the wall.

“Apologize,” roared Nathaniel. “Or I will tear the very tongue out of your mouth you spoke such filth with.”

“I am sorry, Duchess,” William snarled, but there was not a trace of regret in his voice. “Happy?”

“Not in the slightest. Calliope?”

She didn’t think the pathetic *I’m sorry* was enough to atone for the years of humiliation she’d lived under. And Spencer had already beaten him up once, and yet, here he was going at it again. But she didn’t want Nathaniel to fight in a duel. William wasn’t worth getting her husband hurt or killed.

So this had to be enough.

“You must not take a single step in my direction again, Huntingham,” she said.

“Excellent idea,” growled Nathaniel. “And thank my wife for her generosity. If it wasn’t for her word, I’d kill you with the first sun tomorrow.”

William’s dark eyes lay on her with disdain. “Thank you,” he spat.

“Get out of my house,” barked Preston. “I do not want to see you near my family again. As far as I’m concerned, you’re finished in London.”

Nathaniel shook him hard once again and then let go. William staggered to his feet and hurried out of the house.

The next moment, she was wrapped in Nathaniel's arms like in a thick winter cloak, and she buried her face in his chest. William was gone. But would she ever be truly free from him?

19

"COME WITH ME, CALLIOPE," said Nathaniel when the girls retired to their bedrooms later that night.

It was after dinner and Calliope, Nathaniel, and the girls had been sitting in the drawing room. For the first time since Calliope had arrived at Roxburgh, the feeling of being in harmony and being a family enveloped her.

The London night was dark beyond the windows, the square dimly lit with gas lamps, and only the windows in the rows of town houses glowed softly in the dark.

"Where to?" she asked.

They had returned to Roxburgh Place shortly after the terrible scene with William, after which her family hadn't left her alone for a moment. She had refused to tell them what it was about, and Nathaniel had loyally kept the humiliating words he'd heard from William to himself. Although Calliope was still unsure how much he'd really heard.

"I thought I could cheer you up," he said as he stood up, his tall, muscular figure looming over her, his broad shoulders mighty under his navy uniform, his golden hair in its customary tail at the back of his head. He extended his hand out to her, a soft smile on his lips. "You'll like it, I promise."

Calliope wanted to say she really didn't need much, that he'd given her more than he had known when he'd stood up for her...when he hadn't agreed with William's foul words.

She laid her cool hand into his warm one, and his large palm closed around hers, enveloping it. She stood up on wobbly legs.

"You're not going to lock me in a tower, are you?" she said with a chuckle.

He raised one brow, amusement glinting in his eyes. "As much as I would like knowing you're safe somewhere in a tower, guarded by a dragon...no. Not yet, anyway."

Calliope cocked her head. "I'm quite intrigued, Your Grace."

Still holding her hand, he picked up a candle lamp and led her up the stairs onto the first floor. But to her surprise, he didn't stop there, but instead led her to the second floor, which was dark and quiet, only old wood creaking under their feet. The air was musty, and it smelled like dust. Her surprise peaked when they didn't stop there. He took her to the left wing, at the end of which was a door. When he opened it, the candle lamp illuminated circular stairs leading up.

"So it is a tower, after all," said Calliope, both curiosity and a little thrill whirling inside her.

"Not quite," said Nathaniel, looking up. His eyes were full of sadness and, no doubt, memories. "This door was unlocked today for the first time in fourteen years."

His voice rasped slightly, and there was a broken edge to it. He cleared his throat and threw her a glance. "Mrs. Nicholson should have prepared everything by now. Follow me."

Calliope watched him step onto the stairs and ascend them, the light of the lamp illuminating the old wood, spiderwebs, and footprints in the thick layer of dust that lay on the steps. With her heart beating quickly, she followed Nathaniel, who held the candle so that it would also illuminate the way for her.

At the top of the stairs, he opened another door, and moonlight fell through it.

He walked through the door first. When Calliope followed, a gasp escaped her throat.

They were on a roof terrace, closer to the sky than she had ever been, looking down at the endless London rooftops, dark against the starlit sky. Buildings surrounded them, and yet, Calliope had an odd sense of being alone with Nathaniel.

The terrace was as large as the drawing room, surrounded on three sides by the roof itself. On the fourth side, a stone railing faced the distant silhouette of Buckingham Palace. Beautiful golden lights of lanterns glowed all around. In the middle of the terrace lay a large quilt with a little basket and a bottle of wine with two glasses.

And around the perimeter of the terrace were pots and pots of yellow irises.

Calliope's hand shot to her heart, feeling as though it was going to break through her chest and fly straight into the glowing stardust above.

"Nathaniel..." she whispered, tears prickling her eyes.

He watched her with a look of wonder.

"Do you like this?"

She nodded. "This is breathtaking. How did you manage this? When?"

"Ever since you told me yellow irises were your favorite flowers, I keep seeing them everywhere. I saw someone at the market selling them when we were on our way from Newdale to here, and while Mrs. Nicholson cooked dinner, I asked Joshua to go and buy them, then put them here. They will have much more light here during the afternoon than down in the backyard. Then you can decide where you want them."

She nodded and had an overwhelming urge to kiss him, to press her face against his chest and inhale his godly scent, to be surrounded by him and the lanterns and the stars and the irises.

"Come to the railing," said Nathaniel, taking her hand again. "You're not afraid of heights, are you?"

She chuckled as she shook her head. "No."

They went to the time-worn stone railing, and Calliope's breath caught all over again as she watched the dark streets of Mayfair illuminated by the moonlight and gas lamps, and the lights spreading into darkness as her gaze traveled farther. The roofs, appearing silver in the moonlight, were mostly flat, with rows of chimneys poking into the air. The air here was fresh, and the wind played with stray locks of her hair. It was quiet. A carriage passed slowly on the street below, then another one. Servants argued a few houses down the street. Pigeons cooed. A gentleman walked on the street to the left, his dark figure appearing under the light of the lamp, then disappearing into the darkness.

She gazed up into the sky and was lost in the myriad of stars that shone over them.

She looked at Nathaniel, who observed her, his face relaxed and soft for the first time perhaps since she'd met him.

"Why haven't you been here in fourteen years?" she asked softly. "This is such a beautiful place. The gem of this house."

He nodded, his eyes clouding with sadness. He looked at his hands gripping the railing.

"This was my mother's favorite place in the house, too," he

said quietly. “She hid here with me from my father. He never thought to look here.”

Calliope’s face fell. “Hid?”

“My father was not an easy man.” Nathaniel chuckled. “How could he, when he was the richest duke in England, the most powerful man below the king. He was relentless with his expectations of me. Of my mother. And he was persistent in telling us exactly what was wrong with us.”

Calliope’s skin grew cold. Her own father had been strict, too, but there was no doubt in her mind he had loved all his children, and he’d worshipped Mama. “What did he do?”

“He knew the exact words to say that would cause the most damage. He said Mama was too weak and too fat for a duchess. Indulging too much in food. When she started eating less and then acquired the habit of vomiting her dinners, she became too thin, which also greatly displeased him. With him, she was a shadow. When she was away from him, she was the light itself. Before the girls were born, we came here and watched the city from above. We sat on this very quilt she had stitched herself.”

“Nathaniel…” She covered his hand with hers, feeling his anger, his disdain, his pain. “What a terrible man.”

He chuckled. “And I was never smart enough, never well behaved enough. I never finished Oxford. After my mother died, I drank, went to the wrong kinds of soirées, gambled, and wasn’t interested in being a duke in the slightest. Since he had no other heir, he couldn’t just disown me or his line would have died. So his way of getting what he wanted was his will. But it all got so, so much worse when he learned of the true reason for my mother’s death.”

Feeling like she wanted to encompass him in her arms, Calliope stood close to him, so close she pressed against the side of his body. "What was the reason for your mother's death?"

He looked at her and the pain and guilt in his eyes broke her heart in two.

And then the shock froze her into an ice statue when he said, "Me."

20

Nathaniel felt the word escape his mouth, hardly able to believe he had said it.

He had thought it countless times over the years. He'd lived it. Breathed it. He'd gotten himself where he was because of that dark secret.

But saying it out loud was like releasing a demon he had kept under lock and key.

It was terrifying. Painful.

And yet completely liberating.

She'd never again look at him the way she had when she'd seen the terrace, the lanterns, and the irises. The way he wished she'd look at him every day for the rest of their lives.

His confession had wiped the tender look off her face. Instead, confusion and hurt distorted her features.

"You?" she asked. "Whatever do you mean?"

He inhaled sharply, fresh night air cutting through his clenched throat like knives. He looked away from her, into the darkness of the city. "I was fifteen, the twins were one, and Hazel was three. We were on our way to London from our country estate, Kelford Manor, and it was late at night. Papa had summoned us to London because he wanted to throw a ball for the king and queen and required my mama to do it. We rode through the darkness but planned to stop at an inn shortly, where we would retire for the night and resume our way to London the following day. The twins were sleeping, cradled in Mama's arms, and Hazel was nestled against me. The carriage suddenly stopped. I heard the horses neigh and male voices. Then the shots of pistols."

He felt Calliope tense against him, her arm wrapped around his shoulders, although she couldn't encompass the whole width of them.

"The smell of gunpower was acrid even through the glass windows," he resumed, reliving his memory of that dark night. "Then there was silence. They killed our coachmen and our footmen, who were also our guards. Mama's eyes were so white against the darkness. I was terrified. There were muff pistols under the seat of the carriage, I knew, and I told her to stand up so that I would get them. She did, and I grabbed them, hiding them behind my back."

A painful knot gathered in his neck, his chest feeling like it was going to burst.

"Then one of the highwaymen appeared in the window staring right at us and opened the door. He told us to get out and give them all our gold, jewelry, everything. Mama and I got out, but she left the girls inside.

"There were seven or eight of them, all had pistols in their hands. Mama told them she'd give them everything and started to remove her rings, her necklace. Her purse. When one of them told her to also take off her dress, I took the guns from my waistband and fired. I shot one of them in the leg, but the second pistol missed."

His throat felt like it had suddenly shrunk and was as dry as the stone under his fingers.

"They became enraged. Started yelling. Cussing. One of them leveled his pistol and fired at me. I knew I was dead. Saw that blast of fire as though painted against the night. The flash of hot, prickly awareness that I was finished."

He swallowed. It was hard to talk through his tight throat.

"But there was no pain. Nothing pierced me, ripped through me. The bullet intended for me never came. My mother had jumped in front me."

He looked at Calliope, and saw a tear roll down her cheek, her eyes wide on him.

"I thought I would die. Instead, my mother lay dead at my feet," he finished.

And finally, the tears he hadn't allowed himself for fourteen years fell.

Calliope pulled him close, wrapping her slim arms around his large frame, and although she couldn't reach all the way around him, he felt surrounded by her sweet, gorgeous body like a protective blanket. For the first time in his life, he let go and wept. For the first time, he felt like he wasn't alone, like there was someone else who would listen and understand.

Since that night in the moonlit meadow, surrounded by dead people, cradling his beloved mother in his arms, he had felt alone every day of his life.

Until now.

"It wasn't your fault, Nathaniel," she whispered. Her face was pressed against his, and he felt her tears against his cheek. "It wasn't your fault."

"But it was," he whispered. "I had the pistols, and I couldn't protect her. I should have died instead of her."

"No, no." She shook her head, her breath hot and urgent against his face. She took his face in both hands and made him look at her. She was slightly blurry from his tears. "No!" she said firmly. "You are not to blame for those thugs having ambushed you. Several grown men fell victims to those bandits. You were only fifteen—you can't expect an adolescent to have fought off a band of killers."

Warmth spread through his chest. He had never heard anyone say out loud that he wasn't to blame. The only people he had told were his father and the coroner, but he had never told them what it did to him. That, perhaps, he had died with his mother, after all.

"My father thought the same thing I did, Calliope," Nathaniel said. "When he saw me alone and heard Mama was dead, he crumpled into a ball. And in a pained, broken voice I had never heard from him before, told me, 'You should have protected her!'"

"No!" cried Calliope again. "He should have sent more men with you—armed men. He shouldn't have demanded that she travel so hastily that your carriage was on the road at night. It was his expectations and ambitions that killed her, not you, a fifteen-year-old who loved her."

The truth of those words hit him like a cannonball. For the first time since that night, he stopped and considered the truth beyond what he had believed. He felt his tears slowing and blinked. Somehow, it became easier to breathe.

"It was a terrible, unthinkable event," Calliope said softly, still holding his face in her hands, her eyes so full of empathy and love, his breath caught in his throat again. "She loved you very much, and she wouldn't want you to live your life blaming yourself for something she did out of love. She gave you life—twice, as any loving mother would in a heartbeat."

She kissed him then, and he wrapped his arms around her, marveling at the initiative she took. He could taste the salt on her lips, his tears mixed with hers, and he kissed her like there would never be tomorrow, because he didn't want this to end. For the first time since that night, he felt understood. Appreciated.

"Thank you, Calliope," he whispered against her lips. "Thank you."

She chuckled without breaking the kiss. "Thank you, too, Nathaniel. For earlier... And for this wonder."

William...his blood seethed just from thinking of that damned name. "No man can insult you and walk this earth unpunished," he said as he looked at her.

Her lashes were still wet from tears, big eyes shimmering with something. He helped her to sit on the quilt he hadn't used in fourteen years. It smelled musty, but he recognized every pattern Mama had carefully sewn. Not a task for a duchess, but she had enjoyed doing that in Kelford Manor when Papa was in London and she was free to do whatever she wanted. The fabric felt soft and thin under his fingers.

He poured wine into two glasses and handed one to Calliope.

"What happened with that bastard?" he asked. "Why did he dare to call you those terrible words?"

Calliope looked down at the quilt, her face turning red even in the bluish moonlight. "Because he saw me doing things a well-bred duke's daughter shouldn't do."

He frowned, confused. "What?"

"Their family are neighbors of Grandhampton Court, and they spent summers visiting us. I grew up knowing William, and he was the object of my first girlish love. I adored him. Good-looking. Confident. Brave. Smart. A friend of my brothers. When I talked about detective stories that I loved, I thought his teasing was his way of showing he liked me back."

She swallowed.

"There was one book in our vast library...one book I shouldn't have found. You have it, actually."

Nathaniel raised his brows. "Which one?"

"Villains and Velvet."

He was just taking a sip of his wine, and hearing that title made him choke. He barely contained his wine in his mouth. He swallowed. "*Villains and Velvet*? You read it when you were an adolescent girl?"

He could see the beetroot blush on her face. "Yes."

He needed to hide that book better. He imagined his sisters finding it and didn't like it one bit. "What did you think of it?"

"I liked it," she said quietly, her big eyes sheepishly meeting his from under her lashes. So unlike her. He remembered now how she had dropped it when she'd found it in his bedchamber. "It was the first time I realized my body could feel pleasure like I had never felt before."

"I daresay," he said hoarsely.

"But when I was reading it... I tried to do what the people in the stories did. I sat in the library...behind a desk, hidden... and touched myself."

Nathaniel's mouth went dry. She was so pliable, so wonderfully responsive when he caressed her, he was sure she was very sensual. And yet he saw fear in her eyes, and she had stopped him...and those tears... William... Anger started rolling in his whole body, fists clenching. He had an inkling where this was going.

"Let me guess. Did he see you?" he asked softly. "With the book? Touching yourself?"

Calliope looked defeated and nodded. "He did."

Nathaniel suppressed a vile curse. "What did he do?"

Calliope didn't reply for a long time, and her chest began rising and falling quicker and quicker. Her blush spread down to her chest, and her eyes filled with tears again. Goddamn it to hell, the urge to crush the bastard was itching every inch of his body. Instead, he put the glasses aside and pulled her to him, wrapping his arms around her. Her warm, small body fit so perfectly against him.

"He laughed at me," she said. "He called me a whore. He pinched me right here." She indicated a place above her collarbone. "It felt like that pinch branded me. A whore."

"Despicable bastard," gritted out Nathaniel. "I really should murder him."

"Spencer had heard him, although I don't think he saw me touch myself, thank God. But Spencer pummeled him for calling me that and for pinching me. After that, our families fell apart, when William complained that Spencer had hit him. Spencer never told anyone why. It was enough humiliation without that."

She was quiet for a while, fingering the glass.

"And then William appeared the same day I went to the Admiralty. He wanted to marry me."

"I remember you mentioning his name."

"Yes." She looked up at him, and the sadness in her eyes killed him. "But I'm so glad I'm married to you."

What was she doing to him...? It was as though her words hit him right in his core, mending the torn edges of his spirit.

"You don't hate me?" she whispered. "Don't want to laugh at me? Don't think I'm pathetic?"

"He's a piece of swine shit, Calliope, and you couldn't be further from what he called you." He cupped her face and planted a gentle kiss on her lips.

"Even though I was reading and enjoying an erotic book at twelve?"

He looked deep into her eyes. "Darling, you could be reciting bawdy songs at the top of your lungs in front of the queen, and I would still think you're the most desirable woman alive."

He kissed her. He wanted to give her just a sweet, reassuring kiss, but one was not enough. One would never be enough with Calliope. He kissed her again. And again. It must be her scent that always did it for him, stirred his blood with hunger. He came to her lips again and again. Deeper. Deeper. She responded with the same hunger. Her arms wrapped around his neck, and she pulled herself closer to him.

And then he was devouring her mouth, his loins growing tight and hot. She pulled him down as she lay on the quilt, and he was on top of her. And when a beautiful moan escaped her throat, it shot a bolt of desire right into his groin. He pulled away from her slightly, barely able to catch his breath.

"Calliope," he murmured. "If I don't stop now, I won't be able to at all. I want you too much."

She looked at him with her hooded eyes, then gave a sly smile that drove him mad. "I don't want you to stop. I want you to finally show me what it's truly like to be in that erotic book."

21

Calliope's breath caught as a hungry growl escaped his mouth, and something delicious clenched within her.

He came back to her mouth as though he could barely tear himself away. His kiss became so deep, every lash of his tongue reverberated inside her, where she'd wanted him so much.

She was shaking, so hot and needy, her sex aching and swollen. He was a wonderful, heavy, masculine presence, and what he had said about William... She wondered how she could have ever doubted he'd accept her, that, rather than mocking her, he'd be furious with the man who'd hurt her.

Telling him that, all that, was like cracking herself open and releasing the secret she'd held for so long like a foreign presence in her body. Spencer had known about William's words, of course, but it wasn't like she could tell her brother what she'd felt. What she'd read. Or that the whole incident was actually her fault, because good girls didn't read erotic stories or like them so much that they had to touch themselves to find out if all those things were true.

But Nathaniel understood.

And she felt safe. Accepted. She felt like herself. She felt like, perhaps, those things she had thought before William's cruel words and actions could be true.

That her body was good as it allowed her to feel all those beautiful things.

Perhaps...

Nathaniel's kisses made her forget.

She trusted him.

He left her mouth and planted gentle kisses down her chin and her neck. She froze when he approached the spot where William had pinched her. He stilled, too, meeting her gaze with eyes as dark as the night above her.

There couldn't be a person more beautiful than he, all sweeping golden angles, his lips slightly swollen.

"May I kiss you *there*?"

She felt her whole body harden and tense at that. The thought of anyone or anything touching her in that spot brought a familiar wave of fear and revulsion.

And yet, it was Nathaniel. He wouldn't pinch her. Wouldn't humiliate her.

He would kiss her.

And then she knew...his lips on her body wouldn't be hurting or humiliating.

But healing.

"Yes," she whispered, not even believing her own lips. "Yes."

Their gazes still melded, inch by inch, he lowered himself to that spot. She closed her eyes, knowing he wouldn't harm her but unable to relax.

The pain never came.

It was gentle, a sweet touch, then after a few moments, another one. And another.

So soft. Feather-like. Like petals falling on her.

A silky lick of his tongue followed, and she felt herself melt.

"Are you all right, love?" he asked, continuing with those butterfly kisses.

With every loving caress of his lips and tongue against her skin, the shadow receded. "Chase him away, Nathaniel," she whispered as her hands brushed down his hard, broad back.

He moved down then, down her chest just like he had last night, and then to her breasts, kissing the flesh that crested her bodice.

"Good," he murmured and licked at the crease between her breasts with his tongue. "He had no place being part of your life in the first place. You're mine, love. Mine. There will never ever be anything you cannot do or say to me." His arms reached around her and began untying her laces as he looked up at her, leaning over her breasts. "I want all of you. Every thought. Every feeling. Every touch. I want you to know that nothing you desire is wrong or bad."

Every word he said was like a lick of pleasure against her senses, opening her up like a flower towards the first sunlight of spring.

He released the ties at the back of her dress and pulled her sleeves and the bodice down. The air was still warm after a hot summer day, and it was strange but wonderful to feel a slight wind on the bare skin of her shoulders and chest for the first time. He pulled her gown over her hips and off, and she remained in nothing but her petticoats and her chemise and her corset.

He rolled her over onto her side, the quilt soft against her skin.

He undid her corset, tugging at the lacing. Then he planted gentle kisses on her back as he pulled the sides apart.

Pulling it over her head, he tossed it aside, and then off

went the chemise. She shivered, feeling his lips on her skin where no one had ever touched her before. When she lay with her chest bare, his gaze went over her, lingering on her breasts. He let out a long breath, his gaze growing heated.

Calliope's throat contracted. She felt exposed, and vulnerable, and yet...so good. Seeing Nathaniel so affected made her breath hitch and her insides melt.

"Do you like what you see?" she asked carefully.

His eyes darted to meet hers. "Like? I don't think I've ever seen anything so beautiful in my life, darling. Let me see you whole."

His gaze dropped to the petticoats that were still around her waist. She undid the hooks and pulled them down, her hands shaking.

This must be the most exhilarating experience of her whole life, being naked in front of this magnificent man who could have been a piece of art that came to life. He was enormous, blotting out almost a third of the starry sky above him.

He let out a shaky breath when his gaze slowly traveled over her waist and her hips and stopped at the apex of her thighs.

"Heavens, Calliope," he murmured, swallowing hard. "You are perfect."

And he was so much more. She shook, from the feel of air brushing over her heated skin, from his gaze full of liquid desire, from the stunning beauty around them.

"Let me see you, too," she murmured. "Let me see how perfect you are."

He gave a slow chuckle and started to undo the hooks of his coat, then undid his cravat and removed his waistcoat. Off went the white shirt over his head, and while he was busy removing his trousers, Calliope moistened her lips as she looked over his gorgeous chest. The muscles there were large and broad like waves, leading down into a beautifully sculpted stomach with ripples like hills and valleys. The biceps of his strong arms rolled as he moved, his shoulders massive and broad. Soft-looking blond hair speckled his chest, and there was a thin trail leading from his belly button farther down...

The thought of this large body covering her sent a thrill of excitement through Calliope.

And then he pushed down his trousers and a large and hard member sprang from within them. She caught her breath. It was long and pink and straight and thick and looked very, very hard, almost pulsating with veins going along it. She knew where it would go—she'd read it in *Villains and Velvet*—but how would it ever fit inside her? Would it not tear her apart?

As he freed himself from his trousers and stretched himself along her, he kissed her gently. "Do you like what you see, darling?" he asked, echoing her question from before.

Like? She loved what she saw. But she couldn't say that out loud. "I...I'm lost for words."

"Well, we can't have that," he said and brought her to him. His body felt hard and hot against her, his chest hair scratching slightly against her oversensitive nipples. He kissed her again, with so much need and hunger, she lost her breath. The kiss was messy and hard and fast, and yet, she was burning hotter and hotter for him.

She wrapped her arms around his neck, bringing her body closer to his, the feel of his muscular thighs, and the soft hair of his stomach, and the feel of his silky, thick erection against the crease between her thigh and her stomach.

He pulled her leg up and over his hip, and she could feel his erection nudging against her sex, spreading her outer lips. He cupped her breast with one hand, circling her nipple with his thumb, and her nipple hardened and tensed. She moaned and arched her back in a futile attempt to press herself even closer.

The feel of his warm skin against her was like delicious fire setting her blood burning.

He resumed kissing down her neck and gave a special, delicate kiss to that spot above her collarbone that was no longer the source of pain but of pleasure.

And then his mouth was on her breasts. He sucked in one nipple, and an intense pleasure spilled through her, taking her over. She gasped out loud, unable to stop herself, and wrapped her arms around his head, freeing his long silky hair from its tail and digging her fingers through it. His hair fell and tickled her skin. As he sucked her nipple and played with it, rolling it with his tongue, nibbling on it gently with his lips and teeth, his wicked hand made his way down her stomach, leaving a burning trail. His fingers reached the triangle of her hair, and she shivered from need, from aching awareness as her insides tensed and swelled in anticipation. When he parted her folds and his finger dipped between them, a jolt of pleasure made her jerk.

He circled with his finger and explored her, just like she had done herself all those years ago, only it was so wonderfully different to have him do it. She didn't know where his finger would go, how much he would press, and that drove her mad. He played with his touches, as light as a feather, then tapped against her gently, and then he pinched that special spot in those folds in such a way that made her shiver all over and cry out.

"That's right, love," he whispered. "You're so soft and beautiful, and I'm going to lose my mind for you..."

She could feel his cock pressing against her hip, making slight movements back and forth.

And then his mouth left her breast and made a trail down

her rib cage, down her stomach, and finally landed on her sex. She gasped. She remembered in one of the stories one of the villains kissing a lady there...

"Oh Lord, Nathaniel, are you going to... I thought it was nothing but an author's imagination."

"I am, love," he murmured, his voice so deep, it reverberated in her chest. "And trust me, it's not just an author's imagination."

He parted her thighs and dropped to the ground in front of her. And then he parted her folds with his fingers and his mouth was on her...right there. The feel was so decadent, so forbidden, and yet, so right and so exquisite, she burned all over.

She gasped and moaned, unable to contain the hot pleasure pulsating through her. His tongue, his wonderful, wicked tongue played, licking her up and down and circling around that glorious place that made her mindless with bliss.

Whatever he was doing, she didn't ever want him to stop.

Something beautiful was building within her, and when he gently pressed his finger a little ways inside her, she wanted him to be deeper, to fill her completely, to claim her. She knew it would satisfy that need, that deep ache within her.

"Heavens, Calliope, you're so tight, love," he murmured against her sex. "But so sleek and wet and so ready for me."

With a last kiss against her sex, he withdrew and positioned himself between her legs. "I'm sorry, love, but this might feel uncomfortable...but only for the first time, I promise. After that, every time is going to be so good for you. So, so good."

She nodded. She didn't know about the first time, but the ladies in the book always enjoyed it.

He slowly started to push himself against her entrance

while his finger was still on that place that felt so incredible, and she relaxed as he withdrew a little.

He pushed again, a little harder, but she didn't mind at all even though there was a little pressure. This was nothing compared to that hard pinch above her collarbone. This was pleasure and pressure, nothing more. She moaned as his finger rubbed against her.

He gleamed in the starlight like an otherworldly creature, a god who had come down from the night sky just for her, just to make her a woman and show her what her body could do.

He pulled back and pushed forward again, harder, while something within her built, and she arched her back, her breasts pressing against him.

He started making small, persistent movements with his cock, slowly burrowing within her. The pressure kept intensifying, but she was so mindless with pleasure now that she wanted him deeper and deeper. She moved her pelvis forward to meet his thrusts. There was a tiny feel of something popping, and a small pinch of pain, which was swallowed by that satisfaction of finally having him deep inside her.

He groaned as though from pain and froze. "Are you all right, love?" he asked. She felt him shaking.

"Very much so," she whispered.

He kissed her and began moving inside her, thrusting his cock in and out. She arched and moved her pelvis against his, matching his movements. There was a little pain but more pleasure. He retrieved his fingers from between their bodies, and angled his pelvis somehow so that she still felt all the sweet pleasure. Now he was hitting something inside her that brought ecstasy, and she wrapped her legs around his pelvis.

He began moving faster, thrusting harder and harder, and she wanted more of that.

And then finally something was building within her, some

pressure, some tension that was like honey and wine, and there was just one name her blood sang.

Nathaniel.

And then, under the stars and the moon, she fell apart in the arms of the man she knew she was falling in love with. She exploded like a starburst, falling down like rain, and he groaned, bucking against her, and she knew he found his own release. She became those stars, and he became them, too. And together they were one. Among the irises and the stars.

She didn't know how long it lasted, but he collapsed on top of her, and then wrapped his arms around her and brought her to his chest. She felt a slight wind caressing her heated, wet skin, felt the delicious throbbing of her sex, and heard the violent thumping of his heart.

As she listened to it, she realized they had established a small peace between them, a little isle of heaven. She could see how happy they could be together.

He had confided his darkest memory, and she now understood why he was so overprotective of his sisters and her. Because he couldn't save his mother. That was an incredible burden for anyone to carry, and she wanted to make it easier for him.

Only, she still knew she would never comply with his rule and be locked down in a house. Especially not while her brother was missing and needed her.

Perhaps she was a very bad match for Nathaniel. Did he need someone compliant, someone who would sit at home and be safe, away from all danger? She would never be that woman.

He also didn't know about her plan to open her own sleuth agency.

And once he found out, would this happiness and this peace be over?

22

TWO DAYS LATER...

"What are the two of you doing?"

The voice that came from behind had Calliope turn around sharply to stare into Hazel's astonished face, her dark eyebrows drawn together in an expression that looked exactly like Nathaniel's.

Calliope must have been quite a sight. Dressed in Nathaniel's old, musty-smelling coat, waistcoat, shirt, and breeches, Calliope stood in front of the mirror. The twins were on either side of her, their hands deep under the shoulders of the coat as they sewed little pads with stuffed rags, which was meant to make Calliope appear more broad-shouldered. Her hair had been gathered up in a tight bun and hidden under a round hat Violet had found in a chest with Nathaniel's old clothes from when he was an adolescent. Even though Nathaniel had worn these clothes when he was fifteen, they were still too long and too large for Calliope.

Calliope gulped. The twins froze.

"Hazel, please don't tell Nathaniel..." begged Violet.

"Why are you dressed like a man?" Hazel demanded, her frown deepening, her steps stomping loudly.

"It's for a disguise, why else?" Poppy rolled her eyes and returned to her task of sewing the shoulder pad.

"For a disguise?" Hazel shook her head, her eyes like saucers, staring at Calliope in disbelief. "Are these our brother's clothes? And he doesn't know, does he?"

"He doesn't, Hazel, and please don't tell him," Calliope said. "I know you may not like me—"

"So he wouldn't approve, would he?" she demanded. "Does this have something to do with that man who tried to attack us?"

"It has to do with her looking for her brother," said Violet as she knotted her thread. "Don't be daft."

"How could you get my sisters to help with that?" Hazel stepped closer. "I thought you were supposed to be an educated, intelligent lady. Have you not more sense than that?"

Guilt churned in Calliope's stomach. "Hazel, I'm not getting them involved."

"We're not going with her," said Poppy. "We have more sense than that."

"I'm not being daft," Hazel said through gritted teeth. "On the contrary, I know you both, and I know what happens to your brains when you get some mad idea. And this"—she pointed at Calliope—"is madness."

Hazel stormed out of the room, leaving Calliope concerned she may have involved the girls too much.

But they told her not to worry, that she looked like a young gentleman, and wished her luck.

She hired a hackney, and thirty minutes later, she was

walking down the docks, the moon hanging low in the velvet-black sky, casting its gossamer light onto the port. Infrequent lanterns hanging from the beams of storage sheds and buildings emitted dim light that didn't reach far into the deeply shadowed streets and alleys. The cool wind off the water ruffled Calliope's hair at the back of her neck. Ships swayed gently in the port, their masts skeletal against the night. Rigging and pulleys creaked as dark water lapped against the weathered wood of the docks.

The air was heavy with the horrible stench of the river. The Thames always smelled so foul in summer, with the city's human waste dumped there along with waste from mills and factories. Intertwined with this was the sweet, earthy aroma of barrels stacked high, their contents—exotic spices, rum, and tobacco—brought from far-off lands, waiting to be unloaded at the dawn's light.

At the intersection of several shadowy alleyways, three bonneted women of questionable reputation leaned against worn brick walls, looking at her with meaning. One of them had her lips painted red, her eyes gleaming as she followed Calliope with her gaze, no doubt sure she was a man. "Lookin' for company?" asked the woman coarsely.

Calliope shook her head and lowered her voice to resemble that of a man. "No."

Sailors passed by her, the scent of brine clinging to them like coats. Two dockworkers were still busy at this hour as they hoisted crates onto broad shoulders, their muscles straining under the heavy load. A fishmonger rolled a barrel full of catch by her, the scent of fish so strong, her throat scratched.

A beggar sat on the corner of the street, and Calliope went into her purse and gave him several farthings. "God bless you, lad," said the old man.

Calliope allowed herself a little victorious smile. She had

managed to pass as a lad! Hopefully, by lad he meant a very young and short man...not a boy.

She needed to ask around. Chances that this man would remember something were slim, but who knew?

"Forgive me," she said, making her voice as low as she could. "Have you been begging here for a long time?"

The man looked at her with his milky eyes, his face wrinkled with age and weather. "Yes, lad, a year at least."

"Might you remember there were five navy ships docked nearby September of last year. One of them was right here." She pointed at the end of the docks where there was a large merchant ship. It was docked only ten feet or so away from Portside. "Might you remember its name?"

The man chuckled. "I dunno what day's today. Can't recall where I was ten days ago. Don't know nothin' 'bout no ships."

Calliope sighed and nodded. Perhaps she would have a better luck with the sex workers, after all. She went to the one who had spoken to her. Her sizable breasts were very white against her old red frock.

"Changed yer mind, luv?" asked the lady and ran her finger down Calliope's coat. She smelled of stale sweat and old lavender water, no doubt as an attempt to cover her body odor.

"No, but I have a question for you." Calliope went into her pocket and fetched a few more farthings, showing one to the woman.

"Oh." Her eyes widened in anticipation. "What would the young sir like to know?"

"Last year September, there was a raid on Portside. Many men were press-ganged. Do you remember that night?"

The woman pinched her lips thoughtfully. "Coin first."

Calliope nodded and handed her the coin. "Here you go. What do you remember?"

The woman shrugged. "I saw the raid, right from 'ere."

Calliope's heart thumped, and she straightened her shoulders. "Do you remember the names of the ships?"

The woman's eyes narrowed at Calliope. "You're a pretty lad…" she said. "Such big blue eyes…"

Calliope cleared her throat, forcing her voice even lower. "You're not the first to say so. Do you remember there was a good-looking gentleman carried unconscious onto a ship?"

"Most of 'em were struggling. Some were knocked out, yes. I saw all of 'em being brought to the ship docked right close."

Calliope's pulse thumped in her neck. "What was the name of the ship?"

The woman's eyebrows rose sadly. "I can't read, luv."

Calliope cursed. "Can you ask your friends if they remember?"

The woman winked. "They will all need a coin, luv."

Calliope nodded and handed her the coins. She walked with the woman to the other two sex workers, but neither of them remembered anything. Disappointed, Calliope gave them more farthings, feeling sorry for the women.

"Thank you, ladies," she said.

She would need to go to Portside, after all. Worried Nathaniel may be there even though he'd said he had Admiralty business tonight, she wanted to avoid showing her face. But it was the most likely place to find information. It was one block from here, down an alleyway between warehouses. She looked around, but no one seemed to be following her.

She could hear a man and a woman arguing in the distance, and a sudden foghorn from the port made her jump, but the only sound coming from the alleyway was the soft skittering of small creatures. Squaring her padded shoulders, she started walking, careful of where she stepped. She'd made it halfway down the alleyway when a large figure stepped from the shadows, holding a knife that glinted dully in the darkness. Then a second shorter man appeared next to him.

"Well, 'ello there," said the tall, burly man.

Calliope's stomach dropped to her feet. A robber.

Her hand twitched to a pistol she'd taken with her, tucked in the back of her waistband. She didn't really know how to shoot it, but she guessed she could at least threaten them and run away.

"Here's the money!" she said, about to reach for her money purse.

"We don't want money, Duchess," said the shorter man.

"We're told to cut your wee, pretty face," said the tall one.

⁂

Nathaniel returned home earlier than he had expected. The last two days and nights had passed in a strange state of mind and emotions he had never felt before...or expected to.

For the first time in his life, Nathaniel was fully and truly happy.

He had been invited to play cards with one of the captains, and he'd hoped to learn something about Spencer in that informal setting. But it had been a dead end, and he'd found himself eager to return home for a quiet night with his sisters and the woman who had quickly become one of the most important people in his life.

He greeted Joshua, who told him everyone was in the dining room, and, whistling, he went there. Only to see three females instead of four.

His sisters looked up from their plates as he strode in.

"You're early, brother..." Poppy's face flushed, and her eyes widened. "We didn't expect you until very late."

Calliope's place wasn't even set at the table.

"Where is she?" he demanded, already taking a step back, ready to run.

"Who?" asked Violet.

"You know who!" barked Nathaniel, fear for Calliope making him raise his voice more than intended. "Calliope, where is she? Why are you lying?"

Hazel crossed her arms over her chest. "I don't know where she went, but I know she disguised herself as a man."

Cold dread showered over Nathaniel. "Disguised?"

"Hazel!" cried Violet. "We asked you not to tell!"

"She's putting herself and all of us in danger, and you expect me to cover for her?" exclaimed Hazel.

"Where did she go?" Nathaniel bellowed, staring at the twins.

They looked at each other, sighed, and said in unison, "The docks."

"The docks?" Fear for her corroded his insides like acid.

Nathaniel didn't need to ask why she had gone to the docks dressed like a man. He let out a foul curse and had just turned to run when Violet cried after him, "I don't know why you're so angry with her. If you had disappeared like her brother did, we'd be doing the same to find you."

He turned to her, fear and anger tying his tongue.

"I think she's the most admirable woman alive," said Poppy with her eyes burning. "Thank you for marrying Calliope, brother! I want to be her when I'm older."

Nathaniel felt like he was going to combust right here, right now, like a goddamn barrel of saltpeter.

"You are not going to be her!" he roared. "You are to stay away from her, from this investigation, and to sit at home and never show your nose anywhere."

With that he strode out, banging the door with such

strength that glass in the windows rattled and the hallway wall sconce tilted.

"Joshua!" he shouted as he hurried down the hall. "Joshua, don't unsaddle Hermes yet! I need to go to the docks."

He went into his study and grabbed his saber. Then he ran out to the mews and was on his way, galloping through the streets of London as though he were in a horse race.

There were so many carriages in his way, he had to swerve through them, startling a few finely dressed occupants. Another carriage blocked the road completely, and he was forced to turn Hermes around and find another route. All the way, every time his heart beat against his ribs, he died a little inside from fear for Calliope. Images of her hurt and abused flashed through his mind. There could be a band of robbers... just like that night with his mother.

There were plenty of those at the docks. How could he have allowed this to happen? Let his wife walk into mortal danger like that? He should have never let her out of his sight. He should have never believed she'd stay away from this investigation.

Finally, he reached the docks, passing by dozens of dark warehouses, barely illuminated by lanterns. She must be near Portside, probably asking around about those ships, just like they had talked about. He looked into the faces of sailors, whores, workers, one or two regular gentlemen... He passed by every dark alley, rounded every corner.

She was nowhere to be seen.

"Calliope!" he called, desperation clawing at his heart like a thief. "Calliope!"

He kept trying, his eyes darting from dark corner to dark corner, calling her name for what felt like a hundred times.

"Here!" came her voice from somewhere nearby.

That alley, he thought, and with his heart sinking into his stomach, he jumped off Hermes and ran into the dark alley, unsheathing his saber.

Illuminated only by moonlight were two silhouettes of large men and a third one, slim and short in a round hat. His eyes locked on to the two hulking figures, knives glinting ominously in the moonlight as they made stabbing movements, dwarfing the petite figure that ducked, jumping away and cowering.

Calliope...

Horror grasped Nathaniel's whole body in its icy cold claws.

"Get away from her!" he roared as he charged at them.

The two large silhouettes froze. Calliope picked up a piece of wood and swung it at the nearest thug, hitting him on the back of his head.

The man grunted and swayed, swinging his arm with the knife, but Calliope evaded him. The man was clearly disoriented, and Nathaniel lunged at him, his sword slicing through the air with a lethal grace. The thug grunted in surprise, his knife skittering out of his hand as he barely managed to dodge the initial attack. Nathaniel pressed on, slashing, while the man ducked.

The second attacker advanced, attempting to seize the opportunity to strike while Nathaniel was occupied with his companion. Calliope swung her plank of wood at him, but he batted it away as if it were a fly, sending it clattering to the stones. He left her alone and advanced on Nathaniel—thank heavens!

With a swift sidestep, Nathaniel evaded the incoming attack, his saber catching the moonlight as it arced towards the attacker. The dull thud of the blade meeting flesh echoed through the alley, and the thug wailed in pain and staggered backward, clutching his arm.

Nathaniel turned his attention back to the first man, who was now trying to retrieve his fallen weapon. With a roar, Nathaniel launched himself at the man, swinging his sword. It slashed towards the thug's stomach, barely missing it. The thug slashed his own knife across, and Nathaniel counterattacked, but the man was faster. Suddenly, he changed direction, and instead of attacking Nathaniel, he turned away, grabbed his companion by the sleeve and both of them fled.

"Nathaniel, come on!" cried Calliope, who took off after them. "We must know who they work for!"

"Stay back!" he barked at her as he sprinted after them, his lungs burning from running. He had his eyes on the two figures at the end of the alleyway. He was catching up to them, especially the one he'd wounded, who was no doubt in great pain. But just as he was approaching the end of the alleyway, they disappeared around the corner. There was the sound of hooves and of wheels rattling against the cobblestones. And when he turned the corner onto the street, all he could see was a gig disappearing into the darkness.

He put his sword back into its sheath, then stood and doubled over, leaning with his hands against his knees as he caught his breath—not just from the physical effort he had expended but from the shock of seeing Calliope exactly where he had feared he'd see her.

In mortal danger.

Fury mixed with fear was pulsing at the back of his psyche.

He heard the rapid approach of her footsteps and turned to see her, for the first time getting a proper look at her in the disguise of a man. In his old coat and breeches, with her shoulders padded and her hair hidden under a hat, she could be mistaken for a rather feminine adolescent boy.

The sight of her, alive and apparently unscathed, flooded him with a wave of relief.

He straightened his back as the need to hold her close, to hear her heart beating, to breathe in her scent racked his body. He opened his arms and she fell into his embrace. He held her, just letting his body calm down. He'd reproach her later. He knew he would be furious with her, but that would come after she was safe.

For now, his heart beat with a promise. He would always protect her. No matter the cost.

23

One moment Calliope was enveloped in the heaven of Nathaniel's embrace, the next, he shoved her back, at arm's length, frantically looking over her body.

Down the street, towards the river, muffled roars and cheers came from a building standing like a looming silhouette, its windows throwing out fractured glints of candlelight. Across the way, a tattered sign for a tavern creaked in the wind, while a stray cat, its eyes gleaming in the dimness, nosed at discarded fish scraps.

"Are you hurt?" he demanded.

"No." She clenched and unclenched her fist.

He noticed, of course he would, and grabbed her hand, looking it over. The knuckles looked red and swollen.

He kissed her hand, and even despite her recent fear and the rush of danger, a shiver of pleasant awareness washed through her.

"You are hurt," he said in an accusatory voice.

"I'm fine. I punched the smaller one in the nose."

He growled, and her heart broke at the expression of real fear in his eyes. "Calliope!"

"I had to protect myself."

"What were you doing?" he demanded. "I told you to stay at home. This is dangerous."

"And if you hadn't forbidden me from investigating, you'd have come with me and this wouldn't have happened. Instead, I had to sneak out alone."

He gave out an annoyed groan, grabbed her by the elbow, and tugged her after him.

"You could have been badly hurt," he said.

"Where are you tugging me?" she demanded. "Isn't that Portside right there?" She pointed at the looming building from which shouts and cries were still coming. "Let us go and ask around."

"You are going nowhere." He didn't even look at her. Heavens, he was strong—a mountain, not a man. "Good Lord, Calliope, what if I hadn't found you?"

"I have my pistol. I just didn't have a chance to use it."

"But can you even shoot it?"

"No. But I did manage to break his nose." She rubbed her bruised knuckles. "I told you, Spencer taught me boxing."

They reached Hermes, forlorn and untethered. It was unlike Nathaniel to leave his sole horse unsecured on a street, vulnerable to theft. Guilt stirred within Calliope.

"Your boxing can only get you so far against two men," he rumbled. "Up on Hermes you go."

She turned to him. Sex workers looked with interest at them. She didn't bother to lower her voice anymore. "You can't keep me locked in a house forever, Nathaniel. That is not who I am."

He glared at her, his lips thin, his nostrils flaring. He could be the god of war, with that fury thundering behind his eyes.

"I will if I have to. You are a danger to yourself. You are leaving me no choice."

"Leaving you no choice?" She shook her head. "Nathaniel, who do you think you married? A wallflower?"

"Yes," he said. "That was who I had thought you were when we met. A wallflower."

But there was no conviction in his voice.

She snickered. "I just pretended to be one when I went out into society so that everyone would leave me alone. I couldn't care less for appearing to be a rule-obeying duchess."

He sighed, his shoulders slumping in defeat. "I know, Calliope," he said softly. "I don't care if you follow the rules, either...unless it's about your safety. And yet, you keep pushing and pushing against the boundaries I set. My only wish for you is to be safe. I don't want to be a tyrant. But I don't know what else to do."

Her heart broke for him, and she stepped closer, cupping his warm, handsome face with her palm. "You have to trust me to be able to protect and defend myself. I think we can be very happy, Nathaniel. But this marriage will never work if we don't trust each other."

He closed his eyes and leaned into the palm of her hand. When he opened his eyes, they were sad but resolved. "You're right. It's just, every time I think of you alone, in the darkness in the streets swarming with criminals and highwaymen..." His voice shook and trembled. "I am returned to that night with my mother...where I can't defend her and she dies. If you die... If my sisters—"

His voice broke, and Calliope felt as though she'd been struck in the stomach, all of the air kicked out of her.

"I won't be able to live with myself."

She planted a gentle kiss on his lips, and he leaned into her, wrapping his arms around her waist and pressing her against his hard body. "You just defended me," she said.

"But I can't be with you or with the girls every minute of every day."

She leaned her forehead against his. "Exactly. And that's why you should trust me."

He didn't say anything for a long time. They just stood there, with their foreheads pressed together. Then he nodded. "I will try, Calliope. I promise I will try. But you must do something in return."

"What?"

"Promise me you won't go investigating without me."

She saw the ache, the pain, the fear in his eyes. He promised he would try. She should do the same...no matter how hard it would be to try to trust him in return. But she knew why he was like this. Why safety and control were so important to him. And why trusting was so hard.

It was also hard for her.

"I promise," she said, her voice surprisingly small.

"Thank you," he said, relief softening his features. "And to show that I will indeed try, I have an idea."

The next morning, Nathaniel took his pistol from the case Calliope held stretched out for him.

Hampstead Heath was beautiful and quiet this early. After Nathaniel had taken Calliope back home last night, and made love to her twice, he'd woken her up before first light. Normally, duels were fought here in the early morning, so this was an isolated enough place for what he had in mind.

Calliope was a vision. The memory of her the previous night, clad in his old breeches that clung to her shapely legs, was undeniably alluring. Today, her hair was elegantly pinned up, accentuating her striking face under her high riding hat, which was decorated with feathers and silk flowers. She wore a green dress adorned with bright yellow ribbons cinched at her high waist and delicate lace roses on the bodice. She resembled the huntress Artemis, her expression focused, eyes fixed on the tree some distance away where he had set up a round target marked with charcoal rings.

He detested the circumstances that brought them here, that compelled her to learn self-defense. The ever-present fear for her safety cast a shadow over his soul, tearing him apart.

But he had to be a better man. In his mind, he knew she was right. He had to trust her. He couldn't protect her every minute of every day no matter how much he wanted to. She had been trained by her brother to box, and she could protect herself—to an extent.

So in lieu of giving her what she needed—her independence, her freedom—he had to fight down the terror in his soul and teach her to protect herself even more. No matter how much it hurt him to do that.

She was right; he knew it. She was an independent woman, and that was what he admired so much about her—it was incredibly attractive. And yet...

He despised it at the same time. He was afraid of it.

But she was right. If he insisted on locking her up, taking away her freedom, what chance did they have?

What he had thought would just be a transactional marriage wasn't anymore. Not after he had tasted her lips and not after he had started to learn who she really was. No. He wanted all of her or none at all.

And if he wanted them to be happy, he couldn't be like his tyrant father had been to his mother.

He had to be better. He'd promised her he would try, and here he was. Trying.

The cool, solid weight of the pistol felt familiar in his palm, each contour fitting into his grip like a memory. He opened the hammer with a practiced flip of his thumb, revealing the small pan.

"You pour a measure of gunpower here," he said as he did so. "In combat, you don't have much time to reload your pistol, so make every shot count. Take your hand and put it in the pouch at my waist and take out one of the bullets."

Calliope nodded and retrieved a small lead ball, handing it to him. He picked it from her fingers.

"Now, put it at the top of the barrel," he said, indicating. "Press it down."

Using the wooden ramrod, he pressed the bullet down, feeling the subtle give and resistance as it compacted against the charge. He made sure to hold the pistol downward and away from Calliope. He knew all too well how deadly those things could be.

"Now take the stance I'm taking," he said and demonstrated. "Feet shoulder-width apart, angle your body slightly to the side. Distribute your weight evenly."

As Calliope copied him, he nodded. "Good."

He raised his straight arm and aimed at the target.

"You need to brace yourself for the recoil, Calliope. The kickback is going to be strong."

As Calliope mirrored his position, he moved behind her, and pressed the pistol into her hand, putting her finger on the trigger and making sure she held it correctly. He could feel the strong muscles of her arms, the ones he'd admired when he saw her naked. She boxed every other day in one of the free bedrooms. A punching bag had been hung from the ceiling, and she had a jumping rope lying nearby as well as leather fist mitts to protect her hands.

Then he stood close enough that their bodies nearly melded together. His arms reached around her, aligning her elbows and wrists, guiding the pistol into position. He felt her resilient form against him, her softness belying the strength within. Her natural fragrance and her delicious perfume intertwined with the damp, earthy scent of morning dew made his head swim and his blood stir. He should be taking her into his arms and kissing her and making love to her again and again. Instead, he had just put a deadly weapon into her hand and was teaching her how to use it.

He looked at the target. "The key to good aim isn't solely in the hands or eyes."

"Oh?" she asked.

"Take a deep breath and hold it," he said, his chest brushing against her back as he did the same. He could feel the slow rise and fall of her breath synchronizing with his own. He couldn't help the quickened rhythm of his heart, though, threatening the calm he wanted to exhibit.

"Feet apart, good...now, bend your knees slightly, just like this." His free hand pressed lightly on the small of her back, encouraging the subtle shift in her posture.

Her body aligned with his, mirroring his stance. He moved his hand away, placing it back on hers which held the pistol. "Now, extend your arms. Full extension, love," he instructed, the familiar motion of his own arms providing a silent guide.

A terrifying image of her needing to use the pistol against a real foe hit his inner vision and sent a deep chill down his spine.

"Good. Now, line up the sight with your target," he continued, pointing to the small notch at the rear of the pistol and the protruding point at the muzzle end. "When they're aligned, both should point to your target, just there." His finger traced an invisible line towards the tree.

"I see," Calliope whispered, the words drifting into the dawn air.

"Finally"—Nathaniel's voice dropped to a murmur, his lips close to her ear, inhaling her intoxicating scent—"squeeze the trigger, don't pull."

The sharp report of the pistol sliced through the morning stillness, leaves fluttering in response to the echo. A flock of birds darted into the sky, the beating of their wings cut through the silence. He could see that her bullet had hit one ring away from the bull's-eye.

The kickback was strong even in his own body, and he was proud to notice Calliope held her stance well.

As the ringing in his ears subsided, Calliope turned to look at Nathaniel, a spark in her eyes that mirrored the burst of pride in his chest. He knew then their connection wasn't just in the stance, the aim, or the shot. It was in the trust, and her appreciation for his support and instruction.

"Good shot," he said. "Quite close to the mark. Very good, love."

But his voice was still quiet, not ringing with pride and confidence as it should be.

"Thank you," she said, beaming.

He nodded. "I'll give you two muff pistols so that you always have them at hand."

She frowned, her eyes going wet. "Are those the muff pistols...from that night?"

He nodded somberly. He only hoped they would bring her more luck than they had him.

"Now try and reload it by yourself," he said.

As he watched her pour the gunpowder, then put the bullet in, he knew he didn't feel any better knowing she would be able to shoot. He knew he was going against his instincts, against everything he knew to be true, by allowing her to keep putting herself in danger.

Would he ever be able to let her be? She'd promised not to go out and investigate by herself. That should help him not to die inside every time she wasn't where he expected her to be.

But, God forbid, if anything happened to her...

He'd never be able to forgive himself. He'd be completely finished.

He cared for her much, much more than he'd ever intended... She had become essential to his very existence.

Whatever he must do, he wouldn't let harm come to her.

24

THREE DAYS LATER, Calliope watched the team of construction workers in the sitting room using chisels to remove old, damaged parts of windows. A glass cutter lay next to the new windowpanes leaned against the wall.

Several men applied new plaster with trowels over laths, filling the cracks in the old walls and creating a new, fresh layer. Two more men crouched over the parquet floor and hammered in fresh tiles with mallets. It smelled like wet plaster, wax, fresh wood, and dust. The room was filled with the noise of repairs, and Calliope loved every moment of that.

Until a certain tall and broad-shouldered male figure appeared in the doorway and charged towards her like a bull.

"Calliope, what in the world?" he cried.

Calliope sighed. "I knew you were going to be angry with me."

Nathaniel, striking in his navy uniform, came to stand by her side, gaping at the sitting room.

"Then why did you do this?" He swept his arm in an arc, helpless rage darkening his eyes.

"Because it's a beautiful house and it deserves to be restored. I know you want to repair it as much as I do."

"Yes, I do," he declared. "With my own means."

"But it's also my house, is it not?"

He turned to her, eyeing her like a lion on a hunt. "Do not do this."

"What?"

"Ask questions you already know the answer to. I told you I did not want you to spend your money on this. I have a contract with your brother."

Calliope shrugged. "It's my money, and I'll spend it on whatever I want. Besides, it's not just for me, it's for your sisters, too."

Nathaniel gave out a low grumble that made her tense for the first time.

"I cannot believe you," he grated. "After what we agreed on about trusting each other, you go and do this against my wishes!"

Calliope frowned. "Nathaniel—"

But he didn't listen. He marched into the sitting room in three large steps and looked around the room. "Who's in charge here?"

"That would be me, sir," said the man who was working on the window. "Is everything to your satisfaction?"

"Please come for your payment to me, and not to my wife," said Nathaniel, chest heaving with what she knew was anger he could barely contain.

"Very well, sir."

Nathaniel nodded and walked out of the room and passed by her. Guilt twisted Calliope's gut, and she raised her hand to try to catch him by the elbow. "Nathaniel—"

He stopped without looking at her. "Calliope, I am the man of this house," he rumbled in a low voice so that only she could hear. "Do you know how it makes me feel that I couldn't provide a good house or proper life for my sisters? For years, we had nothing. And now I am being rescued by my wife who has everything but simple patience?"

Calliope's cheeks flushed. "I was only trying to help. Are you truly so prideful that you can't accept it?"

He chuckled and shook his head. "Love, I could ask you the same thing when it comes to your investigation."

They stared into each other's eyes, and Calliope couldn't say a thing as the simple truth of his words struck her right in her very core.

"I'll pick you up later to go to Portside," he said and left the house.

Calliope's chest was still tight with worry over their argument when she and Nathaniel walked into Portside later that day, Argos at their feet, sniffing and wagging his tail.

"Stay behind me and let me do the talking," said Nathaniel as he protectively moved her behind him with his large arm, looking around the tavern as though it was full of murderers, vipers, and bears all ready to charge at her and tear at her throat.

Calliope scoffed and pulled slightly at Argos's leash to stop him from sniffing at something sticking to the wooden floor of the tavern, then walked around Nathaniel's back to stand next to him.

"No, Nathaniel," she said firmly, despite her regret about their earlier quarrel. "I am doing everything you asked of me. We've been training for three days until you were satisfied that I could shoot into the bull's-eye three times in a row. I have your pistols right here, in my reticule. We have the dogs. You are with me. Now you must also do what I asked of you. Let me conduct my investigation."

"That is exactly what I'm doing," he said gruffly and pushed her back behind him.

Calliope let out an angry puff of air. For three days they had shot countless bullets at Hampstead Heath until she could reload the pistol in record time and shoot well. They'd also practiced boxing. At the end of their long days, they had spent time with the girls, who had been going out with Grandmama and visiting her for tea.

But at night...oh dear Lord, at night, when there was no shooting and no boxing and no investigation to think of, Nathaniel and she lit the world on fire. At least that was how she felt, like she was burning and evaporating high into that night sky. It had become her favorite time of the day. Sometimes it was fast and needy, to satisfy their shared hunger for each other. Other times it was slow and loving, and they couldn't stop looking into each other's eyes.

She was afraid to believe she was more to him than just the means to get his inheritance. But all evidence showed he may really care about her.

And that was terrifying.

Because he might hurt her no matter how much he wanted to protect her.

Or she might hurt him like she had earlier today.

Besides, he still had no idea what she had in mind for her future. He probably thought that all this danger would be over once they found Spencer... He had no idea she intended to start a business and take on other jobs as an investigator.

She'd enjoyed herself immensely learning how to shoot and was very grateful to Nathaniel for the lessons because they would be indispensable.

"Are you still cross with me?" asked Calliope as they kept moving through the crowd.

"Yes," he said. "But we have a task to do, and I'm a man of my word."

Rough-hewn timber beams overhead, darkened with age, seemed to shudder from the volume of raucous laughter and shouts. And the thick, heady mix of sweat and ale was almost overpowering. The patrons, a motley assemblage of dockworkers, sailors fresh off ships, and a few gentlemen slumming from other parts of the city mingled and jostled, each trying to get a better view of the spectacle that drew them all in tonight.

In the midst of this chaos, a makeshift ring had been set up, delineated by thick ropes and anchored barrels. The crowd pressed against it, some climbing onto tables and chairs for a clearer view, their bets shouted to bookmakers who hastily jotted numbers onto grimy paper.

Two formidable men, muscles slick with sweat and gleaming in the feeble light, exchanged blows in the ring's center. Calliope's heart clenched. It must have been a similar sight last September when Spencer was press-ganged.

Her husband stood like a tall column next to her, his beautiful eyes dark under his eyebrows, his golden hair shining in the slight glow of lanterns and candles.

"You are, Nathaniel," she said as she stepped up next to him again. "But please stop shoving me behind you. We made an agreement, which we both are fulfilling. You're being unreasonable with your overprotectiveness."

His large chest rose and fell quickly as he glared at her. "Unreasonable?" he grumbled. "You have no idea what it costs me to let you stand here."

"You're not the only one making compromises. I would be much better off here by myself without a navy officer looming over me," she said and threw her glance at the sparring men. "Is it always like this during the matches?"

He looked at the ring. "Yes. Welcome to the dangerous and illegal world of prizefighting. Stakes are high, and only the best fighters gather here. Legal gentlemen's matches with no money involved are boring."

"I keep imagining Spencer here," she said. "I think that's why he loved it here. The excitement, the challenge. Put a challenge or a bet in front of Spencer, and he just can't let it go. Besides, his life as duke was full of duties, so I'm not surprised he was here almost every week."

Nathaniel's gaze softened, warming the middle of her chest. "We'll find him."

The gentleness in his voice made her melt. Being here, where she knew Spencer had spent so much time, brought the sadness right back, making her eyes burn. Did he have a brandy at that bar before he went into the ring? Did he have loyal people who came and placed bets on him and cheered for him? How often did he win? What did he feel as he stood before his opponent, his fists clenched tightly, ready to strike?

His absence was a painful hole inside her. "Spencer, hold on, wherever you are," she whispered.

Nathaniel squeezed her hand reassuringly, and she smiled back to him.

His gaze followed one of the servants cleaning the tables. It was a young woman with dark hair.

"Come, let's talk to Daisy," he said. "She has worked here ever since I can remember."

They moved through the crowd, the dogs leading the way.

"Daisy," said Nathaniel when they approached her.

"Ah, the duke is 'ere." She straightened with a wet cloth in her hand and placed her fist on her hip. "What can I do for you, luv? Last time you won me five whole pounds."

Calliope didn't like the woman's hooded eyes when she

looked at him. Not in the slightest. A stab of jealousy made Calliope's nostrils flare. A slight smile on his lips made her wonder if it was only politeness or if they had ever shared more than that. The thought of him with another made nausea rise in her stomach.

"We wondered about one night last September," she said before Nathaniel could say anything, her voice coming out quick and cold. "The night when there was a big raid here. Many men were press-ganged."

Daisy looked her over from head to toe, one eyebrow rising. "Oh."

"This is my wife, the Duchess of Kelford," said Nathaniel.

The woman's eyebrows practically crawled to her hairline. "Your wife?"

"Yes, his wife," said Calliope.

"What is your wife doing in a place like this?" Daisy scoffed and returned to wiping the round table. Patrons lifted their cups from the surface, letting her clean.

"It's her brother," said Nathaniel softly. "He was taken during the raid to be press-ganged, and we wondered if you saw anything?"

She stilled, her gaze momentarily softening with sympathy. "I know what night you speak of," she said as she picked up empty mugs and straightened. "I didn't work that night."

Disappointment felt like a heavy weight in Calliope's chest. "Oh," she said. "Have you heard anything about that night? Something that might be useful?"

"Who was your brother?" The barmaid narrowed her eyes.

"He was the Duke of Grandhampton. Spencer," said Calliope.

Daisy's eyes widened with understanding and a sly smile. Did the woman enjoy a special connection with both her husband and her brother?

"Spencer..." she murmured. "Duke Ironfist. I'm gutted 'e's gone, luv." Her sudden softness to Calliope was a surprise. "Ain't 'eard nothin' except he copped it that night, right there. Broke me 'eart, it did. Always had me back if a punter got too handsy. 'e was a good man."

"Thank you. He still is a good man," said Calliope firmly. "We're trying to find him as we found out he didn't die but was taken onto a navy ship against his will."

"Right," she said and turned away as she walked through the crowd towards the bar. They followed. "Mayhap, Harvey can 'elp. He is 'ere every night."

"Yes, we should talk to Harvey," said Nathaniel. "Come, Calliope."

They made their way to a bear of a man in his fifties. Despite his age, he had hands that seemed capable of crushing stone and arms that had seen their fair share of labor. A dense silver beard covered his square jaw. He had something of a military stance about him. His eyes, deep-set and sharp as a hawk's, missed nothing as they surveyed his establishment. There was an unmistakable aura of authority and respect that clung to him.

"He is a veteran of the American War of 1775," Nathaniel whispered to her.

"Ah, Noble Knuckles," said Harvey, glancing up at Nathaniel with a smile as he wiped the smooth wooden surface of the bar. "Are you fightin' today?"

"No," said Nathaniel.

"He wants to ask you about the night of the press-gang last September," said Daisy. "And this one's hitched now," she added with a quick glance at Calliope.

"Many 'appy years," said Harvey, his eyes scanning Calliope with estimation. "What about that night?"

"Do you remember it well?" asked Nathaniel, leaning over

the bar to hear him better as the crowd roared at something that happened in the ring.

The man's gaze darkened. "Hard to forget the night when every bloomin' thing I 'ad got smashed and a duke copped it 'ere."

Nathaniel nodded. "Right. That is exactly what we're after."

"The duke is my brother," Calliope added. "And we now know he's not dead."

"Duke Ironfist is not dead?" demanded Harvey.

"No. And we're trying to find where he is. Do you remember a man being undressed by someone?"

Harvey nodded. "As it 'appens, I do. Legged it outta the buildin', tryin' to stop some of the blokes bein' dragged towards the ship. In the alley between Portside and that old warehouse, I saw some lads yankin' someone's shirt off. I reckoned it was just some of the ruffians usin' the ruckus to rob someone. I couldn't 'elp as I was too busy scrapping with them press-gang lot. Why do you ask?"

Calliope's heart drummed so fast she thought she would swoon. For the first time in days, she had heard something concrete that might help her find out more. She could feel it. "Because the body we believed was Spencer was dressed in his clothes."

"Ah. I am chuffed to hear Duke Ironfist may not be dead. But I didn't see who it was that they were strippin'. It was chaos. One moment, it was like this—two men boxin', a crowd watchin' them, drinkin', enjoyin' the match. The next, an army of men dressed like Noble Knuckles here barged through the doors, yelling, 'ittin' men, draggin' them outside. No one was safe. People legged it. The whores tried to leg it. The place was 'eavin' with bodies movin' everywhere."

Calliope looked at Nathaniel, who shot a worried glance at her.

"Navy men beat everyone, dragged 'em outside by their shirts. Those who put up a fight? Knocked 'em out cold. I'd bet my last penny some of those wealthier folk who like to come 'here and bet got their pockets picked in all the kerfuffle."

Calliope could feel it—the information was right at the tips of her fingers. She clutched the edge of the bar to stop them from shaking. Nathaniel's body next to her was as rigid as a tree.

"Did you, by any chance, recognize the men who undressed him?"

Harvey's hand, which was rubbing the surface of the bar, went still. "Um..."

"We wouldn't prosecute," Calliope hurried to add. "We're just looking for my brother to try to save him."

Harvey's eyes lingered on her like two dark cherries. "As it 'appens, I remember."

Calliope couldn't breathe. "Who was it?"

He sighed deeply. "I didn't know 'e done that to Ironfist, or I wouldn't 'ave let the bloke back here. I knew 'e was a ruffian, but all kinds of folk come here."

"That's all right. Just please tell me who the man is."

"He comes here every Wednesday to watch the women boxing." He chuckled. "We got our regulars, don't we?"

For the first time in months, a lightness filled her stomach. They had never been this close to finding Spencer. She felt Nathaniel's hand move to her lower back, warm and reassuring.

"Today is Thursday, so it's another week," she whispered. She looked again at the owner. "Thank you, thank you! Do you happen to know his name?"

"No."

"What does he look like?"

Harvey shrugged. "Tall, slouchy. A black eye patch."

"How old is he, would you say?" Calliope asked.

"About forty."

"Any accent? Distinguishing features? Anything that stood out to you?"

Harvey narrowed his eyes. "Yes. He did yell somethin' about his brother being from the rookeries of Whitechapel once. Reckon 'e was givin' someone a warnin'."

"Whitechapel..." Calliope murmured.

She could ask Thorne Blackmore for help. He was Jane's brother and Richard's brother-in-law. That made him family. She'd try to find the man that way first, and if she didn't manage, she'd have to return here next week.

Harvey leaned against the bar with both arms. "If you dare to tell 'im it was me who told you, you won't be steppin' foot in 'ere again. And no one else will talk to you. I don't think whoever it is would take kindly to it."

"Of course," Calliope answered.

Hold on a little longer, Spencer, she thought. *I swear, we'll find you.*

As they walked away from the bar, she squeezed Nathaniel's hand, bubbles rising in her stomach and playing within her. "Nathaniel! Thank you, thank you!" she whispered.

"I'm so glad, love," he said as he looked at her so gently. "I can ask that man next week. You don't have to worry about it."

Calliope had just opened her mouth to say she could do it perfectly well by herself, that she would need to do this work regularly in her sleuth agency.

But he still didn't know...

She should tell him. He deserved to know what he had signed up for... When she'd made the deal with him, he had promised her she would have the freedom to do anything...and yet her *anything* was one thing that would crush him.

How in the world would she ever tell him when, clearly, he was terrified of her being in mortal danger just like his mother had been?

25

"WELL," said Calliope's grandmother two days later as she stroked the white feline menace on her lap and looked around the sitting room. "I like this change."

Nathaniel felt a mixture of satisfaction and annoyance. To all devils, the sitting room looked gorgeous. New windows with fresh paint. Smooth walls of a turquoise color made the space feel warm and sunny. Yellow curtains with a cheerful floral pattern. Fresh flowers in vases. Paintings on the walls. Undamaged furniture that made him think of Mama and how good the house used to look, how much care she used to take maintaining it.

Yesterday, footmen from Sumhall had brought in several chairs, more sideboards, a pianoforte, and a new sofa. Calliope had assured him she had borrowed them from Sumhall and would return everything once he could buy his own furniture.

Calliope sat with a cup of tea, quite pleased with herself. Even his sisters, who sat drinking tea with them, looked cared for, with fashionable hairstyles and in new frocks. They even sat straighter and were quieter. He understood—it was hard to misbehave and not feel the cold stare of the dowager duchess on one's skin...

But when had they started to look like proper little ladies?

But it wasn't just the external things. His own clothes were regularly washed and smelled better. With the cook Calliope had brought in from Sumhall, food tasted better and had more variety. And Mrs. Nicholson had more time to take care of laundry and other housekeeping duties. His sisters had more books, and Calliope had placed an advertisement for a governess for the twins.

He had grumbled with her about all of it, but at least she'd had the decency to ask him first. And when she did, he didn't have the heart to refuse. How could he be so cruel as to say no to a better education and better food for his sisters?

So, begrudgingly, he'd agreed, even if it did mean Calliope spending her own money.

For the first time since Mama died, Roxburgh felt like home.

"Yes," said Calliope as she smiled at Nathaniel. "It has such a great potential. I quite love this house."

Love...

The word made a dark unease move within him. He'd never wanted to feel anything for her in the first place. She was just a means to an end. A wife to give him an heir.

But she'd become so much more. He felt so much for her... and it terrified him.

"Well, it certainly has the right bones to be a duchess's residence, doesn't it?" said the dowager as she stroked Miss Furrington.

"It does," said Calliope, her eyes still on Nathaniel, making his very bones melt. "I trust it will be in its full glory again one day."

Trust...

Another word that burned him like flames.

He wanted to trust her, and he knew if he did, happiness would be in his reach. As Calliope's eyes connected with his again, his goddamn heart softened and drooped like warm wax.

Once they found Spencer, this danger would be done with. And then they'd just be happy together.

Even if she'd never get pregnant and he'd lose his vast wealth to the crown, he'd have her. He'd have his sisters. What else would he need?

"I can just see it," the dowager said as she looked around. "The grandeur of it. The ceilings. The light. The location. And look at the moldings. Just gorgeous." She winked at Calliope. "And plenty of space for the next generation to play."

Nathaniel's gaze dropped to Calliope's stomach as her face went scarlet. The thought of a baby was both a thrill of joy and a tug of dread in his gut. They couldn't know yet if she was pregnant, although it was possible. She could be carrying his child...

And he allowed her to carry a gun; he allowed her to box; he actually took her to Portside! What was he thinking? She was changing him, had him wrapped around her finger, his beautiful little fox.

"Well done, Kelford," said the dowager to him.

"I'm afraid I wasn't given much choice."

"Well, that may be true, but I can see how happy you make my only granddaughter," she said enthusiastically. "And that is all I've ever wished for any of my grandchildren."

Her gaze went to Hazel, Poppy, and Violet. "Now, now." She cocked one eyebrow. "What shall we do with you three? Kelford, I know this Season is almost over, but what would you say if we took Hazel out?"

The three gasps that came from his sisters were a combination of enthusiasm, envy, and shock.

Nathaniel sat up in his chair. “Pardon me?” he barked.

“I think Hazel is ready,” said the dowager innocently. “It’s perhaps a little too early for you two,” she said to the twins with a kind smile. “But Hazel is seventeen.”

Nathaniel’s whole body was ablaze momentarily at the thought of horny sons of marquesses, earls, and viscounts looking at his sister with anything but wonder and adoration. He knew what it was to be a young man in their position, what went through their minds, and hated the idea of them thinking anything of Hazel. His smart, rebellious, pretty sister whom he’d protected his entire life.

“I don’t think she is,” he said, his fingers wrapping around the handle of the teacup so tightly he was afraid it was going to break.

“I am, brother,” said Hazel, straightening her back, then licking her lips. “Not that I care whether I come out this year or the next.”

Calliope exchanged a long look with her grandmama.

“Coming out doesn’t mean she’ll have to marry right away,” said Calliope.

“Nor that I want to marry at all,” said Hazel.

“I’m sure you will, love,” said the dowager, “at some point in the future. Not right away, of course. It merely means you’re showing who you are and that you are on the marriage mart.”

“But she isn’t on the marriage mart at all,” said Nathaniel. “She doesn’t even have a dowry yet.”

Because her dowry, just as the dowries of the twins and his own income, were all dependent on the inheritance that was still out of his reach.

“She doesn’t need a dowry to be on the mart,” said the dowager, and her sly eyes moved to Hazel. “Do you, darling?”

All this time, Hazel had been his young sister, a little girl to protect and shield. The little face he'd seen through the window of the carriage staring at him and their dead mother, wide-eyed. He was sure she didn't remember any of those events that night. She would have told him if she did.

But now, coming out, declaring to the whole world she was a young woman grown enough to marry?

Most of the men who were open for wives would never love them. The thought of someone marrying an amazing young woman like Hazel and not appreciating what a treasure they held made him sick. Made him want to crush something and hit someone.

"I don't mind," said Hazel with a falsely indifferent shrug. "I never even wanted to go out to balls and such."

"Oh, you did, Hazel!" declared Poppy. "You very much did! Don't you lie!"

Hazel gasped, and the dowager and Calliope suppressed amused smiles.

"I did not!" declared Hazel very loudly.

"Darling, your tone," reminded the dowager.

Hazel's face went as red as a beetroot. She put her needlework down, breathing hard. "I remember. And yet, this is another example of why I shouldn't be allowed to come out yet. No one has taught us how to be like you, Lady Grandhampton, or how to be like Calliope. We've been all alone, the three of us, living in Mayfair and yet so isolated from the very essence of the place. Every morning and night, I watch carriages picking up our well-dressed neighbors. Taking them to balls. To soirées. Sometimes they host events right there, and then I see all of them among the beautiful people they know and I..."

She sniffed, and Nathaniel's heart broke as he saw she was fighting back tears.

"And I'm not one of them," Hazel finished.

It was his fault. It was all his fault. She wasn't one of them because he'd failed to provide her with the means and connections and resources to lead the life she deserved.

"Oh, Hazel, but you are." Calliope laid her hand on top of his sister's. "You've always been. Whether you have a frock or not, whether you pick up the right fork, or not, it doesn't matter. You choose your own path, darling. You define where you want to be, who you want to see and who you don't."

"Of course..." he croaked.

The image of someone like that damned William King being as nasty to Hazel as he was to Calliope made Nathaniel writhe with anger. He was losing control. And losing control meant being unable to ensure their safety. Their well-being.

As Hazel grinned at him, her excitement and joy broke his heart. How could he entrust her to another man? What if someone hurt her? The more she was out, the more chances someone nasty would take a liking to her, and he wouldn't be there to make sure she was protected.

He felt his resolve to be a better man crumbling and his instinct to hide everyone he loved in this world taking over. Even if they'd hate him forever, at least they'd be alive.

But no. He was not a caveman. He was a duke. A rational man. A civilized man. He'd be there for Hazel and make sure no one offended her.

Even if he felt like he was about to go completely mad, trying to ensure all the females in his life were safe...

26

"Hazel, darling, are you nervous?" asked Calliope.

The poor thing kept clutching her gloved hands as she watched the room full of elegantly turned out ladies and gentlemen.

"Of course she's nervous," barked Nathaniel, who looked incredibly dashing in his navy uniform and his long hair perfectly combed and tied at the back of his head. Even when he was angry, he didn't cease to take Calliope's breath away. "She shouldn't be here."

"I'm fine," said Hazel, who, pale and big-eyed, didn't look fine at all. "But you're right, brother, I shouldn't be here. I told you I didn't want to be."

"Yes, you do," said Grandmama, who stood proudly by Hazel's side, smiling her wise, eternal smile. "You won't fool me, Lady Hazel. This is your time, and you want this, no matter how much you're trying to tell us you don't."

The salon of Emma, the Duchess of Loxchester, swarmed with people. It was her first time organizing a real soirée for an exclusive number of members of the ton. And, just like Hazel, she was slightly pale. She stood talking to the admiral, next to Penelope and Preston. Richard and Jane were also here, and Jane—standing and talking to Lady Whitemouth and Lady Isabella, her daughter—gave an excited little wave to Calliope.

There were about twenty more people, including Sebastian's mama; the Bishop of London; Penelope's cousin, Alexandria; and the Duchess of Ashton. The presence of Lady Whitemouth and the Duchess of Ashton was especially important for Emma's improving social status. Her marriage to Sebastian had been quite scandalous, with rumors that she was a farmer's daughter whom he'd bought at a village auction.

Which was true in part. Emma had been married to a minor landowner, and it was her husband who'd sold her to Sebastian. However, her marriage had been annulled by the Bishop of London after they'd proved that Emma's former husband had committed fraud when signing the marriage contract.

The scandal lingered, and Lady Whitemouth, a known gossip, was a contributing factor. Sebastian, however, kept defending his wife's honor tooth and nail, and his mama helped as well, as she had come to adore Emma.

"You're going to be fine," said Calliope. "If I know anything about your brother, you're not in danger of getting married off today or anytime soon."

Calliope, Hazel, and Grandmama all looked up at Nathaniel, who threw them a sideways glance, arranging his face to appear cold, his shoulders square, his spine as straight as a pole.

"Quite," he said.

Calliope chuckled and raised her eyebrow as she met Hazel's gaze. "See. Just enjoy yourself if you can."

Hazel let out a long sigh, and, for the first time since

Calliope had met her, gave Calliope a genuine, friendly smile. "You're right, sister."

Sister... Calliope's heart swelled.

"Come, darling, let me introduce you to some people," said Grandmama and led Hazel away. "Indeed, enjoy your coming out."

Calliope turned to Nathaniel, studying him. He looked tense, his gaze never leaving his sister for a moment. "Nathaniel, what is it? Are you really that concerned about Hazel?"

He cleared his throat. "I won't let anyone hurt her."

"Of course you won't. But we're not in the middle of the rookeries. We're at a duchess's soirée in Mayfair. There aren't even many single young men..." She looked around. "Just two. And one of them clearly prefers male company."

Nathaniel followed her gaze to find a handsome blond man who stood talking so close to another gentleman their chests almost touched.

The second young man could be more concerning. Tall, dark-haired, and striking, he talked to Lady Isabella, and so far, was not interested in Hazel.

"I know," said Nathaniel. He was very tense, and Calliope didn't know why.

She felt him pull away from her, and she didn't know what to do about it. Fear crippled her. She felt too much for him, too soon. He was a big, strong, kind man...but if she trusted him, made herself vulnerable, he could break her.

Like William had.

And so instead of reaching out to him, asking what was the matter, telling him she was afraid he would hurt her, she retreated back into what occupied pretty much every second of her life when she wasn't thinking of Nathaniel, the girls, or fixing Roxburgh.

Finding Spencer.

"Right," she said. "Well then, let's use our time wisely. Jane's here, and I want to ask her advice on how to best approach Thorne."

"Thorne?" Nathaniel's attention snapped to Calliope for the first time that evening. "Thorne Blackmore?"

"Yes, Thorne Blackmore. He's Jane's brother, so he's my brother-in-law...and yours."

"Please don't tell me you want to go to Whitechapel—to goddamn Elysium—to talk to him!"

There he was again, the sea devil, his gaze burning.

"Yes, I do, Nathaniel. Harvey gave us some clues, and I don't want to sit back and wait until next week if I could have Thorne's help. Maybe he knows the man. Or he can ask his people to find him. He's like a king over there, isn't he?"

"The king of criminals," Nathaniel spat out. "You promised you wouldn't go there alone."

"And I won't. That's why I'm talking to you about it. As we agreed."

If he reacted this way to her talking to Jane's brother, what would he say to her becoming a professional investigator? Where would this marriage go? Surely he wouldn't go with her every time she'd need to do some sneaking around.

He'd break her heart, wouldn't he? This magnificent man who gave her multiple orgasms and protected her like a large golden bear, and chased away the only shadow she'd ever been afraid of...

"And I appreciate it," he said, his voice softening. "Let's discuss this after the soirée. How about I introduce you to Admiral Langden? He's a good friend who helped me with my commission in the navy and had supported me all these years."

Calliope nodded, a heavy, cold feeling nestling in her stomach. "Splendid idea."

The sun was about to set behind the roofs when Argos stood up from the cobblestoned ground of the mews and growled, looking at the gate.

Violet, trying to ignore the dog, angled Calliope's book so that the last golden rays of the sunlight fell right on the page she was reading. The investigator in the book had just climbed in through the suspect's first-floor window, and as he'd landed, the floor had creaked under his foot!

"Argos, sit!" Poppy exclaimed.

She sat right on the ground in the dirt and unsuccessfully tried to interest Miss Furrington in playing with a dry straw.

Poppy had brought Miss Furrington out to the mews to play with the dogs, and instead, Miss Furrington had joined Cerberus in the dirt, cuddling in between the dog's front legs, happily blinking her sleepy eyes. The straw didn't stand a chance.

Oh, Calliope was going to be cross...all that white fur turning gray... And Mrs. Nicholson was going to have fits at the state of Poppy's dress.

But instead of ceasing his growls, Argos barked. And when Argos barked, walls shook.

"Argos!" cried Poppy, jumping to her feet.

Unfortunately, Orion came running from the other side of the yard, his own barking, though not as tremendous as Argos's, fierce and loud. Argos stood on his hind legs and leaned over the gate with his whole body. Violet laid Calliope's book aside while Poppy continued yelling for the dogs to sit, and walked to the gate, staring at Argos.

Standing, Argos was as tall as she was, his large, meaty

jaws positively terrifying, with those huge clashing, sharp fangs.

"What is it, Argos?" asked Violet.

He wouldn't do this for no reason. Nathaniel had trained him well. Argos kept letting out worried barks, still leaning on the gate, the hardware rattling from his weight. Whatever had him on edge was behind this gate to the mews.

Violet peered through a thin crack. She didn't see anything out of the ordinary at first. The street beyond was empty.

And then she saw them. Three men walked down the street towards Roxburgh looking like that burglar who had attacked Calliope in the alley next to Bond Street.

One of them was taller than the other two. All three had coats and trousers that had seen some wear. They walked about ten feet away, one of them staring at the gate where he, no doubt, heard Argos and Orion tearing their throats out as they barked. Even Cerberus, the little beagle, left his comfy place with Miss Furrington and joined his two friends, adding his howls to their barks.

"Three men, Poppy," she muttered, and Poppy glued herself to the gate, peering through a crack, as well.

Mrs. Nicholson was sick in her bed with a fever and a sore throat. And Joshua was visiting his family.

Nathaniel, Calliope, and Hazel were at the Duchess of Loxchester's soirée. Did these men think Violet and Poppy were out, as well? Or did they know they were home alone...?

One of the men boldly approached the brick wall surrounding the mews.

She saw the largest man take a crowbar from behind a bench he had stopped next to, and the other one had a pistol. Clearly, they were not afraid of the dogs. Violet's blood chilled. The men walked down the fence, watching it in estimation, talking quietly. Were they discussing how to climb over? The dogs were livid by this point—any petty criminal would be running away.

Violet and Poppy exchanged a long, terrified gaze.

"Why do they want to break in?" asked Violet. "We have nothing of value."

"What are we going to do?" Poppy cried. "They're not going to hurt the dogs, surely."

Not just the dogs, Violet thought but didn't say it out loud. Violet had never seen her brave and adventurous sister this pale. It was usually Poppy who'd suggest doing mischief and breaking rules.

Violet thought quickly. They could run. They could hire a hackney and go to Sumhall or to find Nathaniel and Calliope at the soirée. Or they could seek the help of Bow Street Runners... who probably wouldn't believe them, anyway. But the men might catch them as they ran for the street.

"We're going to trick them!" said Violet, a plan forming in her head.

She'd read many of Calliope's inquiry books, about adventures and thugs and investigators chasing them... Sometimes they didn't need any weapons, just a sleight of hand, something clever, to trick the attackers.

"I have an idea," Violet whispered, her eyes darting around. "Get the dogs and the cat inside! The thugs will kill the dogs if they see them out in the open. And don't come out. I'll take care of the stairs."

Poppy, swallowing hard, nodded, determination lighting up her features. She scooped up the cat, who stared at the brick wall with large, round eyes, her tail jerking nervously.

"Come!" Poppy called to the dogs, and they reluctantly stopped barking and followed her inside.

Violet ran towards an old whale oil barrel that had just a little bit left at the bottom, but it would be enough. She scooped up a cup of the stinking liquid. Running back towards the servants' entrance, she could hear the thugs grunting as they tried to jump over the tall fence.

She flew up the stairs. Leaning against the wall was the broken railing from Calliope's near fall. Nathaniel still hadn't found the time to repair it, and they'd all just gotten used to avoiding it as they had with so many things in the crumbling house. She put down the mug of oil, picked up the railing, and set it back into the holes in the stairs as best she could. Then she poured oil over the stairs and the little landing before running back inside and through the servants' corridor.

Poppy and the dogs waited for her at the entrance to the servants' corridor, the dogs held by their leashes but growling, their faces positively terrifying. The cat perched on the stairs leading to the bedroom floor and watched everything with wild eyes.

"Good. Hide the dogs behind the corner over here," Violet said to Poppy. It felt strange to be telling her adventurous sister what to do, but someone had to take charge. "I have something else in mind. Whatever you do, keep the dogs quiet."

Poppy nodded, giving the dogs the command to be quiet, then led them around the corner, out of sight of the servants' door.

Violet ran into the library to remove the board covering the rotten floorboards and saw from the window how the thugs climbed over the fence and raced through the mews towards the servants' stairs. The first one managed to climb three stairs before he slipped and grabbed on to the railing. The railing came off in his hand just as intended. He flailed as he started to pitch backward, then overcompensated and threw himself forward, landing face-first on the stairs and sliding back down, taking both of his companions with him.

Giggling, excited from her first success, Violet ran on tiptoe around the now-exposed rotten boards and joined Poppy. Her sister crouched behind the dogs with big eyes, breathing hard. Violet could hear the uneven, heavy footsteps of limping men as they tried to make their way more carefully up the slippery stairs. The fall must have hurt them.

"Do you remember the rotten boards in the library's entrance?" asked Violet. "I removed the board covering them. Try to lure one of them there. Maybe he'll fall through—and right into the basement."

"Very well. Be ready to attack..." Poppy whispered to the dogs.

The door from the servants' quarters into the master's hallway flew open and one after another, the men came in.

"Attack!" Poppy cried the command Nathaniel had been teaching them for years.

With a tremendous growl, the three dogs launched themselves at the nearest man—who had a gun. He screamed as Argos went for his neck, Orion for his arm holding the gun, and Cerberus for his crotch. The man fell, and his pistol went off with an explosion that filled the hallway with smoke. The thug with the crowbar raised his arm, about to hit Argos.

But the crowbar knocked into a thick medieval shelf bearing the Kelford coat of arms, which hung above the servants' entrance. It was one of the last wall decorations in the house as no one was interested in buying it. As though their ancestors were guarding them, it fell right on the man's head, dropping him to the floor like a sack of meat and bones.

While the first man continued to scream under the dogs' assault, the third one stared right at Violet and Poppy, his eyes bulging and teeth bared. He was the one who had fallen on the stairs, and his nose looked purple and swollen like a potato, with blood oozing from his nostrils.

"Run!" she screamed to Poppy, and the two of them set off to the library.

"Oy, where ya think you're off to?" he shouted. "You're comin' with me, ain't ya?"

They tiptoed around the rotten boards and went farther into the safety of the library, and just as Violet had planned, the man followed them but barged right through the part where the boards were so badly decayed. With every step, they cracked, but he didn't fall through. Violet grabbed Poppy's hand, and they both backed away. She didn't have another plan in mind!

As he reached the last rotten floorboards, they emitted a loud crack, and his leg went through to his knee, but he didn't fall through all the way. It seemed all it had done was infuriate the man even further. He pulled himself up and barged into the library, a knife in his hand.

"Ya reckon yer little tricks can hold me back?"

He grabbed Poppy's hand and tugged her after him.

"No!" Violet cried out as she dashed after her sister.

The man jabbed at her, and a sharp pain sliced through her arm. She grasped the arm with her other hand, blood seeping between her fingers.

Suddenly, the thug stopped in the doorway as another form filled it.

Her brother, with Calliope and Hazel peeking from behind him, their eyes huge. The man let go of Poppy and launched at Nathaniel with a snarl, knife raised. Nathaniel's face distorted, murder written in his expression.

No doubt Nathaniel won money boxing.

The intruder didn't have a chance. One jab in the face with Nathaniel's knuckles, and the man hit the door behind him, his head banging against the wood. The knife dropped to the floor with a clank, but before Nathaniel could grab him again, he ducked and darted, maneuvering between Nathaniel, Calliope, and Hazel.

That did it. With a loud crash, he fell through the boards, wailing as he plummeted, then went silent.

Somehow, the three intruders and her cut, which hurt like it was on fire, didn't frighten Violet nearly as much as the furious and terrified look on her brother's face.

27

IT BROKE Calliope's heart to see Violet's wound, even though it wasn't serious. It could have been so much worse!

She admired how the girls had managed to defend themselves, but she couldn't help but wonder if she'd gone too far lending Violet those books. If, perhaps, Nathaniel was right, and she should stop and make sure the people who were dear to her were safe, too.

Growing up with brothers, she'd never had anyone vulnerable in her life who needed her protection. They'd always been so strong, and she'd needed to be stronger just to catch up with them.

But not everyone was as resilient as the Seaton brothers. And she wasn't independent anymore, whether she liked it or not.

The two other thugs had managed to run away, while the man who had fallen through into the cellar was dead. So they had no answers.

Later that night, after the Seatons' physician had treated Violet, Calliope and Nathaniel were talking in their bedroom.

"I died ten deaths when I saw her bleeding," Nathaniel croaked, staring into the fireplace with the crackling coal grate, his fingers mindlessly chipping at the paint on the mantel.

Calliope's eyes burned with tears. She'd come to love his sisters in the short time she'd lived with them. "I know. Did it make you think about your mother?"

He tensed, as rigid as a tree. "Yes."

His voice was strange, swollen, and a tear rolled down his cheek. It made her chest ache to see him like that.

"If anything happened to them, I'd never be able to live with myself."

The confession was like a boulder that sank into Calliope's soul. She'd brought this on them, on these beautiful girls. On Nathaniel. The intruders had surely come because of her.

"Neither would I," she whispered, standing up from her seat by the fireplace and moving closer to gently brush the tears from Nathaniel's face.

Which meant she needed to be more careful and more considerate. Perhaps, with their enemy so bold as to send men to kidnap Nathaniel's sisters, it was wiser to lie low for a while. And Violet needed care.

"I won't leave her side until next Wednesday," she said.

Nathaniel turned to her, his eyes glaring with unspoken fury. "Indeed, you will not. The investigation must be over now altogether. We put my sisters through enough danger!"

Cold shock washed over Calliope. "No, we cannot stop looking for my brother. Punish me! Do not punish him!"

Nathaniel closed his eyes and sighed deeply. "You're right. Your brother still needs help. Well then." He looked at her coldly. "I will resume the investigation. You may no longer accompany me at all. You must stay at home like I asked. You must not go to Thorne. If there's any investigation before Wednesday, I will do it alone."

"Nathaniel...!"

"And if you disobey me, I will be so heartless as to stop helping altogether. I must look out for my sisters' safety—and yours."

Fury rose in Calliope's chest. "This is not what we agreed on when we married!"

"Exactly. That can be said for both of us. Will you promise me?"

She swallowed hard. It would be difficult for her. If she really wanted to, she could escape and continue her investigation. But there was truth in his words. She was responsible for this. For Violet being hurt, for Poppy almost being kidnapped, for men breaking into their home.

He needed her to stay put. She would give him what he needed, even if it made her feel broken.

"Yes," she said, the word like gravel in her throat.

Over the next few days, Nathaniel came to her, intent on getting her pregnant, but didn't sleep with her in the same bed. It was strange...to be angry with him, to feel guilty, and yet to want him like mad, unable to resist his lips, his arms, his cock. They spoke with their bodies—that they still needed each other, craved each other like air—and yet, they did not talk.

Clearly, Nathaniel wasn't getting much sleep. He had dark circles under his eyes, hollow cheekbones. Seeing him like that, Calliope felt the worry grow in her stomach. She kept her promise and stayed at home, caring for Violet—who was more excited by her success than bothered by her wound. Following her promise to Nathaniel, she had asked him to please let her pay for the repairs to the floorboards, given that the men that had caused the damage had come because of her.

Nathaniel shivered at that, but instead of yelling at her, he simply nodded. He didn't argue. He didn't get angry. It was as though he looked at her from behind ten castle walls, shielded and protected.

It would have been better if he had fought with her. Somehow, this silent compliance was worse.

It was as though he'd given up because that break-in had finally showed him who she truly was. That he didn't want her as a person anymore, just as a vessel to create the heir he needed.

As she looked at the empty place in her bed where Nathaniel used to lie, so happy and so gorgeously hers only a few days ago, her heart was breaking.

Was she nothing but a womb for him?

She ached to ask him that but was terrified of his answer. What if he'd say yes, she was? What if he'd wonder why she was surprised since that was exactly what they had agreed on from the beginning?

Would he think she was silly to have...what? Cared for him? Started to feel like he was essential to her very existence?

The thought was still like a knife in her belly when the day finally came to see the man Harvey had mentioned—the one who may have helped press-gang Spencer. Calliope and Nathaniel climbed into the Seaton carriage to drive to Portside. It was as though he was with her...but also not.

As the carriage rolled down the street, Calliope noticed a man on a horse who seemed to follow them for a while before disappearing a few streets before they arrived in Portside. It was probably nothing, she told herself. But unease washed through her in a chilly wave.

Calliope's heart beat fast as she and Nathaniel walked through Portside, the room packed with men drinking and yelling. She stared with fascination as two women dressed in men's trousers fought each other. Respect rose in her, and she wondered how it would feel to stand in that ring, facing an opponent, and fight...like Nathaniel had fought for years to support his sisters.

When they reached the owner, Harvey shrugged and looked at them with a somber face. "You just missed 'im."

"Just?" demanded Calliope. "When did he leave?"

"Saw a boy come up to him, and then 'e rushed out not a minute ago."

Calliope and Nathaniel exchanged a glance.

"Goddamn it," cursed Nathaniel, and he and Calliope darted through the crowd, pushing people out of the way. They ran outside, frantically looking around. Nausea rose in Calliope's stomach when she got a whiff of stale urine. There was no one outside.

Nathaniel looked at her and sighed. "Come on, Calliope, let's go home. We will try again next week."

"We could go to Thorne—" Calliope started, but one look from Nathaniel and she closed her mouth.

"I am doing all that I can, Calliope," he rasped. "I am at my limit. Men broke into my house and hurt my sister... They almost kidnapped Poppy. And you want to dive even deeper into the criminal world of London?"

Calliope bit her lower lip. All true, and yet, Spencer was somewhere out there, probably fighting the French or the Americans.

The need to act, to do something, was instinctive for her. Being made to sit in one place felt like Nathaniel tying her down with a rope.

And yet, she wanted him and the girls to be safe. Seeing him worried, afraid, withdrawn was worse than her own discomfort. She was no longer angry with him. He was in her blood. He was in her soul. She wanted to make him happy, more like the golden lion he had been when she'd met him at the Royal Navy ball.

She wanted to see that glimmer of flirtation in his rakish eyes again.

And so, even if it went against everything she was, she nodded. "You're right. We'll wait till next Wednesday."

After a curt agreement from Nathaniel, Calliope continued working on the house.

He agreed that having a bigger staff meant increased safety, and so Calliope hired a trained butler, a coachman, and two more footmen, making Joshua the underbutler and increasing his wages to reflect his promotion. Two chambermaids joined the household to help with housekeeping and free up Hazel and the twins from housework. A governess moved in and started teaching the girls all those things they had missed.

Violet's wound was not deep, and after some stitches, it healed well, restricting her only a little. But, as she cheerfully said, she didn't need to use her arm to read.

It was Poppy who noticed a man observing their house the day after Calliope and Nathaniel missed the man at Portside.

Nathaniel sent the footmen to get rid of him, and the man ran away before they could reach him, disappearing in the streets.

To respect his wishes, Calliope didn't break her promise to him to go to Thorne or do anything else for the investigation without him. She wanted to ease his fear and to make sure the girls were safe.

It was because of her they were in danger, because of her meddling that someone had their home under surveillance.

Even though it felt like she was tied to one place by a chain, she hoped she could repair her husband's mood just as she repaired the house, and that he'd look at her with the adoration she'd seen before, on that one night full of stars and irises.

But her sacrifice didn't seem to make a difference to

Nathaniel. He was still angry with her...or afraid... He was withdrawn, still intent on keeping her away from the investigation, which she, like he had accepted her repairs, grudgingly accepted. But her lack of action made her miserable. Itching to do something for Spencer, she felt like she was in prison as she studied a shadow of a man who hid behind a large tree across the street. Every day since Poppy had first spotted him, the man was chased away, and every day, he returned, hiding behind a corner. Behind a parked carriage. Behind the bushes.

Watching.

It must be her passive waiting, but Calliope felt worse and worse every day. She felt nauseated, her breasts ached, and her nipples felt like they were being cut with glass every time something touched them. She was physically exhausted, even though she didn't do much at all, besides talking to the girls, teaching Hazel to play the pianoforte, and making love to her husband.

They still came together like it was the only thing that connected them. Like bringing each other physical pleasure was their only way of communicating. She showed him how much she cared for him. For God's sake, she cared enough to do the one thing she thought she'd never do.

Hide.

It must have been the following Monday that Calliope sat straight up, feeling cramps in her lower stomach in the middle of the night. Certain her courses had finally arrived, several days late, she stood up from the bed to search for the cloth pads she used monthly. Nathaniel, who for the first time in days had fallen asleep next to her, stirred and rose on his elbows as he blinked at her.

"Are you well?" he asked.

She turned to him, his long hair in a mess, his gorgeous face sleepy and so domestic...her heart ached. After her investigation was done, would they ever regain the happiness they used to share? Or would they just drift apart ever further, especially once she gave him an heir. Then he wouldn't need her anymore—

She froze, her hand shooting to her lower belly. She looked between her thighs, expecting to see smears of blood...

Nothing.

She frowned.

She didn't have her courses. They could still come. However, Nathaniel and she hadn't missed a single night, except the night of the break-in, making love.

So, it was possible. Could she be...

"I may be pregnant..." she murmured, more to herself than to him. A jolt of happiness and joy shot through her like sunbeams.

He sat straight up, all sleepiness gone from his face, his muscled chest glowing in the blue moonlight falling through the windows. He stared at her stomach as if it were full of vipers.

That made her heart break all over again. Instead of the happiness she'd expected to see on his face—or even relief that it may be happening, that he may receive his inheritance—there was a look of pure terror.

"So soon?" he croaked out.

She swallowed, suddenly self-conscious, and picked up her dressing gown, wrapping it around herself.

"Yes, so soon."

Still gloriously naked, he jumped from the bed like a lion and darted to the window. He carefully touched the curtain and looked at the street, then picked up his own dressing gown and shoved his arms through its sleeves.

"You wanted this, am I right?" she asked, feeling tears prickling the backs of her eyes.

His eyebrows were knotted, his eyes wide, his mouth a tight line.

Where was the joy of a soon-to-be father? The happiness on the face of the man whose wife may be growing a new life inside her?

"Of course I did," he said without looking back at her.

But it didn't sound at all like he did. He hadn't looked into her eyes since the moment he'd heard the word "pregnant."

She shouldn't talk about it. Shouldn't touch the very sensitive subject. They had enough unspoken secrets, promises neither of them wanted to keep, a paper-thin truce between them that could be broken forever with one wrong word.

And yet, her heart was full of Nathaniel, full of hope for their happiness, for the two of them—maybe for the three of them.

She should just keep her mouth shut.

"Then why aren't you happy?" she blurted out.

Finally, he met her eyes—with a glare.

"Happy?" he snarled. "How can I be happy when—"

He cursed under his breath and closed his eyes, the powerful chest muscles rising in a deep breath. He pointed at the window. "There's someone who surveyed my house for days. How can I be happy that he watches my pregnant wife and my three sisters? How can I be happy if they can invade my own house again? And now there may be an unborn child to protect as well."

Her throat contracted. "But I haven't gone and done anything by myself, just like you asked me. I didn't go to Blackmore like I wanted to. I didn't even breathe in the direction of Portside. I—"

Don't say it, Calliope. Don't say it. There would be no coming back from this.

"You what?" he barked.

It was probably that tone that did it. That fury in his voice, the contempt, the resentment. She knew they had their differences, the big questions between them.

And she snapped. The dam of unhappiness, of tiredness, of anger at him for confining her, and at herself for obeying him, pushed against her resolve like storm-roiled water crashing against a dam.

"I can't do this anymore!" she yelled. "I stopped looking for my brother for you, so that you know I'm safe and to keep the girls safe. Do you think your forbidding me to leave would stop me if I really wanted to go? But I'm suffocating, Nathaniel! I'm suffocating!"

He narrowed his eyes in confusion, in pain. "But I have done the same for you! I have allowed you to do your investigation. I have allowed you to come with me to Portside despite thugs attacking you! Despite my sister being wounded and scared. Despite someone watching our house every day! And what about your books?"

Calliope frowned. "My books?"

"Yes. Your books. The ones about private inquiries. Aren't they what put all those ideas in Violet's head? Poppy and she were excited about the thug who followed you, thrilled to help you disguise yourself! And because of that, instead of running away and looking for help, they decided to fight three grown men alone!"

Tears welled in her eyes. The worst of it was, he was right. She was wrong for him. Wrong for his sisters. She thought he was one man who wouldn't reject her independent spirit, her odd ideas.

She should have never opened herself up to him. She should have given him her body but not her heart.

Too late. He was already in her very bloodstream. Just like the girls. But it didn't mean they had a future.

Calliope shook her head slowly. "We will never be happy, Nathaniel, will we?"

He glared at her, angular jaw muscles working.

"We're opposite," she said. "I need freedom and independence. You need to know your family is safe. I will never be able to give that to you, no matter how much I might try."

He swallowed hard. "What are you talking about? This will all be over once we find Spencer. I'll keep you safe until then if you just hold on and stay put a little longer."

It was time to tell him the whole truth.

She slowly shook her head, nausea rising in her stomach. "It won't, Nathaniel."

The concern on his face was so sharp it looked like horror. "Why not?"

"Because I have always dreamed of running my own sleuth agency. And once I find Spencer, I will start one."

He crossed the distance between them in three long strides and grabbed her by the shoulders. "What in the world are you talking about?"

"When we agreed to marry, I asked you for freedom. Once I give you an heir or an heiress, you promised me I would be able to do whatever I wanted."

"Within reason."

"Reason being, I won't have other men in my life."

"Yes. Reason is also not putting yourself in constant danger!" he roared.

She freed herself and stepped back. "I am prepared for danger. I'm smart enough to avoid it, if I can, because I take calculated risks. I can protect myself. And men underestimate women. I will also hire other sleuths who will help. But this is my dream, Nathaniel. I've wanted this for years. And very soon, finally, I will have the freedom to do it."

He shook his head. "I never agreed to this. You should have told me. Had I known, I'd never have married you."

There they were, the words that could not be unsaid, the discussion that could not be forgotten. He had stabbed a knife straight into her heart.

She nodded. She was so stupid. Had she not fallen in love with him, this wouldn't have hurt so much.

Fallen in love... The sensation, the realization was as crystal clear as a mirror. She loved her husband. She loved him enough to go against her instincts and sacrifice her true, independent nature for him. Try to make herself someone she'd never be.

An obedient wife.

"I agree," she said, holding her neck straight. "We should have never married. I will never be a woman sitting behind four walls, hiding. And you can never support me in my dream."

He glared at her, his breath accelerating with every second. He looked like he was a cauldron of water coming closer and closer to the boiling point.

She saw the moment something within him snapped. He darted to the bellpull and tugged at it.

"That's it," he barked. "You are forbidden to go anywhere near the docks, do you hear me?"

"Not this again, Nathaniel. We agreed."

He pulled at the cord again several times and looked at her like he was in pain. "Will you obey me or not?"

"Of course not. We're so close to finding out what happened to Spencer. We'll meet that man on Wednesday, in two days—"

"That's it." He threw her chemise into her hands. Panic seemed to be radiating from him like body heat. "Dress. We're leaving."

Calliope clutched the chemise to her stomach. “Leaving? Leaving to where?”

He charged out of the room and into the hallway and yelled, “Abigail! Joshua!” so that the walls shook.

There were footsteps pounding from downstairs. Joshua appeared at first, rumpled and barely able to open his eyes. “Your Grace, is everything all right?”

“Go get Abigail to dress the duchess, please, and pack her things. Right this minute. Then come and dress me.”

“Very good, Your Grace.” Joshua ran downstairs.

“And tell the new coachman to get the carriage ready!” he roared after him.

“Nathaniel! Where are you taking me?” Calliope’s stomach twisted in helpless rage.

Nathaniel took her by the elbow and dragged her back into her bedroom. He locked the door and stood with his arms crossed, his back pressed against the door.

“I’m taking you to Kelford.”

28

When Nathaniel could see the roofs of Kelford village, his chest squeezed with the pain of memories. This was where he'd spent most of his childhood; every tree and every bush was familiar. He'd come here with his mama to visit the tenants, bringing treats from the kitchen and inquiring about everyone's health and well-being. Mama liked to organize village fairs and games, and he'd enjoyed playing with the village children.

The Tuesday afternoon sun was slowly sinking, coloring the sky in oranges, reds, and violets. Calliope's face was cold and distant, her fury with him understandable and yet as painful as a knife in his heart.

He knew he was hurting her. He knew he was making her hate him. He knew he was going against everything that she was.

But he couldn't help himself.

What had happened to Poppy and Violet was bad enough.

Last night was the last straw. It was as though every single thread of strength that he had to control himself, to try to overcome his terror at the thought of losing her, snapped and was gone. And he could no longer force himself to go against his instincts.

The reason was one word.

Pregnant.

He couldn't have known that he would fall in love with his wife. He couldn't have known he'd want this baby like he wanted nothing else in his whole life. That the thought of a small human being that was part her and part him would bring this feeling that was close to benediction. As though he had touched something divine with his big, unworthy fingers.

But he knew one thing.

A wife who would despise him her whole life was better than a dead one.

Sleuth agency...he scoffed inwardly as he watched the new footman open the carriage door.

Why was he surprised? It was so like Calliope. Admirable. Honorable. Courageous. Smart.

And absolutely mad.

He descended to the dirt road. Streets meandered through rows of quaint stone houses with thatched roofs, their chimneys releasing tendrils of smoke that melded with the evening mist. Crimson and pink geraniums spilled from window boxes and sills. The distant hum of village life—the laughter of children playing, the clinking of glasses from the local tavern, the soft conversations of neighbors—created a tranquil backdrop.

Nathaniel turned to his wife. Auburn curls spilled down, framing her face under her bonnet as her eyes blazed with fury. Her cheeks were red and her lips tight and thin.

He hated himself for doing this to her. But sixty miles away from London would be the safest place for her.

At one point, a gig had started following them from London, but he and his footmen had stopped and descended, telling Calliope to stay in the carriage. As they'd walked towards the gig, the driver had jumped down and run away, after which Nathaniel and the lads had broken the wheels of the carriage with axes.

No one had followed them since.

"Come on, Calliope," he said as he stretched out his hand to her. "We're here."

She sneered. "In my prison, you mean?"

"No. It's not a prison. I'll put you in the home of the housekeeper of Kelford Manor. It's a safe place no one will look for you."

She laid her hand in his and descended, looking around. "What about the manor itself?"

"It's locked in the will," he said as they walked towards a small redbrick cottage. "I can't touch it until the heir or the heiress is born before my next birthday, but I know the housekeeper will take you in as a favor to me."

"Nathaniel—" she started as they stopped before a low door.

"Don't," he said. "There will be no more discussion."

Sleuth agency...he thought again. He couldn't imagine living in terror every day while his wife went out and put herself in danger. He'd lock her in here for the rest of her life if he had to. The very thought that he could now lose both her and the baby was like death to him.

He couldn't lose them like he'd lost his mother. He just couldn't.

"How long are we going to be here for, then?" asked Calliope.

The coldness in her words drained the color from the picturesque world around him, making the charming village appear bleak and desolate.

He knocked and the door opened. Mr. Howitt, the housekeeper's husband, opened the door. He was of medium height but with a stout, solid build. Sparse strands of silver hair lay combed back, revealing a receding hairline. And deep-set gray eyes under bushy salt-and-pepper eyebrows assessed Nathaniel with caution that shifted to recognition.

"Your Grace?" Mr. Howitt asked, frowning. "Goodness, I haven't seen you for so long! Please, come in."

He led them through a short hallway into the small sitting room. Mrs. Howitt hurried from their dining room, still chewing. Mrs. Howitt was of slender build, slightly shorter than her spouse, with a graceful posture cultivated from years of managing a household. Her face was framed by waves of soft gray hair tied back in a neat bun, and her bright blue eyes bore the gentle weariness of age. She wore a simple yet tidy blue dress, its faded fabric showing signs of frequent washings and impeccable mending.

"Your Grace!" she said with a warm smile. "Forgive me, we were just having dinner. What can we do for you? Are you back?"

"I'm afraid not yet," he said. "But this is my wife, Calliope, the Duchess of Kelford. I was wondering if she could stay with you here."

"Whatever do you mean, *she* can stay?" asked Calliope, staring at him. "Are you leaving me?"

He didn't reply, couldn't face the hurt in her voice. Of course he wanted to stay with her, knowing it may be months before he'd see her again. He wanted nothing more than to see her grow round with the life inside her, see her glow, feel that first kick, hear her talk about the baby and what she felt, and wait for it to arrive together.

And keep her safe.

But he couldn't stay. His sisters needed him. Besides, the sooner he found Spencer, the sooner she'd be safe.

"Please, will you take care of the duchess while I'm away?" he asked.

He couldn't look her in the eye knowing how much she must hate him for taking her freedom and independence away from her. If he saw that hatred in her eyes, it would shatter his heart.

"Of course we will," said Mrs. Howitt. "But wouldn't it be quite...modest here for a duchess? Your Grace, would you be comfortable?"

"I don't mind the discomfort," said Calliope. "I'm sure this will be perfectly pleasant. Especially since His Grace won't keep me here for long...will he?" she asked him icily.

"I don't know how long the investigation will take," he replied, staring at the small watercolor of Kelford Manor hanging on the wall. "I will go and see that man at Portside tomorrow. I will return to you once I find your brother."

"Nathaniel!" she cried, her voice ringing with indignation and hurt.

"Keep her here, Mrs. Howitt," he said. "Do not let her out of your sight. Abigail, Her Grace's maid, will stay with her. If you could find them both a room, I'd be most appreciative. I'll be back as soon as I can."

Then he finally had the courage to face her. He looked into her beautiful eyes for a long time, aching to take the woman he loved into his arms and kiss her. The thought of leaving her tore at his heart. He hadn't spent a day apart from her for three weeks now, and had thought he'd spend the rest of his life with her like that.

But he knew if he did take her into his arms, he wouldn't be able to leave her.

And he must leave.

Feeling like he had to physically tear himself away from her, he turned around and left the house. Her footsteps sounded after him, and he accelerated, running to the carriage like a madman. As though chased by death, he climbed into the carriage and shut the door, yelling for the coachman to drive.

In the descending twilight, he didn't even look at her from the window. His heart was shattered. He hated to leave Calliope there like that, trapped, against her will, but he had no other ideas of how to keep her safe...her and the baby.

She was right. She was too fearless and independent, and had she stayed in London, she would still go investigating and putting herself in danger the second his back was turned.

The most important things in life for him now were her, the baby, and his sisters.

His family.

And he would destroy his own happiness to protect them.

29

Early Wednesday morning, Calliope sat on a small settee in the Howitts' sitting room, drumming her fingers against the windowsill and watching the village through the slightly imperfect glass. Tiny bubbles and subtle ripples in the pane distorted the view, giving the outside world a dreamlike quality.

Beyond the window, Kelford village looked idyllic with the soft glow of morning light. Women in bonnets chatted by the communal well, drawing water in wooden buckets. Children ran about, playing with hoops and sticks, their laughter echoing through the streets. A few men tipped their hats in greeting as they headed to their work, some leading horse-drawn carts filled with produce or goods for the market.

Every so often, a horse's hoofbeats would break the steady hum of village chatter, and a rider or carriage would pass.

She hated how much she loved it. This may be her home in one year, the village she'd come to visit as the Duchess of Kelford who lived in Kelford Manor nearby. And she craved coming here with Nathaniel.

Last night was horrible. Not because of the bed or the room or anything in the house. But because every fear she had about her and Nathaniel's relationship had come true.

And she felt rejected. Set aside. Controlled.

Imprisoned by the man she loved.

And so, so alone.

She still felt tired and nauseated; she couldn't eat much except for Mrs. Howitt's pickled walnuts, which settled her stomach.

"May I bring you something else, Your Grace?" Mrs. Howitt asked with a kind smile.

Calliope returned her smile. "No. I'm quite all right, thank you, Mrs. Howitt."

"Very well. If I may inquire...you seem upset... Whatever happened, I know my master. He's always been a kind soul. After his mama died...he was never the same. Neither was his papa."

Calliope nodded, unsure how to respond. What was she supposed to do? Sit here every day, watching the village, the people, while she slowly died inside?

No. That was not who she was. She'd let Nathaniel bring her here, which was a mistake. She would show him that this was not the life she wanted with him. He was hiding behind fear—and, whatever their agreement, she was not just a womb. She wouldn't let him lock her up like this.

She would know how to keep the baby safe. And besides, there may not even be a baby yet; it was too early to tell.

She stood up, an idea making her straighten her shoulders and keep her head high. "I'd like a walk," she said. "A bit of fresh air would suit me well."

"That sounds like a marvelous idea," said Mrs. Howitt. "There's a ribbon and fabrics shop on the market square. Perhaps a new shawl would cheer you up?"

Calliope nodded. "Yes, precisely. Thank you! I'll go up and get my money purse."

"Very well. I'll tell Abigail to accompany you."

"Please do."

Abigail was a good sport. She wouldn't mind Calliope's plan. Calliope went up to the room that had been provided for her and took her money purse as well as all her jewelry. She thought she'd need as much as she could take for what she had in mind.

As she and Abigail strolled through the village streets, Calliope asked a woman to direct her to a farmer who bred horses.

They walked for about ten minutes and reached a farm at the edge of the village. There, two men, one in his forties and one around twenty, forked hay from a cart to a large haystack. Calliope introduced herself as their new duchess.

"Would your son like a trip to London?" she asked. He looked like he was a strong young man, and she had her pistols with her. And if they left now, they wouldn't need to travel after dark.

"I'll pay for his time, of course," she said.

The younger man looked up at her with great hope in his eyes. "I would, Your Grace."

"My lady, what are you doing?" asked Abigail quietly.

"Finding a way to London," said Calliope.

"But His Grace was clear—"

A wave of anger hit Calliope at the mention of Nathaniel. "His Grace is delusional if he thinks I'll let him lock me up."

Calliope looked at the farmer's son. "Do you know the way?"

"Yes, I do. That is, I know the way to Bramblebrook. That is halfway to London. We can ask for directions from there."

"But wouldn't His Grace send a carriage with footmen for you, my lady?" Abigail asked. "The roads may not be safe."

"Begging your pardon, Your Grace," said the farmer. "I need my son here, and he's never been so far from the village."

"I'll only be gone a short time, and I know the way, Pa," the young man reassured his father. The farmer studied his son for a moment and then clapped him on the shoulder with a warm smile, a little worry still lingering around his eyes.

"My lady, I wish you would reconsider..." whispered Abigail hotly. "What about our things?"

"We can have our things brought later...besides, I don't want Mrs. Howitt to know. She may do something to stop us."

"But, my lady—"

"Excellent," said Calliope to the farmer with a broad smile and pointed. "I'll take your best horse and that gig."

She handed the farmer her ruby and sapphire necklace. The farmer's eyes widened. "Your Grace, this is too much."

"No, it's not. It's just right. And perhaps your son may know another young man who could act as my bodyguard and would like a trip to London. And perhaps your wife could pack us enough food for the journey. I must be in London by seven this night."

As the farmer and his son nodded and started to prepare the horse and the gig, Calliope sighed with relief, even though Abigail was clearly uncertain about this.

Nathaniel's rejection was painful. She loved him, but she was not willing to be open with him anymore if this was how he planned to treat her. She'd keep her thoughts and feelings to herself from now on, as she always should have.

30

"Is the man here?" Nathaniel asked Harvey.

Portside was, once again, lively and bustling around him, thick with the pungent scents of sweat, ale, and the rush of anticipation. As usual for a Wednesday night, two women boxers were the main event.

The first, a fiery redhead with her hair tied back in a rough bun, bore a look of fierce determination. Her opponent, a beautiful dark-haired woman with piercing green eyes, was slightly taller and had a reach that seemed to give her an advantage. They danced around the boxing ring, their bare feet kicking up clouds of dust from the well-trodden wooden floor. Every jab, hook, and uppercut was met with roars, jeers, or gasps from the audience.

Nathaniel's chest ached. He missed Calliope like he missed a limb. Every minute of the day he'd thought of her, wondering if she could eat, if she had nausea, if she was tired, if her nipples still hurt like she had told him they did. Her absence in the house was felt everywhere: in the empty space on the new settee in the sitting room, in the dining chair she usually used, in his bed, and even in the silence that hung over him and his sisters when they sat together as a family last night.

His sisters looked sadder. The servants walked around with seemingly no direction. The goddamn cat came into his bed and he cuddled against it, its presence like a small mercy.

The man watching his house was still there, returning every time they shooed him away, like an annoying fly.

Not for long. Hopefully.

Harvey nodded and pointed behind Nathaniel with a cup he'd been cleaning.

"He is. Only, your wife is already talkin' to 'im."

Nathaniel's stomach sank. With a horrible sense of dread, he turned to where the owner pointed. Sitting at one of the round tables was Calliope, dressed in a spencer she used for road trips and in her green bonnet that made her hair such a striking red hue his heart ached. She leaned over a mug of beer, speaking with a man who looked like a proper thug.

Nathaniel didn't think he could ever feel so furious and yet completely terrified at the same time. He had been feeling this way to varying degrees practically every day since he'd met her, and he didn't like it, not one bit.

He marched through the room to the table, and she looked up at him, cool and collected. And so beautiful he couldn't breathe.

He looked her up and down. The sleeves of her spencer looked a bit dusty, her curls slightly fuzzy. She was a little pale, her eyes somewhat puffy. Had she been crying?

You made her cry, you oaf.

Goddamn it!

"Are you well?" he asked.

"I am," she said, the chill in her voice sending a shiver through him. "How's Violet?"

"She's fine."

Calliope didn't ask about him.

He could feel the thug's frowning gaze upon him. He didn't care.

"How did you get here?" he demanded. "When?"

"I bought a gig and a horse and hired two men who guarded me, and I drove myself here. Abigail is already on her way to Roxburgh Place."

"Drove yourself?" His chest was so tight it felt about to burst. He pulled over a third chair and dropped himself onto it. Around them, a wall of onlookers bellowed at the boxers, shook their fists in the air, drank, and chatted. The noise was overwhelming. "Are you out of your mind?"

Calliope gave the thug a smile so charming, she could be speaking to the prince regent himself at a ball. "Forgive my husband, Mr. Rawkins. Please continue. You were saying?"

"Um..." The man looked unconvinced. "Mayhap it's better to meet another time."

"No," she said and put a purse full of money on the table. "Please. It's a matter of life and death."

Nathaniel's stomach was churning. His gaze darted around the crowd, looking for someone who may be watching her, someone with a knife, someone who might fall upon them and take his wife away. Hell, Mr. Rawkins could be the biggest danger.

"Calliope—" said Nathaniel and stood up. "Come. I'll drive you home."

"In a minute," said Calliope without looking up at him. "We need to finish our conversation with Mr. Rawkins. He only just got to the good parts. So, you were paid by a man with a walking stick that had a handle made of walrus ivory, and it had an emblem. But you can't remember what emblem."

"Yea. He was one o' them fancy blokes. Some baron or duke or summat."

Nathaniel sat back on the chair, listening, but his eyes continued to scan the people nearby, his senses so alert he could feel every thread in the fabric of his shirt against his skin.

"But you don't know the name?" Calliope asked.

"No."

"And what were you asked to do, exactly?" she asked.

"Give the duke a good thump. Paid us to deck 'im and stash 'im on that ship. Thought we'd nick 'is posh rags, too. Worth a few bob, those. But one o' the lads got big ideas, put 'em on when the rest of us was chinwaggin'. So we gave 'im what for. By the time we was tryin' to get them clothes off 'im, we 'ad to leg it."

So that was why a different man was buried instead of Spencer.

Nathaniel watched his wife now. He could see how nervous and excited she was underneath her perfectly collected mask of a well-bred lady. This was the most information they'd gotten in weeks. He admired how she could get Rawkins to talk, her calm demeanor not making the man nervous, even though he had harmed her brother and she could want retribution.

She was neutral. She was polite. She was attentive. She made him feel at ease and provided the right motivation—plenty of coin.

Calliope nodded. "And you're sure the duke was still alive?"

Rawkins nodded. "Me mate checked 'im out. Bloke was still takin' breaths. Chucked 'im in the ship's 'old with the other lads."

Calliope's face went very, very pale, her lower lip trembling for a mere moment. Her eyes watered slightly, destroying Nathaniel's reserve. He found her hand under the table and squeezed it—so cold and small. He thought she'd retrieved it from his grasp, but she squeezed back.

This information was important. *Vital.*

This was the first time they had heard good news.

She nodded to Rawkins and swallowed hard. "What was the name of the ship, Mr. Rawkins?"

The man took the purse from the table and tucked it into his jacket, throwing her an estimating look. The hair on the back of Nathaniel's neck stood. He straightened his back, gently releasing Calliope's hand, his other palm going to the dagger hidden in his right boot.

Maybe the thug had sensed her desperation. Rawkins reclined slightly, a smug expression painting his features. "Seems me memory's a wee bit foggy. Per'aps ye can jog it, Your Grace."

A fiery rage blazed within Nathaniel. Swiftly drawing his dagger, he slammed it into the table's wooden surface, just inches from Rawkins's hand. "I'll jog that memory for you," he snapped.

"Nathaniel, calm down," said Calliope with a soft chuckle. She dropped a second money purse full of coin onto the table. "How's this, Mr. Rawkins, does it scratch the itch?"

Rawkins glared at Nathaniel while his hands slowly moved to the purse to grasp it grudgingly. "Your wife is smarter than ye," he said without taking his eyes off him, and put the purse into his coat.

"Don't I know it," said Nathaniel.

Rawkins looked at Calliope. "It were *Concord*."

He didn't think Calliope's face could get any paler, but it did. She looked positively ashen. "*Concord*." Her wide eyes met Nathaniel's.

Nathaniel's own body chilled. "Captain Dean. Bound for America."

"This is the worst outcome," Calliope whispered. "The

French war is coming to an end, but the American is only beginning! And he's an ocean away, Nathaniel!"

31

Holding Calliope's elbow, Nathaniel walked her towards the carriage that was waiting on the next street.

Calliope was quiet. So was he. She'd finally found out where her brother was, which meant he could make inquiries at the Admiralty about *Concord*. They could discuss what next steps to take to recover him. They would definitely need to tell Preston and Richard.

Even though fury with her seethed in the pit of his stomach, he hesitated to reprimand her for leaving the safety of Kelford and putting herself in danger against his instructions. Truth was, she had managed to get that information from Rawkins with her gentle approach...and plenty of money.

Not force.

Had he been alone with Rawkins, would he have been able to get this information?

He didn't know. He admired her bravery, her courage, her skill. This woman was so fierce she didn't need him. Didn't need anyone.

And yet, he needed her in his life like he needed his next breath.

A sleuth...

To all devils, she was right. She would be good at it.

And yet...she may be expecting their baby. She had purposefully put herself and possibly their unborn child in danger. She should have known better.

"How could you do this, Calliope?" he asked.

"No! How could *you*, Nathaniel?" she cried out. "Abandon me like that in some village I've never been before? You put me in exile!"

There was no one on the dark streets around them, despite Portside bustling with patrons. And Nathaniel caught a flicker of movement in the deeper shadows cast by the lantern above the door to a warehouse. Cold unease crawled up his spine.

She was still in danger. He needed to get her out.

"Get into the carriage, now," he commanded.

"Do not dare bark at me!" she exclaimed.

"Get in," he said.

Her eyes still wide in shock, she climbed in, her face dark in the dim light of the little lantern over her head. Nathaniel looked over his shoulder, the hair at the back of his neck standing as he had an odd sensation someone was watching him. But at least she was now in the carriage.

"It is almost over," he said, softer. "We know where your brother was shipped to. We can now track him down."

She nodded. "We know everything but who wanted Spencer press-ganged—and why. And that may be the most crucial piece of the puzzle."

He looked back in the direction of Portside. Rawkins was their only connection to the man with the walking stick, who Nathaniel needed to find.

She leaned forward, placing her hands on the sides of the door. "What do you have in mind?"

"You're right, Calliope. The person who ordered Spencer's disappearance is the key. And until we find him, we cannot know if you'll ever be safe. Rawkins is still in Portside, but who knows if he'll be there next week. We must go back and find out something about that man with the walking stick. Maybe he can remember more about the man's appearance."

"You're right," Calliope said. "I'll come with you."

She had already risen from the seat, but Nathaniel put his arm before her like a barrier, helplessly knowing she'd still probably do whatever she wanted.

"No! I'll ask Carl to drive around the corner. Please, if you care for me at all, for once in your life, do as I ask and wait in the carriage."

He may have said it too loudly. Too angrily. But it had an effect.

Looking perplexed, she nodded. That melted his heart a little. Did she care for him, after all? Was he not just a husband to her, the man who had promised to give her freedom once she bore him a child?

A promise he didn't know if he could keep the way that she needed him to.

He nodded and said softly, "Thank you. I'll be very quick."

He walked to Carl and told him, "Take the carriage around that corner and wait for me. I will be back in just a few minutes. Hold on to your pistol. At any sign of trouble, drive. Drive for your life. Save Her Grace."

The man nodded somberly.

With his heart drumming hard against his rib cage, Nathaniel turned and walked through the empty street. He heard the shoes of the horses clicking and the rattle of the carriage wheels against the cobblestones, going into the distance. Good man, Carl. Then there was the sound of only his boots clicking softly against the road.

He had just turned the corner and could see Portside when he heard a drum of shoes behind him. He whirred around to see six navy officers storming towards him with sabers drawn.

He unsheathed his own saber with a metallic whisper, lantern light flashing off the blade. His body tensed, muscles strung taut, eyes narrowed on the men. The first officer lunged, a swift jab aimed at his midsection. Nathaniel sidestepped, his saber slicing the air where the officer had stood. A grunt echoed in the narrow alley as his weapon met resistance, grazing the officer's arm. No time to relish the small victory.

The second officer closed in, a large man with a thick neck. He was strong but lacked technique. Nathaniel met him head-on. Steel clashed against steel, ear-piercing in the quiet night. The shock traveled up his arm, jarring his bones, but he pushed back with equal force, his teeth gritted.

Then three officers attacked all at once, their sabers a blur of deadly silver. Nathaniel ducked, rolled, then came up behind them. He split his focus, anticipating and calculating their attacks. His saber parried one strike, and he kicked another officer in the stomach with his boot. But the rest of them kept charging at him. He continued slicing, hitting, whirring. But he simply didn't have the strength to fight all of them at once.

From the corner of his eye, he saw a glint of metal. The saber came swinging down, handle first. He tried to evade, but his body didn't respond in time. Pain exploded at the side of his head. The world tilted, and darkness encroached his vision.

He tasted the iron tang of blood in his mouth. His knees hit the cobblestones hard. Then, the darkness swallowed him whole. His last thought was of Calliope, and the promise he'd made to keep her safe.

Nathaniel slowly blinked open his eyes through a skull-crushing pain that clamped around his temples in a viselike grip. It pulsed with every beat of his heart, each throb echoing like a heavy, distant drumbeat.

He was sitting somewhere, his arms tied behind his back. A slightly musky, briny scent permeated the air—tar, wet wood, and old canvas. Rough-hewn planks were beneath his boots. Dust particles danced in the sparse shafts of moonlight piercing the high, narrow, grime-covered windows, but the dim light didn't do much against the darkness and many shadows.

Stacked high against the walls was an organized chaos of barrels, crates, and bundles. Rope, coils of tarred hemp, lay haphazardly beside bolts of sailcloth, their fibrous textures standing out in the muted light. Copper nails, destined for ship hulls, glittered dully in wooden bins.

He must be still in the docks.

Is Calliope here? Please, no!

Frantically, he looked around himself, but his gaze halted when he saw seven figures standing and watching him from the shadows.

Then a familiar figure stepped forward, sending a visceral shock through Nathaniel. It was like the ground beneath him cracked and gave way. Admiral Langden? A rush of memories—shared confidences, mutual support, and countless moments of camaraderie—flooded Nathaniel's mind, making the present moment even more inconceivable. A cold, queasy sensation settled in the pit of his stomach, as if he'd swallowed a stone of betrayal. Every ounce of trust he had vested in the man, who had been more like a father than his own, now seemed a cruel joke, and the weight of the truth threatened to crush him.

The rest of his attackers also stepped forward from the shadows, making a semicircle around him.

Nathaniel looked at their faces, but he didn't know any of them. They didn't even look like real officers, just thugs wearing uniforms, with rough scars on their faces, untrimmed beards, tangled hair. The uniforms fit poorly, either too big or too small.

Please, let them not have Calliope! They'd never wanted him; they'd always tried to stop her.

Nathaniel jumped up from the chair, but one of them hit him in the face while two others darted to hold him down.

"Nathaniel, my boy," the admiral said. "Respectfully, I must ask you to stop digging around the disappearance of the former Duke of Grandhampton."

Nathaniel's mind raced. He could ask why Langden was doing this, how he could betray Nathaniel like this, if the memory of Nathaniel's father meant nothing to the man...

But he had a more important question on his mind.

"Where's my wife?" he rasped.

"The beautiful, if bothersome, Duchess of Kelford is safe," said the admiral. "For now. Her continued safety will depend on your cooperation today, friend."

Nathaniel scoffed. "You attack me and threaten my wife and then demand my cooperation, *friend*?"

Langden's face straightened into a serious mask, any traces of his usual kindness gone. "I never knew you would become entangled in any of this, Nathaniel!" he barked. "Were it anyone else and their wife, they'd long be dead."

Nathaniel's gut squeezed. Had he ever truly known this man? "Well, you certainly fooled me with your act."

Langden sighed. "I'm doing you a favor, believe it or not. I'm asking you to cooperate, showing myself to you as the last resort. I have tried everything to persuade the duchess and yourself to stop...but nothing helped."

He had tried everything... Nathaniel's mind flew, remembering all the moments of terror as he saw the dried flowers being delivered to Calliope, the man with the knife attacking her and his sisters in the middle of the day in Mayfair, the thugs trying to harm Calliope in an alley at the docks, his sisters trying to fight off the intruders, someone watching his house for days, and finally Violet's wound...

All Langden? He was not surprised or astonished anymore.

He was enraged. "You have known my sisters since they were born. Do you realize Violet could have been seriously hurt because of you? As it is, she will bear a scar."

Langden sighed and shook his head mournfully. "I'm sorry for little Violet. Truly. This was never supposed to lead to such drastic consequences. It could all have been over with the flowers."

Yes, it could have. If it was about any other woman but Calliope.

Calliope was a force of nature. A storm that may lead to devastation but also brought healing rain and nurtured the earth.

He felt an urge to growl. "All this to hide a duke's press-ganging. Why? Why did you want Spencer gone in the first place?"

"That does not concern you. Like I said, stop asking questions and leave the matter alone."

"You were the one that issued the press-gang order. But I don't remember you owning a walking stick with a walrus-ivory emblem."

The admiral's jaws worked. "Nathaniel. What you don't understand is that I'm on your side. If I wanted you or your wife dead, you would be. I'd like to resolve this so that you don't have to die."

To Nathaniel's surprise, the admiral didn't look like a victorious villain. He looked like a man who had a dirty job he didn't want to do.

"And if you promise you will stop digging and stop your wife from digging, I will let you go and you can return to her."

"Why are you doing this? I've never known you to get entangled in despicable business."

The admiral swallowed hard, his nostrils flaring. "Sometimes you have no choice but to do what a powerful man asks of you."

Nathaniel knew if he let this go, if he didn't get answers, there would be no end to it. Calliope would never be free. They would always live under a shadow of fear and uncertainty.

"I know you don't want to do this. You serve your country. You're not the man to threaten an innocent lady only because she wants to find her brother."

The admiral slowly walked to him, boot heels clicking slightly against the floor in the warehouse.

"I know you want to be free from whoever is forcing you to act, just as much as I want my wife to be safe. Who is that powerful man, Admiral?"

Langden swallowed hard, indecision behind his eyes. Then he looked at the thug who had stood by Nathaniel's side and gave him a curt nod. The thug hit Nathaniel in the stomach, knocking the air out of him, pain bursting through his insides. Nathaniel doubled up, gasping for breath.

"I told you I will not have you ask any more questions," said the admiral coolly. "Either you give me your word of honor, in which case I'll leave you and your wife alone. Or I will need to have one of these men kill you. Which will it be, Your Grace?"

32

Calliope waited and waited. He had said it would be only a few minutes.

The street was quiet. She saw the sex worker she had talked with on her first visit walk around the corner and lean against the wall, looking around. Someone passed by at the end of the street.

With every minute that passed, her worry grew.

She knew she promised to stay put, but something must have happened to Nathaniel. She could just feel it.

Retrieving her two muff pistols from her reticule, she opened the carriage door with a shaking hand.

"Your Grace," said Carl, who heard her and descended. "Please go back into the carriage."

She checked both pistols. Loaded. The hammer was in a half-cocked position, which prevented the guns from discharging unless the trigger was intentionally pulled.

She tucked them under the ribbon of her dress, beneath her spencer.

"I'm afraid I can't. I'm worried His Grace is in trouble."

"Your Grace, let me go into Portside and see if he needs help. Please, stay in the carriage."

Calliope hesitated. She had already put Nathaniel and his sisters through enough. She needed to be more careful now that she may be pregnant. She did think it would be wise for Carl to go and see if anything was amiss. Besides, she had given Nathaniel her word. And if she had any hope of happiness with him, she should better give him what he needed. Her safety.

Unwillingly, Calliope nodded. "All right. Go on and take a look, please. I'll wait here."

Calliope was just about to climb back into the carriage to wait for Carl when the blond, busty sex worker said loudly, "You're right, luv."

Calliope looked at her. She still stood with her back against the wall of the building, fingering her nails.

"Excuse me, what did you say?" Calliope asked.

"You're right. Somethin' 'appened. If you're lookin' for that pretty duke, I saw some navy officers beat him and drag him into a warehouse."

A cold shadow cloaked Calliope's heart. She couldn't feel the ground under her feet.

"Where?" she demanded, her voice raspy and low.

"Two warehouses down that way." She pointed in the direction opposite of where Carl had gone.

Calliope broke into a run. As she approached the building, she walked quieter, her breath heavy in her chest, her stomach churning with bile. Terror for Nathaniel made her legs feel limp and cold.

Lord, was this how Nathaniel felt when she was in danger? This was horrible.

The warehouse loomed ahead, its dark brick facade battered by time and weather, casting long, foreboding shadows in the faint moonlight. Cranes and pulleys jutted out from its upper levels, hinting at the hard labor done during daylight hours. A few dim lanterns flickered at its entrance, revealing an occasional rat scurrying past, while from a small, high-set window, a muted conversation drifted out.

"Either you give me your word of honor, in which case I'll leave you and your wife alone..."

Calliope had an odd sensation of falling. The voice sounded familiar, although she couldn't place it. The speaker sounded well-bred, and the "word of honor"...he could demand that only from a gentleman.

She frantically looked around and noticed some crates and barrels nestled against the wall.

"Or I will need to have one of these men kill you..."

Her hands shook, her ankle twisted a little as she heard that, and she stumbled. *No, Nathaniel!*

"Which will it be, Your Grace?" said the voice.

Your Grace! That must be Nathaniel.

She needed to look through that window. With trembling fingers, she pushed a barrel to stand under the window. Thankfully, she needed to move it only a few inches. Then, she picked up an empty box and placed it on top. That should be high enough.

She heaved herself to the top of the barrel, then climbed onto the box and looked.

Her heart shuddered. Three officers... Two of them held Nathaniel down on a chair while the third one beat him. There were three more officers, one of them holding his wounded arm. The admiral she'd met at Emma's soirée stood watching. It was dark, and only the candles in the candelabra directly above them had been lit.

"Which will it be, Kelford?" demanded the admiral.

Calliope's hands shook.

"You won't kill me," growled Nathaniel.

"Ah, but I will. There's much more at stake than your life. And I will sacrifice it, even if I don't want to."

Nathaniel said nothing, just glared at the man. His lip was cut and bloody, his right eye was swelling, and blood dripped from the side of his head. The admiral nodded to one of the thugs who took out his saber and stood behind Nathaniel. He grabbed Nathaniel's head, pulled it back, then pressed the blade against Nathaniel's neck.

Calliope felt the crate under her feet wobble. No!

This was what he must have felt like that night when he watched the highwaymen threaten his mama. The fear, the desperation digging at her, making her entire body go numb, invisible pain tearing at her very soul. If they killed him, she would never be the same.

A big part of her would die with him.

"For the last time, Kelford," said the admiral. "What is it going to be? Your silence? Or your life?"

She couldn't take it anymore. She had to act. Do something.

There was a row of very large, iron-hanging candelabra along the length of the ceiling of the warehouse. Each of them had twenty or so candles in the large circle to illuminate the work in the dark months.

She just needed to scare the men, to give Nathaniel a chance to run. She took out her first muff pistol and aimed at the chain of the candelabra above the admiral.

Her hands trembled, and she told herself to breathe. Just like Nathaniel had taught her. She needed to breathe. She aimed, calming her nerves.

Removed the safety.

And pulled the trigger.

The force of the explosion sent a jolting recoil through her body. As the ground seemed to sway beneath her, Calliope's feet skidded on the uneven surface of the crate. Desperately, her arms flailed in the cold air, grasping for something, anything, to steady herself. Her fingers managed to catch the worn edge of the window just as the weight of imbalance threatened to tip her over. Using every ounce of strength, she hauled herself up and braced herself against the window's frame, her heart pounding fiercely in her chest.

Below, a wild interplay of shadows and dim light drew her attention. The chains of the heavy candelabra groaned, weakened by her shot. Then it split and started a nightmarish fall. Every candle flickered wildly as it spiraled downwards, casting an eerie dance of light across the large space of the warehouse. With an ear-splitting crash, it found its mark. The admiral, perhaps too stunned or disoriented to react, had remained rooted to the spot.

Now he lay sprawled beneath the weight of the twisted iron candelabra, its heavy arms pressing him into the wooden floorboards. His uniform was marred with melted candle wax. A few, still lit, cast a flickering glow on his pallid face, highlighting the shock that was frozen in his wide-open eyes. His tricorn hat had been knocked askew, revealing strands of silver hair slicked with sweat and seeping blood.

In their panic, the other officers' gazes darted about, trying to piece together the situation. Seizing the opportunity, Nathaniel pushed himself up with the strength of his legs. Despite his hands being bound behind him, he launched himself shoulder-first at the nearest officer.

The man was caught off guard, and the force sent him reeling backward onto the fallen candelabra. A sharp spike from the iron fixture penetrated through the breast of his coat, immobilizing him with a combination of pain and shock.

As the room continued its descent into chaos, Nathaniel managed to maneuver himself to the admiral's side. With a swift movement, he used the tip of the admiral's own saber to slice through the bindings, freeing his hands.

An officer attacked him, and Nathaniel hit him with his fist, the man collapsing into the crumbled mass of the candelabra. Grabbing a dropped saber, Nathaniel brought the blade up as another officer lunged. Metal sliced through the air, Nathaniel's saber drawing a red line across the officer's chest.

From the corner of her eye, Calliope saw movement. Another officer, pulling free his pistol. The world slowed. She had to protect Nathaniel! She fumbled with the ribbon of her dress, frantically pulling at the second loaded pistol. Finally, it came free and she took the position Nathaniel had taught her.

Breathe, aim, pull. The explosion of her second pistol shook the window frame, and the officer dropped, saber clattering against the warehouse floor.

Nathaniel looked up and saw her in the window. Their gazes connected, relief...love...fear...all mixed in her chest, and she saw the same in his eyes. He ran, the remaining officers at his heels. He opened the door of the warehouse and disappeared behind it. She heard his running footsteps against the cobblestones.

She quickly descended from the crate, and there he was, appearing from around the corner, eyes wide, saber dripping red. Relief shuddered through her, potent and sweet. And together, they sprinted back to the carriage.

Thankfully, Carl was nearby, his eyes mad with worry. Calliope looked over her shoulder. Three officers were running after them, sabers glinting in the light of lanterns.

"On the box!" called Nathaniel. "Be ready to drive!"

Calliope's legs burned with effort as they approached the carriage. Carl swiftly opened the door of the carriage and climbed onto the driver's seat. Nathaniel helped her climb in, and as he followed her, he roared, "Go!"

He closed the door behind him, and hooves pounded against stone as they escaped into the night.

33

She was alive...

And not only that, but she had also made sure *he* was alive.

Nathaniel's limbs couldn't stop shaking as he climbed the stairs to his bedroom two steps at a time, holding Calliope's hand in his.

Back in the warehouse, he had been terrified the next time he'd touch her hand it would be forever cold. His heart had thrashed against his ribs like a wild creature ensnared. A familiar chill had snaked its way up his spine, each vertebra locking into place, leaving him as rigid as an ice statue. The ghostly pallor of Calliope's face, framed by the darkness of the warehouse window, had plunged him into an abyss of memories best left untouched—the agonized moment he had watched his mother crumple from the bullet.

That same paralyzing dread had returned, gripping his mind in iron claws. The metallic taste of fear flooded his mouth, and a cold sweat formed on his brow. The muffled echo of his own blood rushed in his ears, drumming a relentless rhythm.

Would Calliope's laughter, her touch, the very essence of her, be stolen from him in this hellish cavern of darkness? Would he be forced to listen to the fading beat of her heart? With each passing second, visions of her graceful form being pursued, caught, and silenced threatened to shatter his mind.

The thought of his world without her radiant presence threatened to crush the breath from his lungs. The void she and their babe would leave was so much worse and more devastating than his mother's death could ever be.

He'd forever be a shell of a man.

But that didn't happen. Her warm hand was alive and right where it belonged—in his.

And she was right where she belonged.

By his side.

God in heaven, if he'd known at the beginning of this all how she'd have transformed his life...how happy she'd make him...

And how miserable with terror for her.

Would he have married her?

She was supposed to be a bluestocking wife who'd bear him the child he needed. He would restore his wealth and reclaim his rightful position, and then they'd lead their lives separately like so many aristocratic couples did.

Instead...

He closed the door to perhaps the only place in the whole house that hadn't changed—his bedchamber.

Turning to the wife he'd never imagined but now couldn't live without, he slowly approached her. Her auburn locks were in disarray, her blue eyes shimmered with hope and uncertainty. He noted her petite frame, seemingly fragile yet emanating an undeniable strength. She had taken over his heart and soul so completely, they belonged to him no more.

And whatever happened, they would never belong to him again.

During the carriage ride home, he had frantically looked back at the dark streets, making sure no one followed them. In between those quick glances, he had reloaded Calliope's muff pistols, ready to shoot if he saw a shadow of danger.

She'd fussed about his lip, about his eye, about the pain in his side, but he'd brushed her off. He didn't even feel them, his mind feverish with one thought...

Take her to safety.

And now she was safe. Carl was rousing Joshua and the footmen from their beds to keep watch and to report to Nathaniel the moment they saw someone suspicious near the house. Joshua would take the dogs into the house, ready to protect if someone tried to get inside.

Calliope and his sisters were as safe as they could be, given the circumstances.

He wrapped his arms around her and brought her to him, sealing his mouth with hers. His bruised lips protested, but he didn't care. The pain was nothing compared to the relief of connecting his lips to hers, his skin to hers.

He loved her.

No, love was nothing to describe what he felt for her.

He worshipped her. He lived for her. He breathed for her. She was necessary for his heart to pump blood, for his lungs to take air.

He was hers.

She retreated. "Are you in pain?" she asked.

"No," he said. "I was no longer in pain the moment you were safe."

She was shaking in his arms, her tremors like convulsions. He looked for a wound, a scratch he hadn't noticed. Her skin was unblemished, but her eyes were wild.

"What is it, love?" he asked.

Her jaw trembled, teeth clattering as she looked at him with blue eyes so dark they could be bottomless wells.

"I just killed someone."

The realization hit him like a storm wave crashing into a ship. Admiral Langden was dead. The longtime friend of his family, or who Nathaniel thought was friend... The man who had lent Nathaniel money, who had supported him in his navy career. The man who had commanded the first ship Nathaniel ever served on. The man who, despite his high rank, had personally taught Nathaniel how to tie the lines and dock the ship.

The man who was one of the few connections to his father Nathaniel had.

He was behind everything...

Why? *Sometimes you have no choice but to do what a powerful man asks of you.*

Did this have something to do with the man with the walrus-ivory walking stick?

The question was buried in his psyche the moment another tremor ran through Calliope, and he brought her to him. She had killed Langden...

For him.

He swallowed and wrapped his arms around her like a protective blanket. "I'm sorry, love," he rasped. "I wish I could take that dreadful deed away from you. Especially since you did it for me."

She looked up at him as though he'd offended her. Her lips were a lush strawberry there for his picking. They were both alive, and her heart beat against his chest.

"Whatever do you mean?" she said, her eyebrows drawn together. "Of course for you. I l—"

She closed her mouth. She...what? Lightness engulfed him at the possibility of what she was going to say.

Love.

Goodness, could this miraculous creature love him? She had protected him.

As his mother had.

Protection he didn't deserve.

He returned to her lips. The hunger for her body, the need to feel her, warm and soft and his, against him was a constant ache in his muscles.

He clung to her mouth, drinking from her and unable to get satisfaction. *Alive...you're alive...*

He picked her up, sliding one arm under her knees and the other under her back, and carried her to his bed.

He laid her down, their gazes connected, and a similar desire to that raging in his own blood glistened in her eyes. He kissed her again and cupped her breast through her dress, so round and soft. He ached to taste her skin, to feel her bare against him.

But what he yearned for the most was to be inside her, to feel surrounded by her, warm and tight, to know that she was still his.

His...

He moved down her body, his tongue tasting the salt and the sweetness of her skin as he licked his way down to her neckline.

He then raised her skirts and her petticoats to her stomach, exposing those long, sculpted legs clad in stockings. Just the sight of the dark auburn curls between her thighs had his balls tighten in anticipation and his hard cock jerk in his trousers.

Spreading her folds, he sealed his mouth with her sex and moaned in satisfaction when she gave a long, sweet gasp of pleasure. He loved how she tasted. Sweet and pungent. Just the taste of her and the soft, velvety feel of her against his mouth was enough to make him stiffen even more.

He knew where she liked to be teased, how much pressure would bring her the most pleasure, and how fast he needed to move his tongue. He sucked in her clit and suckled it gently, and she rewarded him with an adorable little squirm of her hips, closing her thighs around his head. When he inserted his finger and hooked it so that he could reach the sweet spot inside her, and started moving it just how she liked, she moaned and arched her back, her fingers digging into his hair.

When she began moving her hips, rubbing herself against him, he almost came. He loved it when she did that, practically using him to bring herself pleasure.

He moved his finger inside her faster and harder, and he felt her tighten and shrink around him. She was close, he could feel it, but she stilled and pulled herself away from his mouth and pushed his hand.

"I want you inside me..." she murmured, her eyes hooded, her cheeks and neck red. "I must feel you, Nathaniel. You and I connected. One..."

He must be inside of her, feel her, alive and well and in his arms.

"Yes, love," he replied. "That is what you shall have."

He rose against her, removed his trousers, and hugged her, lay on his back, and pulled her on top of himself. His cock twitched and ached, impatient to get inside her. Her folds were right there, but he wanted her to have all the control now.

He wanted to see her riding him, on top of him, see her face once she claimed her release.

She reached back and grasped his cock, directing him to her entrance. She was so wet he slid in quickly and shuddered as her tight, hot walls took him in, wrapping around him. Then she began to move, and he lost it. Feeling her sex pump him like that, own him like that was his undoing.

"So good, Nathaniel," she murmured as she rode him. "You feel so good..."

"You're gorgeous," he whispered, barely able to stop himself from coming. He felt his release tighten his balls and fought to contain the tidal wave of pleasure he was about to spill.

He grasped her hips, moving her faster, harder against him, as her own movements grew more urgent.

And then, as their hips moved in unison, he felt her quiver and tremble around him, her entire body shaking. He couldn't stop himself. She was his undoing. His fearless woman. This gorgeous creature he knew he would always love.

He bucked, his body as tense as a tree, and then he was coming and coming, exploding into her, and they were on the edge together, and he couldn't stop looking at her.

His precious wife, who was his salvation and his destruction.

She crumpled on top of him in a delicious heap, and he wrapped his arms around her, burying his face in her beautiful locks, inhaling her scent like it was air and he couldn't get enough.

He could feel her back moving up and down against his arms as she breathed, and he was still inside her and never wanted to leave her body. He longed to be forever intwined with her, connected like this, skin to skin, soul to soul.

He felt so heavy and warm and sated, her soft weight like heaven on top of him. Her silky hair tickled the side of his face. As he came back to awareness, he listened to the sounds of the house, alert for intruders. He could be lying dead on the floor of that warehouse. Instead, he was alive and holding the love of his life in his arms. The mother of his future child.

Who had risked her life and the life of their future child—for him.

Who would still be in danger.

"I could have lost you and the baby," he rasped against her neck. "You were so reckless."

He could feel her muscles stiffen under his fingers, and she raised her head and looked at him. An emotion rose in his throat at how beautiful she was, her lips red and full from his kisses, her eyes glistening, a healthy blush on her cheeks. "I wasn't. If I had to barge into the warehouse and fight the seven of them with my bare fists, I would have. But thanks to you, I can shoot, and I could act without endangering myself."

Anger rose in him like a wall of fire, and he sat up with her still on top of him. She blinked and frowned.

"We do have quite different definitions of 'reckless,' then," he said. "I told you to stay in the carriage. You promised me."

"Aren't you glad I didn't?" she demanded.

"You could have been hurt! So could the baby!"

"So could you! He almost killed you, Nathaniel!"

He moved her aside, jumped up from the bed, and swiftly put on his trousers and boots. Tiny snakes of fury shot up and down his body. "I don't care about that. I wouldn't be able to forgive myself if you died to save me, just as I will never forgive myself for my mama's death. I would have gladly exchanged places with her, just so that she would live. And I would have gladly died for you."

The look of shock on her face made him swallow his tongue. "Well then I wouldn't have been able to forgive myself," she said. "Your mother wouldn't want you to live your entire life thinking it was your fault she died. That is not why she protected you. She protected you so that you would be happy. Live your life with no regrets. She gave you a precious gift, Nathaniel. A gift you're throwing away by blaming yourself when there was nothing that you could have done against a band of highwaymen who killed your bodyguards!"

He was shaking. Her words were like a hammer against his heart.

"You have no idea what you're talking about!" he roared. "I have lived just fine until you came into my life. My sisters were safe. My heart—" He stopped himself before he would tell her the whole truth.

That he loved her so much, he couldn't stand the mere thought of something happening to her.

That he wouldn't be able to survive.

That she was the best and the worst thing that had happened to him.

He pushed out a lungful of air in a sharp exhale and collected himself. His heart beat so hard, he thought she might hear it drumming against his ribs.

"I can't stand to do this anymore, Calliope. When I saw you there in that window... I thought now that you may be pregnant, you would understand that you are risking not just your safety but also the safety of our baby."

She frowned. "Of course I understand that! But I had to help you. You have to trust me to make my own—"

Trust her? How could he trust her? He couldn't even trust himself.

He interrupted her with a sharp gesture of his arm. "You won't stop, will you? You'll never stop. Your sleuth agency—that lunacy—"

She gasped, and her face lit up as though on fire. Her eyes widened, her hand clutching at her stomach. *"Lunacy?"*

He was too harsh—he regretted the word the moment it left this mouth, but hurtful words were better than a broken neck.

"You'll never listen to me and try to avoid danger. You're

too independent, too strong." He failed to tell her that was what he admired and loved about her...though it also terrified him. "I would have never married you had I known. I wouldn't want to limit your freedom. Do you think I enjoyed driving you to Kelford and leaving you there when all I wanted was to never leave your sight?"

Her face softened. "You didn't want to leave my sight? But—"

"But I just can't stand the fear and worry."

His whole body grew cold. These dangers, they would never end. She would be putting herself at risk every single day. He knew he needed to trust her to defend herself. He'd seen her do it. But what if the next time she couldn't?

It was as though a shard of broken glass pierced his heart, and an icy realization hit his brain. He had lived alone, not allowing himself to fall in love, for this exact reason.

He looked at her precious face and felt the distance between them grow into a vast chasm. "You are too dangerous for me."

Calliope slowly stood up from the bed, her sex still sleek and wet, her body warm from the fire he'd lit within her. She could feel him withdraw, could see the cold in his eyes like a wall of ice. They were still turquoise, only not the warm turquoise of the Mediterranean but the turquoise of the eternal ice in Norway.

It was confirmation of something she'd feared her whole life.

Their shared warmth and joy was an illusion.

From an early age, Calliope had known she was fiercely independent, perhaps to a fault. William King had only reinforced that belief when he'd discovered her reading mature literature and engaging in private explorations far too young.

She had always thought she might be too formidable, too self-reliant for a partner. Sometimes she even felt a pang of shame for being so. Who could truly love her with such a resolute spirit?

For a few wonderful weeks with Nathaniel, she had harbored this mad hope that she may have done the impossible: married a man who would love her...who would cherish her *because* she was so different, so strong and independent.

Not in spite of it.

She was so wrong. He was just like the rest of them. He didn't trust her to know her own mind. He didn't trust her to keep herself and her baby safe.

He didn't trust her.

What a complete and utter idiot she was. She had fallen in love with a man who thought her a lunatic.

Perhaps he hadn't called her a whore as William King had. But the very same feeling of shame and embarrassment crept through her body, prickly heat making her want to crawl out of her own skin and disappear, dissolve, hide.

Because he made it worse. He'd made her feel ashamed of her own dream. Of her passion.

Lunacy...

"You could have died," he kept going, "and our child."

"We don't know that there is a child yet," she said.

"Perhaps not yet. But you're my wife. We still have an entire life in front of us, Calliope. And I've never envisioned my role as a husband to be a jailor."

"And I have never envisioned myself being locked away in a country estate," she snapped. "If I wanted that, I'd have accepted William King."

She spat the name like it was a curse. Nathaniel's eyes

darkened even more at the mere mention, his jaw muscles working.

"How low have I fallen if you compare me to him?" he spat.

Calliope shook her head, pinching the bridge of her nose with her thumb and index finger. "This is pointless. You'll never support me," she said. "If you think my dream is *lunacy*... You're never going to stop trying to control me, are you?"

He closed his eyes, jaw tightening.

"That is what I am with you," he said as he met her gaze again, his voice broken. "A tyrant. I don't want to be this man."

Silence fell between them as they looked at each other, not moving, not breathing. Something had just broken between them; something had reached the point of no return.

"We have been unfit for each other from the start, have we not?" she asked, tears prickling her eyes.

He didn't reply, didn't contradict her.

She straightened her shoulders.

This was the end. It was her own fault, really. She should have never fallen for him.

She'd always thought herself a smart woman. How could she have been so stupid to open up to him and fall in love with him?

How could she hope for happiness with this man, for the same wonderful marriage her mama and papa had?

"Now you and I have completed our deal," she said coldly, her heart dying in her chest. "I know where Spencer is. And most likely, you have your heir. If you feel I'm a lunatic and I can't give you the compliance you expect from your wife, there is no more reason for us to torture ourselves and be together."

He blinked; his jaw worked but he didn't say anything. Then he nodded. His chest barely moved as though he had a hard time getting any air into his lungs.

"Where do we go from here, Calliope?" he asked, his voice quiet, his body rigid.

"We cannot divorce," she said. "So we must remain husband and wife. I will carry your child. I will not start my agency until the child is born. As we agreed in the beginning, once the baby is here, you will get your fortune. And I will get my freedom."

His Adam's apple bobbed as he swallowed. Then nodded again.

"I will return to Sumhall and live there," Calliope said. "I think it's best we don't see much of each other."

It killed her to say it, the pain tearing apart her insides.

"No," he said, and a small jolt of hope sparked joy in her blood. "The girls love you and would be heartbroken if you left. More so than if I left. Violet needs you especially. They have missed a female presence their whole lives. And they're used to me being away for days. It is I who will find an alternate accommodation."

It felt like the floor careened and slipped from under her feet. Needles pricked at her skin. Her heart was just a tiny reticule of broken glass.

He picked up his clothes, walked to the door, then stopped and looked at her. "Just promise you will not put yourself in more danger..." Then he looked at his boots and chuckled. "Oh wait. You already promised me that. And look where we are now."

And then he left her forever.

34

Three weeks later...

Hyde Park was far too hot for Calliope... The sun shone too brightly, frying her skin under her light muslin gown and petticoats. The vast, open meadows were slightly yellow after the heat of the past ten days. The breeze, which Jane had called pleasant, was far too faint for Calliope as she walked along the gravel path, refusing to succumb to the weakness that had taken over every inch of her body.

The shouts of children running around in a shadowy grove sounded too loud, the crunch of gravel almost hurt her ears. Her sense of scent drove her mad, overwhelming her with the odors of horse manure, roses, Adam's needle, dahlias, and grass.

In front of them, Calliope's brothers conversed with Poppy and Violet, who were leading Orion and Cerberus. A bit behind them, Hazel accompanied Grandmama. Richard would be departing on a ship in a few days, heading for America to search for Spencer.

What not a soul from her family knew was that Calliope was going on that ship as well. She had to finish this and save her brother who had saved her when she needed him most.

But also...the urge to run from the pain left by Nathaniel's rejection, by him leaving her, was too much. She needed to distract herself, to do something active. She couldn't stay and show him how much he'd truly hurt her. She couldn't give in and lower her walls for him, show him her underbelly just to get another blow.

No matter how much she wished it, she could not return to the night of stars and irises when they both bared themselves, and not just physically.

The entire procession was concluded by four footmen who walked behind Calliope and the ladies. Before Nathaniel had left the house, he'd ordered the footmen Calliope had previously hired to always follow her whenever she went out. She didn't fight him on that. She simply had no energy to do so. She knew he needed to make sure his heir, and therefore Calliope, would be safe.

Even though their romantic relationship had ended, she would still be his wife and the mother of his child.

"Are you all right, Calliope?" asked Jane. Hercules, her foxhound, happily trotted in front of her on his leash. Calliope held Argos's leash as he walked in front of her, his giant tail moving fast.

"You look quite pale, darling," said Penelope, who strode on Calliope's other side, "and green."

Both of her sisters were too observant. Unlike Penelope, who looked glowing and radiant in her pregnant state, Calliope had never felt so sick in her life. Raising her legs to walk was hard physical labor, like there wasn't enough air in the whole of London to fill her lungs. The constant feeling of nausea she'd had for the past three weeks got stronger every day to the point where she couldn't keep most food down, save for salty bread and slightly sweetened, weak tea.

These must be the symptoms of pregnancy... Her monthly bleeding still hadn't come and was already three weeks late. She couldn't have been sick from something bad she ate for three straight weeks... And yet, she didn't know for sure. Nor did she know if this pregnancy would stick.

The thought was a little concerning. Calliope hated feeling out of control, despised being dependent on anyone, feeling vulnerable.

And yet, it seemed, she couldn't do a thing about changing any of that.

The only thing she could do was to keep her head high and pretend she was fine. That she had no wound in the middle of her chest that ached from the absence of her husband, no bile constantly trying to rise up her throat, and no dizzy spells so strong she sometimes had to grasp on to furniture so that she didn't fall.

"I do feel a little queasy," said Calliope, "but that's why I came here for a walk, to get some fresh air."

"No word from Nathaniel?" asked Jane gently.

"Not since he sent me the letter," said Calliope, the mention of her husband like a knife between her ribs.

Three weeks had passed since Nathaniel had left. Since her whole world had shattered and broken apart.

The very next day, she'd received a letter from Nathaniel outlining every detail he'd learned about HMS *Concord*. In April it was protecting York on Lake Ontario, but the town was captured by the American forces. Luckily, HMS *Concord* managed to escape. The last thing the Admiralty had heard was that it was headed to Boston after that.

"I'm sure he'll let you know if he hears anything," said Penelope carefully. "News from America doesn't come often, does it?"

"No, it doesn't, given that it can take anywhere from two to six weeks for the ships to cross the Atlantic."

"That means," said Penelope cheerfully, "if the ship was captured or sunk, we would have heard by now. So it's good we haven't heard that."

"Unfortunately," Calliope said, "it doesn't mean Spencer is safe. We don't know if he's still on that ship. All we really know is that he was taken there with no money or possessions, dressed only in smallclothes, with no way to return home, and we haven't heard from him since."

"I still hope he returns," Penelope whispered. "However much I think he'll be in shock to learn that I married his brother."

Calliope swallowed. "Poor Spencer. You were his first and only love. The only woman he seriously considered marrying."

Jane, who had only heard about this briefly as she'd joined the family recently, bit her lip. "Oh. Your poor brother."

Penelope sighed, her eyes on Preston's broad back. "Yes. Poor Spencer. I don't know if he's ever going to be able to forgive me...or Preston."

"But everyone thought he was dead," argued Jane.

"It wouldn't make it easier, I imagine," said Calliope. "Actually, I'm a little worried what it could do to our family."

"We won't let it break us," said Penelope. "I won't let the brothers become enemies because of me."

Jane raised her eyebrows. "I'm afraid it's not up to you, love. You will have to let them resolve it themselves."

"But first, we need to find him," said Calliope.

"Speaking of, Nathaniel has helped a lot with this investigation, hasn't he?" asked Penelope. "He cares...even if he left."

At the reminder of Nathaniel, a sudden onslaught of nausea rose in Calliope, and she pressed her gloved hand over her lips. She inhaled deeply and slowly, and it subsided. "I am thankful he took time to find out everything he could," she said. "But he couldn't even face me...couldn't stand to see me and deliver all this news personally."

How would they ever keep a pretense of being married if the very sight of her repulsed him?

"I'm sure that's not true!" said Penelope. "Clearly he cares about you. I think he loves you, darling."

"But why did he leave?" asked Jane.

Calliope looked at Jane and pursed her lips, thinking of how to reply.

"Because we shouldn't have been together in the first place," said Calliope. "It was just a matter of time before he would see me for who I really am and realize he had made a mistake."

Jane and Penelope exchanged a worried look, and Calliope shook her head. "There's truly no need to look at each other that way," Calliope said.

"There's every reason," said Jane. "He was obsessed with you at the Royal Navy ball, and at your wedding he looked at you like you were a treasure he'd found and was afraid to lose."

Jane could have no idea how those words hurt her. Because the memory of those first happy days was far away.

Lost. Never to be found again.

"He may have looked at me so once," said Calliope, looking at the faraway bushes but not really seeing anything, "but he certainly won't look at me that way ever again."

"Calliope..." said Penelope, reaching for her hand and squeezing it. "If that is so, he is the blindest man alive."

Tears began burning her eyes, and she looked up into the sky and blinked rapidly in an attempt to chase them away.

"I'm fine," she said with a smile she hoped looked bright and cheerful. It was strange to try to stretch the corners of her lips apart when inside she felt as if she were collapsing on herself like a sinkhole. "I've always been fine. Do you remember us walking in Hyde Park just a few weeks ago when I told you I never wanted to marry exactly because of this reason?"

"And what reason was that again?" asked Penelope.

"Because no man would know about me dreaming of having my own sleuth agency and love me for it. I'm too odd. Too independent. I can't be any other way, and I don't want to be."

"Nor should you," said Jane.

"Yes, but that just means there's no man who would love me for me. *Lunatic* ideas and all."

Jane and Penelope squeezed Calliope's hands from both sides.

"That couldn't be further from the truth," said Jane softly. "The right man will love you for who you are."

"Is Nathaniel that man?" asked Penelope, then looked at Calliope carefully.

Calliope could feel it in her heart that he was the right man. At least, he had felt right. He had accepted her when she'd told him about William—and that was the most embarrassing and humiliating moment of her life.

And yet, he loved her for it. He'd kissed that spot that had hurt before, and made her feel like she was made of stars...

So what had gone wrong? Was it when he had learned about her wanting to be a sleuth that everything broke?

She laid her hand on her lower stomach.

"I don't know," she said. "We didn't marry for love. It was a marriage of convenience. He helped me to find Spencer. I am carrying his child."

Both her friends gasped, and Hercules and Argos looked back at them in surprise. Argos gave a questioning bark.

"Shhhh!" Calliope threw a worried glance at her brothers walking in front of her. "It's not yet certain, and I don't want those two to start a fuss."

"That's why you look green!" said Jane. "And thin."

Calliope sighed and nodded in silent surrender.

"Oh, congratulations, darling," said Penelope. "Our children will be cousins...and play together!"

Calliope smiled at her. "I hope they will be. I hope this pregnancy sticks."

"Of course," said Penelope, so beautiful and peaceful, Calliope's heart soared. "Look, sister. Preston and I are another example that a marriage started without love doesn't mean a loveless marriage. Ours was a marriage of hate, after all." She threw a loving glance at Preston's broad back. "And look at us now. He's the love of my life."

As though hearing her thoughts, Preston turned to look over his shoulder, and the most tender expression crossed his usually stark features. When he saw Calliope and Jane staring at him, he wiped the look from his face, but Calliope knew now how her ice-cold brother melted when he was alone with his wife.

She remembered a special look on Nathaniel's face. The one that was just for her, when there were no footmen, no officers, no friends or family around. Just him and just her.

She missed it so much, tears burned her eyes all over again. She wished she could walk like her sisters-in-law, with her own husband just a few steps away. She wished Nathaniel would throw her that special glance that was just meant for her and no one else.

Especially now that she was pregnant, and both of their lives were going to change once again.

"And my engagement started fake," said Jane with a chuckle. "As a ruse. We weren't supposed to be married at all! And yet, Richard is exactly the man who made me realize I belong where I want to belong. And that where I want to belong is with him."

They both looked at Calliope, whose heart beat hard against her chest.

"You deserve to be loved for your dreams, Calliope," said Penelope. "Everyone does."

"You're lucky your husband supports your art," said Calliope. "And Richard never once thought of stopping your school, Jane. And yet, Nathaniel took me to Kelford village and left me there."

"Was it not because you had men following you...and thugs trying to attack you?" asked Jane carefully.

Calliope sighed. "Yes. He did panic, I know. I had just told him I may be pregnant."

"Look," said Penelope. "I'm not trying to excuse him by any means. That behavior is abhorrent. I'm just saying...if he left you in the countryside to protect you, that doesn't scream to me that he disapproves of your dream. Or that he doesn't love you. On the contrary, in his strange and twisted way...maybe he does. And he's so terrified for you, he doesn't know what else to do but to hide you away."

Silence fell upon them, and only the gravel crunching under their feet and the faint sounds of conversation from their family members before them reached their ears.

"Not because he doesn't want you or love you. But because he really, really does," added Jane.

Calliope couldn't really believe any of that. Logically, she believed that all of this might be true. And yet, she'd always thought of herself as someone who was too strong for a man to love.

She needed to think like a sleuth. Did she really have sufficient evidence to suggest Nathaniel did not love her? Or was he terrified to lose her—like she had been terrified of losing him when she'd seen him held hostage?

Knowing what he'd gone through when he'd lost his mother, could she imagine it was not about herself but about him? Could it be her own belief that stopped her from fighting for him?

Could the right man love her and still believe that her biggest dream sounded insane?

The sound of hooves behind her made her stop and turn around. Argos turned and growled, dashing past her, tearing the leash from her hand.

"Argos!" she cried. "Stop!" But when she saw the rider on the horse behind them, any further commands died on her lips.

Looking positively regal, William rode on a beautiful tall brown thoroughbred. He stopped the horse abruptly when his dark eyes connected with hers, his expression growing very, very cold. Argos kept barking and growling at the man, and his horse got nervous, prancing and rolling its eyes.

"Duchess of Kelford," he said as he looked at her. "Duchess of Grandhampton," he greeted Penelope. "Lady Seaton."

He lingered, the face Calliope had thought long ago to be so handsome, so irresistible...now showing her what he truly was.

A coward.

Something was odd about him. He had said Seaton with a slow slur of the *S*. His eyelids were heavy. He swayed slightly in the saddle. His hair was disheveled, and not just windswept but positively tangled.

His gaze went over her and stopped at her chest. She didn't wear her spencer today because of the heat. Neither did her sisters-in-law. But, unlike any of the meetings before, when she had dreaded the very memory of him, of his fingers reaching for her neck, of that one word, "whore," that had made her cower and tighten up in a little, weeping ball...

She felt nothing.

Not the burning of that spot over her collarbone. Not the heat of shame that the very sight of him brought. Not the word itself that had made her feel dirty and like she was all wrong. Who would love such a whore as she? Who would want such an odd woman who was supposed to be all grace and poise and manners but, instead, hunted for danger? Protected her loved ones. Uncovered mysteries.

And enjoyed herself in her marital bed with her husband... sometimes feeling like a whore with him...and loving it.

"Huntingham," said Calliope, stepping forward and staring straight into his eyes.

Drunk, she thought. He was drunk!

"I hope your husband is well and your matrimony serves you well," he said, his eyes still lingering on her chest.

Previously, that lingering would have brought her shame, had her face flaming.

No more.

He had no power over her anymore.

"Get away from my sister!"

She turned around to see Preston running towards them, fury written across his handsome face. "I told you to never come near her again!"

"I was just leaving," said William, but before he could spur his horse, Calliope grabbed its reins.

"No," she said and turned to Preston. "Thank you, brother. One day I will tell you the true story of what happened, and you will understand. Then, it was Spencer who protected me. Just a couple weeks ago it was Nathaniel and you." She looked straight into the dark eyes of the man to whom she had given far too much attention and power for years. "And now, it is me."

As both her brothers froze, she turned to William. How small he looked to her now, even sitting on his horse, so tall and mighty. How could she ever think he was anything more than tragic? He visibly shrank under her gaze.

She squared her shoulders. She knew had Nathaniel been here, he'd applaud her. She wished he could see this. She was free from William. From the power he had held over her.

She actually wanted to go back and reread *Villains and Velvet*. There were a few scenes she would have liked to try with Nathaniel.

"William," she said with her biggest smile. "I pity you, dear boy."

He glared at her but said nothing.

"I pity you," she repeated. "Calling a young girl what you called me during a very vulnerable moment few get to see. And yet you caught me... It must have been quite a shock to you, feeling what you did then, wasn't it?"

He swallowed hard, and his eyes bulged, but he said nothing—which told her she must be quite right.

"Did you want to marry me because you wanted to understand that forbidden thing you felt when you saw me?"

Silence fell around her. She was very aware of several pairs of eyes on her, that she was letting her family in on something extremely private—something she should have told her parents about back then. Her mama, at least.

She was not ashamed anymore. There was nothing to be ashamed about.

"You made me feel like dirt," she said. "You destroyed years of my life when I thought I was not worthy, not lovable for who I was."

His nostrils flared. "Served you right."

She shook her head and stopped Preston, who had launched at William on her right side.

"No, Preston," she said. "I will handle him. You have mistreated me, William," she said, coming close to his horse, and he flinched back, his eyes widening. "You hurt me. Not just emotionally but physically. But thanks to you, I'm now married to a man who wanted me. Who thought the fact I had that book was exciting. The man I love."

William shrank into the seat of his horse so much Calliope wondered if he could get any smaller. She quickly looked him over. Could he be the one who had ordered Spencer press-ganged and sent to war? Spencer had beaten him up. Was it, perhaps, revenge William sought? Was he the man with the walrus-ivory walking stick?

But the walking stick he had attached to the saddle of his horse was just a simple mahogany. And he wasn't brave enough to take such bold action. He went after only those weaker than himself... But she was no longer that little girl.

She didn't really care to teach him anything. Nor did she need a victory over him. All she cared about was the feeling of freedom she'd looked for ever since that day William had seen her in the library. The feeling she had thought Nathaniel would give her if he confirmed he loved her by supporting her dream.

The feeling she now knew no one could provide but she herself.

That realization was like a ray of sunlight shot straight into her heart. And something expanded inside, like a giant air balloon, growing and growing in her chest, making room for more wonderful feelings.

"Leave now, William," she said, looking straight into his

dark, cowardly eyes. "And do not ever come near me or my family again."

"Duchess, I still have information—"

"I do not care what you say to anyone, William," she declared. "My husband knows exactly what you have done. It's just a matter of a short conversation before I tell everything to everyone who loves me and will stand behind me. Telling more people will only make you appear to be a dirty lecher, looking at young girls. Do you really think there's anything you still have against me that may be advantageous?"

"You might be strong now, Duchess, but time will tell if this confidence of yours holds."

As Calliope watched his horse walking down the path, she felt a sense of peace. And she knew the right man would love her for who she was. She didn't need to prove to Nathaniel the worth of her dream, nor anything else.

A dizzy spell made her sway a little, and the onslaught of nausea made her hand shoot to her mouth. She didn't manage to hold the contents of her stomach this time but turned and emptied it right on the path. Her family crowded around her, holding her hands, rubbing her back, asking what was wrong, offering her handkerchiefs.

But the only hands she wanted soothing her and rubbing her weren't there.

She imagined going to call on Nathaniel and telling him how horrible she'd been feeling. How she wished he would just lie in bed with her, cuddling her, whispering soothing words of encouragement. Her nausea would be better, she just knew it.

But he had left her, not the other way around. How could she go to him and risk being hurt like that again?

No. All she could do was continue on and hope that he would be able to set aside his fear one day.

Even though part of her doubted if it was the best thing for the babe that she was going on a transatlantic journey, she told herself she didn't know for sure she was pregnant. And even if she was, many women had done those journeys countless times and they were fine. She would take money; she would be prepared. Her nausea would subside soon enough.

She was still going to find Spencer.

35

Pain was the only thing that could keep Nathaniel sane.

He'd been at Portside every night since he left Calliope, picking up every fight he could. Even brandy didn't do much to numb the mental flogging meted out by his own heart.

Where was Calliope? What was she doing? Was she wearing one of the yellow dresses that made her skin and hair glow so beautifully? Did she feel nauseated? Was she tired? Could she eat well?

There wasn't one moment when she wasn't on his mind.

Not even the bachelor lodgings on Curzon Street in Mayfair did anything to make him forget her. He'd thought being alone and not knowing Calliope's every risky move would return the feeling of lightness and fun he'd experienced from time to time in the past ten years. On the contrary, seeing single men come in and out drunk, laughing, sometimes with ladies of questionable reputation on their arms, made him miss the things he had never imagined would bring him happiness.

He missed his wife. He missed his sisters. He missed his dogs.

He even missed that fluffy white monster otherwise known as Miss Furrington who loved to wrap her warm body around his feet during the night as he slept next to Calliope.

He wondered what plan Calliope and her brothers had come up with to locate Spencer and bring him home. No doubt by now they had something in mind.

He was afraid there could still be someone following Calliope and his sisters or watching Roxburgh Place. Unable to stop himself, just like a lurking footpad, he often went to stand behind a tree, watching his own home...which was lunacy. The irony of thinking *that* word about himself made him cringe...

But he'd never discovered anyone watching the house but him.

That calmed his worries and brought him some happiness, even though seeing his wife's silhouette behind the curtains at night made his arms ache with the desire to reach out to her, to feel her warm skin under his palm. She was so close and yet so far. He just needed to walk up the stairs and enter the house and find her.

He loved her, goddamn fool that he was. He loved her so much he felt sick without her. He woke up every morning in the narrow bed, his hand brushing against the place where she was supposed to be and finding only cold air.

At the Admiralty, he had inquired after *Concord* and wrote Calliope a letter. He'd considered delivering it to her himself but the thought of facing her...

She hated him, no doubt. He'd offended her when he'd disrespected her dream. He'd kidnapped her and left her stranded far from home. He'd intended to keep her away from the thing she loved the most.

Not because he wanted to change her but because he loved her and was afraid to lose her.

He wanted to be close to her and the baby he was sure she

carried. He wanted to see Calliope grow, touch her big, round belly and hear every little detail of how she felt.

He kept going to the Admiralty.

The day after their breakup, the admiral was found dead, the victim of what was assumed to be an accident when the candelabra fell while he was at the docks. Nathaniel wondered about the other man who had fallen onto one of the candelabra's spikes and been impaled as well as the one Calliope shot. Had someone removed that body? Nathaniel was quite sure they weren't real navy officers; they had looked and sounded like thugs dressed in uniforms.

He never suspected his close friend being behind all that—attacking his wife, trying to kidnap his sisters, taking Nathaniel hostage and threatening to kill him. This was the man Nathaniel had thought was a loyal friend. Someone thanks to whom Nathaniel still had a roof over his family's heads.

The grief of losing Langden first as a trusted friend, then to death made him question everything he knew.

Though he went about his work at the Admiralty as if nothing had changed, Nathaniel kept his eyes and ears open. Who was the man with the walrus-ivory walking stick? What did he have against Spencer? The admiral had known about Calliope snooping around, but did that more powerful man? And was she still in danger?

One week passed.

Then another.

But he didn't hear anything suspicious. No one approached him or followed his wife or sisters that he was aware of. Everything was quiet.

He settled into a routine. Working at the Admiralty during the day. Then eating at Portside and getting himself beaten in the boxing ring.

On the morning of the seventeenth day, there was a knock on the door of his lodgings. The room, typical of Mayfair bachelor lodgings, had tall, narrow windows that allowed diffused morning light to pour onto the richly polished mahogany floor. The furniture was serviceable and sparse: a four-poster bed with plain hangings, a small writing desk positioned to catch the best of the daylight, and a single well-worn leather armchair by the fireplace. The walls were lined with muted plaster and a solitary framed painting of a hunting scene. It was a place for a man to rest, not to live.

Nathaniel could hardly move a finger without some pain piercing his flesh. Purple, red, and yellow bruises covered his torso like a disturbing painting. Five days ago, he could hardly open one eye; now he sported a black bruise around it. He had a thick lip. And his knuckles were open, with a dark crust covering his wounds.

He hissed in air as he tugged on his shirt and trousers, then opened the door.

At first, he didn't recognize his sister. She was a pretty young lady dressed like a little duchess, with her curls perfect and a pale turquoise bonnet framing her concerned face.

"Brother..." she gasped.

"Hazel." He looked into the hallway behind her. "Are you alone?"

"Yes."

He cursed and grasped her arms, pulling her into the room and closing the door behind her. This painfully reminded him of another female who had come searching for him in a building full of men with no chaperone.

"What were you thinking coming to bachelor lodgings alone?" he said.

She looked around, her gaze taking in the sparsely furnished room with curiosity and a little pity in her eyes.

"What were you thinking?" she demanded. "You are a bachelor no more. You have a wife."

"I might as well not have." He swallowed hard and winced as he put on his waistcoat, which touched a particularly tender place under his ribs. He threw a quick glance at Hazel, waiting for her to say a word about Calliope. When she offered none, he asked, "How's Violet?"

"She's fine. The stitches were removed."

He nodded. That was good. "How's Poppy? How's...Calliope?"

Hazel's eyes were as sharp as two shards of ice cutting through him. "Everyone's well."

There was a strange note at the end of her "well" that raised an alarm in Nathaniel's gut. "What? What is it?"

"It's just that Calliope...she's well, really..."

He gripped the back of the single chair he had in the room. "Except?"

Hazel sighed out deeply in resolution. "Except she can't seem to stop emptying her stomach, brother."

He stilled. "Oh."

"She's pale and weak, and the only thing she seems to tolerate somewhat is salt and bread."

"Did you call a physician?"

"No, she refuses."

He sat down in the chair as his knees suddenly felt too weak to hold his body. This could be a sure sign she was pregnant...right? And if she was...

Regret slashed at him. He had wanted to be there for her, to ride out to fetch a physician despite her protests, to bring her water, to hold her hair if she needed to vomit, to take care of her.

"And she's not going out and trying to find her brother...do any more investigations?"

Hazel shook her head. "She couldn't even if she wanted to, being sick like that."

Nathaniel nodded, fighting the urge to jump up and run through the door to help his wife.

"Why are you hiding here, anyway?" Hazel asked.

He was so tired he put his head into his hands and dug his fingers into his hair. He was tired of fighting his love for Calliope, tired of imagining everything that could go wrong and all the things that could take her from him. He was tired of keeping himself away when his body, heart, and soul ached to be near her.

"I can't stand seeing her in danger, Hazel," he said, feeling like his throat was full of gravel. "It seems I'm unable to keep people I care about safe. I've tried to do what I thought was best to make sure she was unharmed, but I only ended up hurting her. She doesn't deserve to be treated like I treated her. It's best I remove myself from the situation."

Hazel sat down on the edge of his bed.

"Brother, is this because you couldn't save our mother?"

He looked at her so sharply his neck clicked painfully. "How did you know?"

She pursed her lips and looked at her hands. "I remember everything."

He went cold all over. "What?"

"I remember. I thought for years it was a bad dream."

His eyes blurred from tears, and he wiped them away quickly. "Oh, Hazel. I thought you were too little to remember."

"It's all quite blurry and strange. I was in a carriage alone with the twins. It was dark. I looked out of the window and there you were...fighting the highwaymen like a hero from a book. But you were alone. There was no one else to fight beside you but Mama. And she protected you."

Nathaniel sighed deeply. He couldn't deny it. Couldn't tell her she had imagined it all. That would be a lie.

All he could do was surrender to the truth.

"I'm sorry you remember it," he said.

She sighed. "It is the only thing I remember about Mama. I'd rather have that memory than no memory at all like the twins."

Nathaniel walked to the bed and sat down next to his sister, taking her hands in his. They were small and cold, and he cupped his hands around hers to warm them.

"You're quite right, darling. She was a wonderful mother, and she loved you very much."

Hazel's eyes met his. "She loved you, too. That's why she threw herself between you and the bullet. Because she wanted you to live. To be happy. It was a wonderful gift, brother. A gift that you're wasting by spending another moment torturing yourself when you have a wife and a baby on the way."

Nathaniel swallowed hard. Her words were so similar to Calliope's, which he had dismissed in anger and fear. But now that he had some distance from the terrifying events of the night at the warehouse, he could see that Calliope and Hazel were right. A gift...his mother had given him the gift of life, and he was wasting it.

Hazel gently rested her hand on Nathaniel's arm, her fingers soft and warm. She looked deep into his eyes, her gaze unwavering. "Thank you, Nathaniel, for all you've done for us, for all the nights you've stayed awake, worrying and planning, trying to keep harm at bay... For every time you went out boxing and did other things I'm sure you're not telling us."

She paused, and her words sank into him as if he were a sea sponge absorbing water. He never expected his sisters to notice anything he did for them or feel any gratitude at all. He did it because he couldn't do it any other way.

And yet, hearing Hazel acknowledge what he had done warmed him like a bed warmer on a winter night. It also meant one more thing that worried him.

His sister had grown up. And, perhaps, like the Dowager Duchess of Grandhampton insisted, it had been the right time to have her come out.

His all-too-grown-up sister smiled and continued. "But, you see, life is unpredictable and fleeting. Safety is like smoke and mirrors. It means nothing. I learned that when I saw our mama die. Then when we lost Papa, and with him, all the comfort and money and privileges... And then only recently, when we returned from the soirée to find our home invaded, one of our sisters being kidnapped, and the other one injured..."

Nathaniel couldn't fathom it. His dear Hazel, whom he'd considered something akin to a porcelain doll, was talking to him about death and the unpredictability of life...

He slumped forward, elbows on his thighs, but kept his gaze on his remarkable sister.

Hazel's eyes sparkled with tears as she looked over at him with a smile. "We chase this daylight, this safety, believing it's the sure way to keep darkness at bay. Just a few steps ahead, yet it always eludes us. Does it not? It's a thing that doesn't truly exist, not in the absolute sense you wish for."

Drawing a deep breath, she added, "We are all given a limited amount of time on this earth. Instead of living in constant fear, we should embrace every moment. Love deeply, help others, and follow our passions. After all, the quality of our days matters more than their number."

Nathaniel blinked, absorbing the wisdom she'd just imparted. It felt like a weight was slowly being lifted off his shoulders, replaced by a new understanding of what truly mattered.

"Good Lord, Hazel," he muttered. "You're just seventeen. How is it that you are so wise and...somber?"

Hazel chuckled softly and reached over to squeeze one of his hands, then let it go. "See? You really needn't worry about me marrying, brother. I can't imagine anyone wanting to marry me."

Oh, Nathaniel highly doubted that. Any man would be lucky to breathe the same air as his sister.

"What do you truly want, brother?" Hazel asked.

Nathaniel leaned back on his elbows. He wanted the pain in his body to stop. And once it did, for the ache in his soul to cease torturing him. For the constant barrage of questions at the back of his psyche to end.

"Peace..." he breathed out.

Peace of mind would be all he needed for a long while. Perhaps it was all he had ever needed. Perhaps the ton had considered him a confident rake, but no one knew the constant agitation and worry that lay deep below the exterior.

"When did you last feel like you had complete peace?" asked Hazel.

He thought about it and knew exactly when. The night full of stars. The roof terrace. The irises illuminated by lanterns.

The most beautiful woman in the world giving herself to him.

His wife.

Perhaps that was the night they conceived their baby.

"With Calliope," he rasped.

A cool and calming sense of peace had enveloped him like a beautiful blanket. He had felt peace with Calliope just as he had felt peace with his mama when they'd retreated there to hide from his father.

Just like his mama, he had tried to do the impossible, to ensure that those he loved never came to any harm.

But it was impossible.

It was simply not in his power to ensure anyone's safety.

"Calliope is well, brother," said Hazel. "Well...besides her vomiting. You can find peace with her again, I am certain. But first you must find peace in yourself."

After that, Nathaniel accompanied her to the end of Roxburgh Square where he watched her enter the house safely.

He spent the next week in the same routine, except for going to the boxing matches. He no longer felt the need to get himself beaten to diminish his pain.

There was not so much pain anymore. He kept thinking of Calliope, but not as the source of his ache.

As his source of happiness.

The night of stars and irises was, perhaps, the best day of his life...after the day he married Calliope, of course...or the night of the Royal Navy ball when he first met her. It was hard to pick.

But as days passed by and his bruises healed, he kept mulling over Hazel's words and his own thoughts.

Safety was an illusion.

A lie.

He was not God and could never fully protect his sisters and his wife...and his future children.

All he could do was love them and do his best to help them.

The thought filled him with such a deep and powerful sense of peace he felt it through the crust of the Earth and through the whole planet. He lingered, feeling a sense of calmness.

What would it feel like, to always have that peace he'd felt? To feel like he could trust her to protect herself and to know her own mind? To let go and let her be who she was and who he loved her for?

Fierce. Independent. Sharp. Beautiful. Someone he couldn't help but admire.

Someone he could support.

And love.

And see shine beyond her wildest dreams. And be so, so proud of her, watching her with pure adoration.

Something like a benediction came over him, and he felt light and vast and warm.

How would it feel to be the kind of man who had the peace of mind that came from the love that he felt for her and from his trust?

Perhaps it wasn't rational. But he could feel it just like he could feel his own heart beating.

Because his love for Calliope was bigger than his fear.

Just like his mama's love for him was bigger than her fear of death. She had been blessing him all this time, and he didn't even notice. Perhaps it was she who had led Calliope to him and given him the biggest treasure in his life.

He grabbed his coat, feeling strange and almost ethereal as love and peace spilled through his blood, and he said out loud to the room he hoped to never see again, "It's time for me to go home."

36

NATHANIEL WALKED into Roxburgh and saw no one. It was strange, given he had instructed Joshua to make sure at least one footman watched the door at any moment.

There was no chatter of the twins as he walked through the hallway, which now looked beautiful, with a vase full of yellow irises and the contrasting navy blue paint over the plastered wall. Like the navy of his uniform against the gold of her dress.

With an unsettling feeling that something was very, very wrong, he passed through the hallway in just a few long strides and headed towards the stairway. He climbed up two steps at a time until he finally stood on the bedchamber floor. He rushed to Calliope's door and opened it.

Empty.

Quick footsteps sounded behind him, and he turned around.

"Brother." Violet beamed.

His heart shattered at the sight of the red scar on her forearm. He pulled her into his arms and engulfed her, wishing with every part of his being he could shield her from every single drop of harm.

"How are you feeling?" he murmured against her head.

"It still hurts," she said. "But I'm feeling well otherwise. One more excuse to never have to wear fancy dresses."

He leaned back and looked her over at arm's length. "What are you talking about?"

She chuckled softly, sadness in her eyes. "Well, I don't have to wear sleeveless dresses anymore, the ones that are so fashionable now. Therefore, I'll be deemed unfashionable and won't be invited to certain social events, or to dance at balls, or be called upon by gentlemen."

He blinked, not ready to contemplate young bachelors pursuing any of his sisters. "Any young man would be lucky to call on you, love," he said. "You're a beautiful, intelligent, kind person, and I'm very fortunate to call you my sister. I'm very sorry I failed to protect you and shield you against this."

"You didn't," she said softly. "And I never wanted to get married, anyway. My way will be in the world of intellect."

"And I will support whatever you want to do," he said, squeezing her small, warm hand.

He looked back at Calliope's room.

"She's at the docks," said Violet.

His stomach lurched. "Where?"

"At the docks. About to board the ship to America."

Nathaniel's heart fell. She was going away—she and the child she carried. On board that ship, she would surely face seasickness, the danger of unwanted male advances, and the reality of heading to a battlefield.

But he loved her. And he understood now that if he loved someone, he had to let them choose their own path.

Danger was real, but he couldn't control what happened.

And in trying to do so, he'd alienated those he loved and kept them at a distance.

No one knew what might happen to cut their time short. But with the time that he had with his loved ones, he chose to support them and help them achieve their dreams rather than hold them back.

Even if it meant losing them.

Losing Calliope.

He wouldn't try to stop her from going to America. Instead, he would go with her to support her. Not to control her. Not to limit her. But to help her and witness her brilliance.

Nathaniel's mind raced quickly, calculating. He just needed to write a letter to the Admiralty. He was sure his rank would mean something on the ship, and in Quebec.

"I must go there, darling," he said. "I must go with her."

Violet's eyes widened, but then she nodded with understanding.

"Good luck, brother," she whispered. "And Godspeed."

In thirty minutes, he was at the docks and pushing through dockworkers, passengers, and whores to get to the ship that was boarding.

The docks of London were a hive of frenetic energy, even under the scorching August sun. The heat created a shimmering mirage over the worn cobblestones, blurring the outlines of ships, large and small, bobbing in the Thames. The salty tang of the sea mixed with the musky scent of laboring bodies, barrels of fish, and tarred ropes. Men heaved crates onto wagons with sweat dripping down their foreheads, leaving their shirts darkened with dampness. Seagulls cawed overhead, swooping down to grab scraps of food discarded by dockside vendors who shouted their wares, their voices echoing above the constant drone of bustling activity.

Children darted in and out of the crowds, playing tag with

one another, while pickpockets saw an opportunity in every unsuspecting traveler. Women with colorful shawls draped around them touted their services or goods, and the hum of negotiations permeated the air.

Suddenly, there she was. Calliope.

He could die at that moment, and he would know he'd lived a worthy life and would have no regrets but one—being apart from her for even a single day.

Her blue eyes were two oceans, so bright and beautiful, his breath caught in his throat.

She stood upright, but something was wrong. She was thinner than he remembered, her hand clutching at her stomach. Her shoulders weren't squared like usual, and her back wasn't straight. She was breathing too hard.

And then she swayed.

Her knees buckled, and she was crumpling to the ground.

Nathaniel's own heart dropped like a boulder. He dashed forward and caught her before her head would connect with the cobblestones.

With his whole being screaming from inner terror, he stared into her pale face, her eyes closed and unmoving.

Calliope was in heaven...or in a dream. She was sure the strong arms that held her were Nathaniel's. She could smell him; she'd know his scent anywhere.

She opened her eyes, so weak she didn't feel like she had strength to lift a single finger.

And there he was, his turquoise eyes luminous against the blindingly blue summer sky.

"I love you, Calliope," he murmured, tears welling in his

eyes. "How I missed you. Holding you. Smelling you. The feel of you against me."

He gave her that smile...that Nathaniel smile that was just for her, not for his sisters or his dogs or his mates.

No one but her.

"Did you just say you love me?" she asked.

"I did," he said, his voice rasping. "I should have told you I loved you the moment I felt it in my heart. I love you, Calliope."

He kissed her then, a gentle, loving peck on her lips, but she was already melting.

And then she knew it. She didn't need to go to America to run away from pain and from vulnerability. There she was, weak and incapable of moving, completely dependent on him.

And she didn't want to run, to fight it, to close herself off. She wanted to dissolve in his embrace and let him hold her. There was something so oddly reassuring and even freeing, knowing if she fell, he'd catch her.

And then it was so easy to say the truth that had been in her heart for a while now.

"I love you, Nathaniel," she whispered against his lips.

"I never want you to change who you are." He leaned back and looked at her. "You. Fierce and courageous. Smart and resilient. Gorgeous and...so independent you don't need me at all."

She let out a long puff of air. "Except that I do. I need you." She chuckled as she looked at her body, which he still held in his arms. "Clearly."

"How are you feeling?" he asked.

"Better now." She smiled. "I think I was too self-confident. It is, perhaps, too warm today for a pregnant lady to be outside. I thought I'd shake this nausea off and would soon be able to eat and drink properly. But, I suppose, I am wrong. My body is telling me to slow down...for the baby I'm carrying."

The grin that bloomed on his face had her melt all over, excitement dancing in her stomach...not nausea.

"The baby you're carrying..." he murmured. "Is this for certain?"

"No," she said, unable to stop her own grin. "But all of the signs are there."

"I am sorry for calling your dream lunacy," he said. "I certainly do not think you're a lunatic. I will support whatever you want to do, love. Even if I will worry every minute of every day while you keep doing whatever sleuths do. I will also trust you to be able to protect yourself. To use your intuition. To be smarter than anyone who's against you. I've seen you do it. I trust you."

The words created a warm, sizzling effect in the middle of her chest.

"I want to come back to you," he said. "To love you. To love our baby. To help you set up your agency when the time comes. To be the first one to tell you how proud of you I am. Proud enough to be your husband. To be your loved one. To be in your life at all."

Tears welled in her eyes, and she kissed him with such vigor, she almost knocked her teeth against his.

"Yes," she whispered against his lips. "Come back to me... I love you so much..."

"I've craved you for weeks, love," he murmured between gentle, but insistent kisses.

"We should go, Nathaniel."

He frowned. "I thought you didn't want to go anymore."

"I don't. But I do want to say goodbye to Richard. He is going to look for Spencer."

He smiled. "Of course. Are you able to walk?"

"I think so."

He lifted her and set her feet on the ground, holding her for a moment to make sure she was steady.

"Good. Then let us go and say goodbye to Richard. And then I'll take you home and spoil you rotten."

Calliope walked by Nathaniel's side through the throng. She felt much better now, though her head was still spinning, and her legs felt weak. Even though part of her felt saddened to not be able to help Richard and not be an active part in the search for Spencer, deep down she felt right and she felt complete.

She felt like she had just shed the last of her old skin, that now unnecessary and unwanted barrier that had protected her heart. She was someone else now. The person, perhaps, who she was always meant to be. A woman who was both strong and vulnerable. Independent and yet relying on her partner.

One part of a whole. A whole that had three parts now.

HMS *Ares*, the thirty-six-gun Apollo-class frigate, was swaying gently at the end of the dock that protruded several feet into the River Thames.

In the midst of the Thames, she saw another navy frigate with the Union Jack flag flapping in the wind, its bold red, white, and blue colors stark against the backdrop of a clear sky. The sun's rays caught the gleam of the polished cannons on the frigate, signaling its might and the empire's far-reaching grasp. A tender, bearing the same emblem, cut through the waves, making its way towards the coast.

There were so many people on the dock, Calliope grasped Nathaniel's hand to make sure they weren't separated from each other. Somewhere among this crowd was Richard, no doubt, as well as Preston and their wives.

They walked through the crowd and closer to the ship. Her hand clenched around Nathaniel's when she saw her grand-mama's straight back, Preston's square shoulders, Penelope's blond head, and Jane's dark locks shining in the fierce sun. Now that they were even closer, the stench of the Thames, reeking of excrement and offal, was almost unbearable.

"Here they are." She released a long, deep breath, wishing she didn't have to inhale again. Her nausea was back, and she swallowed hard against it.

She reached her family and poked Richard's broad shoulder gingerly.

He turned. So did Preston and Grandmama.

And their gazes fell on her.

"Ah, sister." Richard beamed. "Came to say goodbye. Thank you. I didn't think you'd make it."

His eyes landed on Nathaniel, and he nodded, as if in some secret understanding between men.

"Yes, dear brother," said Calliope. "And wishing you best of luck there. Get Spencer back home."

Richard nodded, smiling warmly to Calliope and to Nathaniel.

"Any word of advice from you, Kelford?" he asked. "As a navy man."

As Nathaniel talked, Calliope inhaled the sickening air, marveling at the new sensation that everything was right inside of her for the first time since she was a little girl. It would take some time for her to get used to, but she was looking forward to it.

From the corner of her eye, she saw the tender full of sailors and officers in navy uniforms finally dock at the jetty. Most of them were wounded, and several others were helping them get out to the boat.

One of the figures that had stood up and climbed out of the tender was taller and more broad-shouldered than any of his counterparts. Even from her side vision she felt there was something familiar about the man, and her head turned fully in his direction.

Twenty feet away, he walked towards them in a navy uniform, his dark hair tied at the back like Nathaniel's, the sharp, chiseled features of his face straight and familiar...the ones she'd known her whole life.

Her stomach dropped, tears welling in her eyes with every step he took towards them.

The hubbub of the people around her died out, and all she could hear was a loud beating of her heart.

"Is that—?" asked Richard.

"Spencer?" finished Preston.

Grandmama wrapped her arms around herself, her handkerchief at her mouth. "My vinaigrette," she demanded. "I need my salts."

While Jane searched in Grandmama's reticule for the vinaigrette, Calliope, Preston, and Richard all hurried towards their brother.

"Spencer!" cried Calliope, her chest aching, her eyes burning from tears. "Oh Lord, it's Spencer!"

Her brother's dark eyes widened and searched for the source of the voice, finally landing on her.

She couldn't really see the expression on his face, the detail of him—if he had any scars, if he was in pain, if he was all right...

All she knew was that he was finally here.

She ran towards him, pushing aside everyone who was in her way, until she finally reached him and fell into his hard embrace, the sheltering arms of her older brother she'd loved her whole life.

"Spencer..." she whispered as she looked up into his face, wiping her tears away, finally able to see every detail of him.

He had scars. New wrinkles. A beard of several days. He smelled like brine and the sea and the ship.

Her brothers now found him, too, and she and Spencer were both enveloped in their strong embrace, finally the family they were supposed to be.

Preston and Richard clapped him on the back, on the shoulders, shook his hand. She wondered what Preston thought now that Spencer, who had loved Penelope, was back. What would Penelope think?

And as she looked into his eyes, she knew this was no longer the brother she had known. She saw hardness as well as sadness and pain. This was a different Spencer, and she needed to get to know him once again. Anew. But he would need time to open up.

For now, he was safe. He was alive. He was back home. But the mystery of who had gotten him press-ganged was still unresolved. Did he have any idea who was responsible? Was the danger to him still present? Had he been safer fighting a war than he would be walking the streets of London?

She looked up at him. "You must tell me everything!"

"Of course," he mumbled.

But he wasn't looking at her.

With a gaze full of surprise, ache, and hope, he was staring at Penelope.

EPILOGUE

Eleven months later...

"Happy birthday, Nathaniel," said Calliope, looking at him with so much love.

They stood in front of Roxburgh Place. It was his thirtieth birthday, and his heart was squeezing with joy and love—and not because he'd finally received his rightful inheritance and his sisters their proper dowries. Nor because he was now the richest man in the whole of England.

But because the two people who constituted the greatest happiness of his entire life stood by his side: his gorgeous, brilliant wife holding their two-month-old son, Ethan. The little bundle, its sweet face peeking out from folds of white lace swaddle, gurgled with tiny, cute sounds. Those big blue eyes looked at Nathaniel, making his heart lurch and sending currents of joy through him.

"Thank you," he replied, watching how the slight breeze

played with Calliope's auburn hair. "What a difference this year has made. Not because of my inheritance. But because you're my wife. And because you gave me Ethan."

Calliope beamed at him. "This day one year ago you caught me at your office."

"And that was just the beginning," he murmured.

"Please, give me my nephew," said Hazel, who reached out to Ethan, her appearance almost regal and absolutely stunning with her gown of the latest fashion and her hair done in a perfect chignon by her personal maid. "Or you'll suffocate him in your embrace. I know you two."

Calliope chuckled and gave Hazel the little bundle, Hazel's eyes warming up and melting as she cooed over the tiny face.

"I'm next!" said Violet, who held Miss Furrington on a red velvet pillow in her arms. "As soon as I deposit Miss Furrington on her favorite chair."

"It's been moved to Roxburgh, right?" asked Poppy, who could barely keep hold of the leashes of three very agitated dogs. "Miss Furrington got used to it during the last ten months in Grandhampton Court."

"It's moved, darling," said Calliope. "Everyone's baggage has arrived. We can finally see our home in all its glory!"

After Nathaniel and Calliope had made up last August, he'd stopped caring so much about whose money they were spending, his or hers. He just wanted to give the best home possible to Calliope and his sisters, and so he'd agreed to do a proper floor-to-ceiling renovation of Roxburgh, which had taken almost a year. Calliope, the girls, and he had moved to Grandhampton Court during the process, to give Calliope plenty of fresh air and quiet to cope with her pregnancy, and for Violet to recover in peace. Grandmama had moved in with them to help Calliope and to continue guiding them in the art of manners and navigating the social life of the ton. The girls adored Grandmama.

"Right," said Nathaniel, "let us go, then."

They passed through the grand wrought iron gate, which opened onto a carriage driveway that, with its sweeping grandeur, could easily accommodate multiple carriages in a manner befitting royalty. The tall brick walls enveloping the estate were freshly plastered and washed, standing as steadfast guardians of the property.

Fresh gravel crunched pleasantly under his feet as he walked, having been raked to perfection. No weed dared to mar its surface. Surrounding the estate, what had once been an overgrown forest had been transformed into a manicured garden. The house itself, previously an eyesore, was now the pride of the street. The stonework of its classic architecture was now meticulously restored, each stone seemingly imbued with the dignity and grace befitting a home of its stature.

Freshly painted in an elegant shade of white, the window frames seemed to glow in the daylight. Every glass pane was flawlessly transparent and intact. The roof over the three-story building had been immaculately repaired.

The twin stone lions that flanked the grand staircase leading to the double doors had been carefully restored—one brandishing a newly carved tooth, the other sporting a skillfully reconstructed ear. Both the double doors and their regal knocker had received layers of fresh paint. The knocker itself was securely affixed, ready to announce the arrival of esteemed guests. And above the door, the restored Kelford coat of arms served as an enduring symbol of the family's legacy.

They climbed the stairs towards the double doors. Mrs. Nicholson and female servants stood along the right side of the hallway. The male servants lined up on the left, a row of ten footmen with Joshua as the underbutler. At the head of the line of footmen stood Foster, the butler whom Nathaniel had known his whole life and who had served in Kelford Manor all these years. The old man's face lit up with pride and a hint of joy under the obligatory mask of a loyal servant.

"My lord," he said. "My lady. You are very welcome."

He gave a bow and opened the grand double doors before them.

Nathaniel's heart drummed hard in his chest as he and Calliope stepped into the entrance hall.

The once barren navy blue walls now showcased Penelope's paintings, handpicked by Calliope, alongside sweeping landscapes brought over from Kelford Manor. Nathaniel stood in front of one of them. "Papa bought this one in Delft," he told Calliope and the girls, feeling tears prickling his eyes. "He took me with him. I was eight, and it was my first sea voyage. I fell in love with the sea then, and it was one of the reasons I enlisted with the navy when I had to find an occupation."

"I love hearing that about Papa," whispered Hazel, and she gently rocked the baby while looking at the painting with soft eyes.

Calliope nodded. "They're beautiful."

Violet leaned forward and read the name. "*Evening in the Meadows* by Aelbert Cuyp. I read about him. He's well known for his river scenes in the golden hour."

"I can't wait to have the whole family here!" exclaimed Poppy, running through the hallway with her arms outstretched. "Penelope would go mad from delight seeing all this art."

At this loud outcry, the dogs ran after her, the cat jumped off the pillow and ran after them, and Violet followed the crowd.

Nathaniel chuckled. They may be sixteen, but they were still his little sisters.

"Girls!" hissed Hazel as Ethan started to stir. "Shh, darling," she shooshed and walked with him, rocking him, to the sitting room.

Nathaniel and Calliope smiled at each other. He looked at the painting from Delft again, taking her hand. "Papa negotiated so well then," he said. "That trip was perhaps the single time when I didn't feel like he was constantly disappointed in me. Like he taught me things."

He felt Calliope's warm eyes on him. "Do you still resent him?"

He chuckled and smiled at her. "Strangely, no. None of the events in our past have changed, and yet, a year ago, I despised him, resented him for torturing me and my sisters. Today...I have forgiven him. Perhaps the requirements in the will were a gift that he gave me, even though it was hard to see. Because it led me to you. And gave us our little man." He gently cupped her cheek. "And I became a better man for that. So, no, Papa, wherever you are, I hold no more resentment. Just forgiveness. And love."

Calliope grinned at him. "I'm proud of you."

Nathaniel grinned back and thought of little Ethan playing in this house now that it was so beautifully restored. And maybe he would even have brothers and sisters to play with. He remembered running through this space as a six-year-old, his mama chasing after him as he slid across the marble floor with his shoes, carried by the force of his run.

The floor was, once again, resplendent, the once-faint pattern now vivid and freshly polished. The intricate designs seemed to come alive as they caught the light from above.

The sweeping staircase had been fully restored, every

balustrade fitted perfectly in place, the wood gleaming with fresh polish. And flanking the staircase, the ornately carved niches were no longer empty. Some of the statues and vases had also been sent from Kelford. One or two were Papa's particular pride as he had gone to Greece himself hearing there had been an excavation and wanting to make sure he got them. Perhaps, Nathaniel thought, it was not Papa's pride as much as his care to leave such treasure to his son and for generations to come after him.

Others were picked by Calliope, vases showing flowers, and the Greek statues of beautiful and soft-formed women with full lips and curls around their heads and fabrics flowing in the wind around their curves. They were sensual and feminine and yet strong and so like her.

Hanging from the middle of the ceiling in the hall, a chandelier of crystal and gold was Calliope's particular pride. It dazzled, casting radiant prisms of light across the room. Wall sconces, fitted with new glass covers, brightened the hallway with a warm, inviting glow.

They continued their tour. The sitting room, the drawing room, the dining room, the ballroom, the library, every room grand and beautiful, ornate with gilt, bustling with artwork, intricately carved furniture, and soft carpets. Everything was in perfect order and waiting for the family to arrive and fill it with lively chaos. Calliope's touch was in every room, with her whimsical and yet harmonious choices, but so was his touch and reminders of his ancestors as she had asked him and the girls what they would like to have in every room. It was fresh and yet timeless, modern and yet rooted in their common history.

When they climbed the stairs and proceeded to the room that would be theirs, Calliope gasped in awe. Sunlight bathed the room, filtered through vast windows, painting everything in a soft, radiant light. Long yellow curtains framed the windows, pooling at the bottom in a display of quiet elegance. Paneling stretched high up the walls, carved in gorgeous designs and painted turquoise.

The fireplace featured a new marble mantel intricately carved with patterns of flowers. Atop the mantel sat a vase filled with yellow irises, alongside porcelain figurines.

Against one wall stood Nathaniel's heirloom bed, the old wood newly varnished and polished, swathed in opulent linens of yellow satin. A yellow draping hung over the bed. The inviting bed was big enough to get lost in, and Nathaniel couldn't wait to christen it with his wife.

Opposite the bed, a wooden cot stood, its craftsmanship equally exquisite. Calliope had ordered it from an old London master months before the baby was due.

Everywhere he turned, he saw home. Calliope had transformed the broken house into a beautiful oasis. She had transformed his unruly sisters into young ladies.

She had transformed his mere existence into a life worth living.

"Nathaniel," she exclaimed as she walked in. "This is everything I wished it to be!"

"You have done splendidly, love." He grinned. "I couldn't have imagined a better home for us. I have a surprise for you."

On the little round table by the fireplace, and flanked by two beautifully carved chairs, lay a square box, wrapped in yellow silk with a white ribbon tied around it. Good. Mrs. Nicholson had made sure his present for Calliope was here, as instructed.

He picked it up and went to her.

"This is for you," he said.

She raised a brow, taking it. "A gift?"

He nodded, unable to wipe the grin off his face. She weighed it in her hands and shook it slightly. "I'm quite sure it's a book," she said, and he watched with his breath held as she untied the ribbon and unwrapped the silk around it.

"You'll have to see."

She opened the wooden box and gasped. Cushioned on the blue silk was a golden name plate.

"Calliope Fitzgerald. Private Inquiries."

He hadn't included her title because he suspected announcing that it was a duchess doing private inquiries may not be beneficial for business.

Her eyes sparkled as she looked at it. Then she met his gaze, and his heart completely melted at her teary but happy expression.

"Thank you, Nathaniel," she whispered, smiling broadly but wiping away a tear.

Then he kissed her, slowly and deeply, his hunger for his wife seething through his blood like fire. He pulled her to him, forgetting everything... She had been allowed to lie with him two weeks prior, when Ethan was six weeks old, and Nathaniel had been careful with her, even though she had assured him she was fine and there was no need to treat her like a fragile flower. Still.

He was always going to put her first.

"Calliope! Nathaniel!" came Violet's voice from behind the door, and he leaned back with a groan. "Come see the library!"

Nathaniel sighed deeply and shook his head with a chuckle.

"We're coming!" called Calliope, her face lifting in the most beautiful smile.

"I look forward to this chapter of our lives," he said to Calliope. "Living in this beautiful home with you, my son, and my sisters. Taking care of my estates. The tenants. Doing some good with the fortune that I received."

"Me, too," she said and laid her head against his shoulder. He kissed her head, inhaling her dear scent.

"Are you absolutely certain you wish to wait with your agency?" he asked. "You can start it anytime you want."

"I know," she said and grinned. "And it brings me so much joy that you support me like that. I think it's knowing I have the freedom and the choice—the option to be a mother and a wife and then start working on my dream—that makes me so confident I want to spend this time with you and Ethan."

The sense of peace he felt now was trust, he knew. The trust that came with knowing the woman he loved was an extraordinary woman who was born to do extraordinary things. Trust in her. Trust in life. Trust in his little family.

"You came into my life," he said, "and turned everything upside down. Then you put everything in order again. A new order. You made me and everything around me better."

He was a new person thanks to her. He would never have believed he'd have the courage and the strength to become a loving husband or a father.

"And so did you," she said. "Thank God."

He chuckled. "You know, love," he said. "For the first time in my life, I know I'm right where I'm supposed to be. With the exact person I'm supposed to be with." He gave her a deep, sweet kiss that made him ache to test out their new mattress right now. "And, thanks to you, I'm exactly who I was always meant to be."

Thank you for reading PROJECT DUKE. If you enjoyed Nathaniel and Calliope's story, make sure to get your exclusive bonus epilogue here:

https://mariahstone.com/project-bonus/

Find out what happens with Spencer in book 4 of the DUKES AND SECRETS series, BETTING AGAINST THE SCOUNDREL.

Read BETTING AGAINST THE SCOUNDREL now >

GET A FREE MARIAH STONE BOOK!

Join Mariah's mailing list to be the first to know of new releases, free books, special prices, and other author giveaways.

freehistoricalromancebooks.com

ALSO BY MARIAH STONE

MARIAH'S TIME TRAVEL ROMANCE SERIES

- Called by a Highlander
- Called by a Viking
- Called by a Pirate
- Fated

MARIAH'S REGENCY ROMANCE SERIES

- Dukes and Secrets

VIEW ALL OF MARIAH'S BOOKS

Scan the QR code for the complete list of Mariah's ebooks, paperbacks, and audiobooks in reading order.

ENJOY THE BOOK? YOU CAN MAKE A DIFFERENCE!

Please, leave your honest review for the book.
As much as I'd love to, I don't have financial capacity like New York publishers to run ads in the newspaper or put posters in subway.

But I have something much, much more powerful!

Committed and loyal readers

If you enjoyed the book, I'd be so grateful if you could spend five minutes leaving a review on the book's sales page.

Thank you very much!

ABOUT MARIAH STONE

Mariah Stone is a bestselling author of historical romance novels, including her popular Called by a Highlander series and her hot Viking, Pirate, and Regency novels. With nearly one million books sold, Mariah writes about strong modern-day women falling in love with their soulmates across time. Her books are available worldwide in multiple languages in e-book, print, and audio.

Subscribe to Mariah's newsletter for a free historical romance book today at mariahstone.com/signup!

facebook.com/mariahstoneauthor
instagram.com/mariahstoneauthor
bookbub.com/authors/mariah-stone
pinterest.com/mariahstoneauthor
amazon.com/Mariah-Stone/e/B07JVW28PJ

Made in the USA
Monee, IL
13 April 2025

15701413R00204